ALL THINGS HIDDEN

THE TERRITORY SERIES
BOOK 2

D.L. BUNCH

STRIGIFORM PUBLISHING

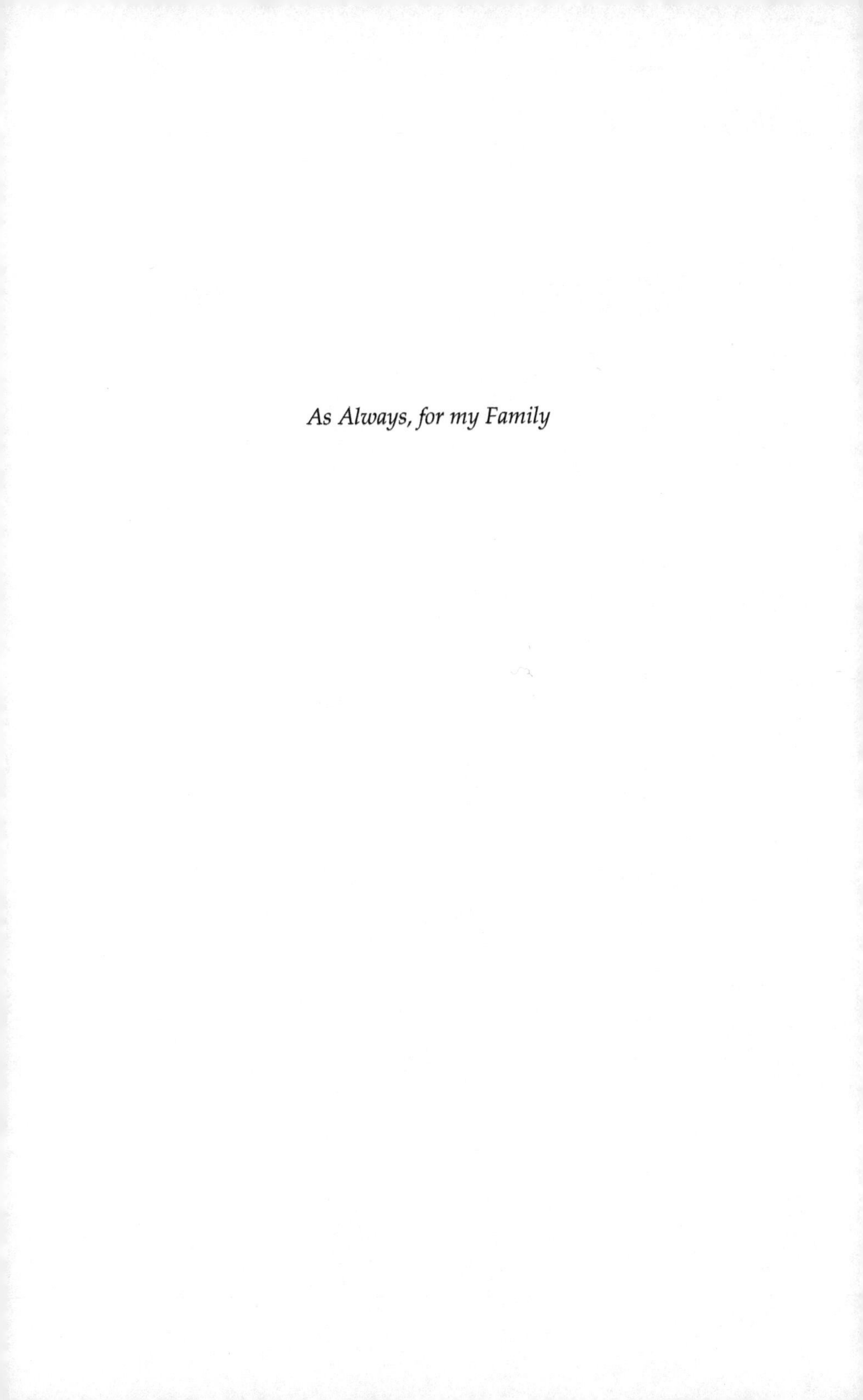

As Always, for my Family

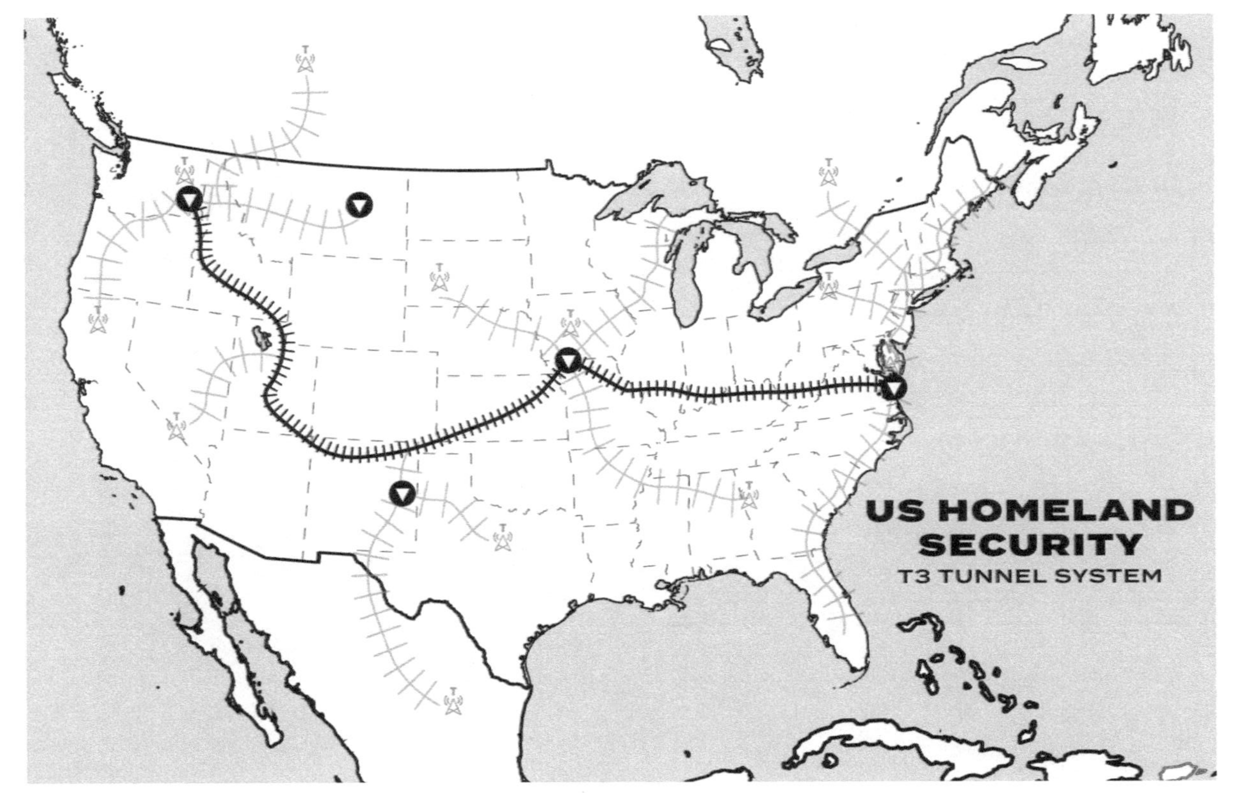

US HOMELAND
SECURITY
T3 TUNNEL SYSTEM

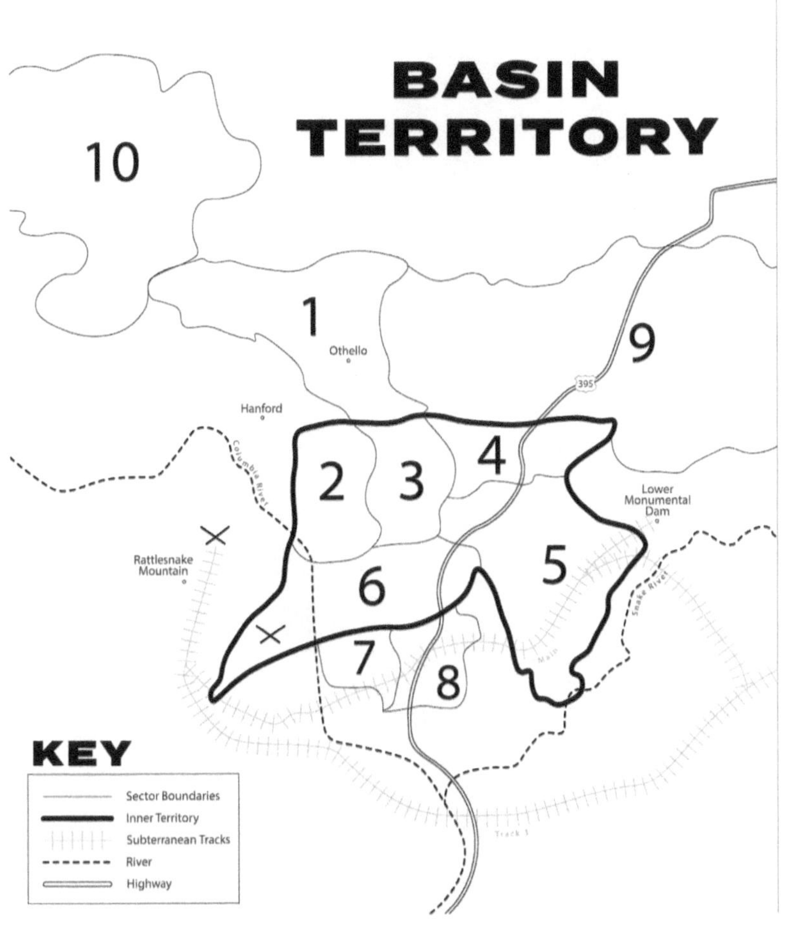

BASIN TERRITORY
10
1
Othello
9
395
Hanford
Columbia River
2
3
4
Lower Monumental Dam
5
Rattlesnake Mountain
6
Snake River
7
8
Main
Track 5
KEY
Sector Boundaries
Inner Territory
Subterranean Tracks
River
Highway

PROLOGUE

The Dig
May 2055

I f Chloe ever made it back to the Basin Territory, she'd never steal again.

Compared to her current surroundings, her home in the Pacific Northwest was heaven. Here, enormous mountains of debris lined the double-tracked railway tunnel for as far as she could see. A by-product of clearing two miles of a massive cave-in, they closed in around her, suffocating.

Chloe shoved the ever-present claustrophobia aside, and picked up a heavy rock with gloved hands. The musty dust tickled her nose and she sneezed. Snot spackled the rock. Tossing it onto the growing pile next to her, she wiped her nose on her sleeve. Yep, stupid decisions never paid off.

Pickaxes clanged all around. Curved walls, cracked and broken, towered above while roots and globs of dirt hung between the concrete slabs still holding the tunnel together. Rebar poked out like shadowy, skeletal fingers, the girders like a giant's ribcage. Kansas City's dead and buried carcass. Chloe shuddered. Her mother had always told her she had too much of an imagination.

Pools of light dotted the already cleared tracks here and there, highlighting the other workers in their worn jeans and cracked leather boots. Their supervisor and guard, Neil, leaned against the tunnel wall by one of the emergency lights, flipping through an old paperback he'd picked up topside along the way. A rifle hung on his back to stop them from escaping, and Chloe snorted. As if any of the workers wanted to leave this hellhole for the hellscape above.

Kansas City had fared worse than others in the Collapse.

And except for those first few days her crew spent clearing the underground tunnel somewhere beneath Nebraska, they hadn't had any run-ins with scavvies. The nickname suited the almost feral humans that Neil and the other guards called *hostiles*. Even better, *local hostiles* like they were in some freaking old war movie. The long days spent here in Kansas City hadn't produced a soul from topside. Thank God. She hated huddling in the makeshift mining carts with the other workers while bullets whizzed overhead.

Kerchunk. The pile next to her grew.

One more hunk of the dense concrete and she could take a break.

The crash of rock against rock, followed by a sharp curse shook her out of her pity party.

"Aaah! Help!"

Torrance.

One of her few friends in this shithole.

Clambering over the rubble, Chloe's feet hit the exposed ground running. She rushed over the double tracks, a median, and past mountainous piles of excavated debris. Others in the general vicinity did the same and they all converged on a slim man, bloody rivulets trickling from a head wound.

She and Neil reached him at the same time.

A huge black hole yawned above them all, the giant sections

of concrete Torrance had dislodged lying atop one of his legs. That wouldn't have been too bad except for the slender shaft of rebar pinning his other leg to the ground. Blood seeped out around the metal sticking out of his torn jeans. Teeth clenched and face set in a pained grimace, he panted out breaths of pure agony.

"Grab the other side." Neil directed, picking his way around the gravelly earth beneath where Torrance lay. Chloe gingerly placed her foot next to the downed man and found the edge of the table-sized hunk of concrete. Two more sets of hands grabbed the rough edge next to her, and they hoisted it together. Groaning and swearing, somebody moved Torrance from under the rubble, lifting him from the rebar in a swift jerk.

He howled and then fell silent in unconsciousness.

Please don't die.

Chloe's group lowered the slab, careful to miss gloved fingers and leather-covered toes.

"Anybody see what happened?" Neil tore the jeans further, revealing that the rebar had just missed the femoral artery. She closed her eyes for a beat, relieved, and then moved to help. Neil batted her away.

A murmur of 'no's' circulated through their group.

"Looks like he moved an unstable piece," A thin, scraggly-haired woman named Colleen said.

Neil quirked one bushy eyebrow. "This entire blockage is unstable. This is why we have a spotter, people."

Feet shuffled and everybody avoided eye contact. Nobody wanted to spot. A spotter would have to watch every move, every piece of debris for movement, and yeah it made things more safe, but it also made the day drag by at a snail's pace. Some had volunteered or been ordered as guards for this mission, and others, like her, were here as punishment.

She would have much rather got wall-building duty back home.

"Don't touch that. Ally, go get Saul and the med kit. Dan,

bring the cart down here so we can load Torrance up. Colleen and Chloe, check the wall and that hole. If we've finally found the end of this blockage, we need to shore up the opening so we can send a crew to check the other side. The rest of you, back to work," Neil ordered.

Torrance moaned, his hands reaching for the source of all his pain. Neil gripped the other man's hands to keep him from touching his leg.

Nobody moved.

"Now!"

The crew jumped as if electrocuted by a cattle prod and moved to their various locations. Colleen and Chloe eyed each other.

Colleen wrinkled her nose and turned toward the gaping maw above their heads. "You're young. Climb up there and see if you can make out anything on the other side. I'll spot ya."

"Seriously, Colleen? You're not that old."

"But I have more experience spottin'. Now, get your skinny ass up there. I'll let you know if anything shifts."

Chloe glared at the other woman but turned on her booted foot and mounted the chunk of concrete they'd pulled off of Torrance. Pieces of subway tile clung to it like a reminder of a more structured world. It wobbled a little but didn't tip. The rubble, like an alluvial fan, spread out below her as she climbed higher. Nothing shifted. *Thank God.*

"You're doing good," Colleen called behind her. She resisted the urge to flip the other woman the bird.

Slipping a bit on some of the loose gravel at the top, Chloe caught herself.

Something clattered on the other side of the blockage. She froze.

"I think there's something over there."

"What did you say?"

Chloe gripped the edges of a table-sized hunk of concrete,

rebar shooting out of it like mutated porcupine needles. "Hello?" she called through a narrow opening.

Stupid. Chloe chastised herself.

Seriously? Was she really announcing herself to some unknown presence on the other side of a barrier dividing them from what was most definitely hostile territory?

"Local hostiles," she murmured to herself and ducked down for a moment, heart pounding.

"Who you talking to? Get up there and scout it out." Colleen shouted.

Chloe pulled herself to the top of the ledge and peered over to the other side. Stale air met her nose, musty and stagnant. Darkness punctuated by more darkness. She squinted her eyes. Was that a flash of light? Couldn't be. There. Again. Farther away this time.

She tried to climb higher, head craning forward over the edge of the rubble. One more time. In the distance down the tunnel. Twin sparks of—of something. Like the small narrow luminescence in the eyes of some small animal.

Her foot slipped.

Arms and legs spun to grasp at the nothing of thin air, her ass and then head crashing against the rough slab. The tumble to the base of the pile of debris wasn't as dramatic as Torrance's, but it was close. Breath wheezed out in painful gasps and stars danced in her eyes, every muscle screaming.

"Ow." She rubbed at the back of her head.

Colleen smirked down at her. "Serves you right for not paying attention. You know better than to climb through those holes before we stabilize them."

"You told me to look! And I wasn't trying to climb through. I thought I saw something."

"I said peek, not climb. Your imagination is getting away from you. There's nothing over there but years of dust and whatever the old government was hiding. You were probably just seeing reflections from the emergency lights." Colleen extended one muscular arm.

Chloe looked at the hand and then back up at the older woman. Grimacing a bit at the motion, she grasped it and wobbled to her feet. "I know what I saw."

"Uh-huh. Best keep your fantasies to yourself. Now come on, Neil's probably going to have us working overtime now that we've almost got this section cleared."

Chloe held her pounding head with one hand. "I hope not."

She glanced one more time up at the gaping hole. What had those lights been?

CHAPTER 1
EVA

August 2055

Eva brushed a strand of hair away from her sleeping daughter's brow. The dark waves slid through her fingers, silky smooth. God, she would miss her. With a quick kiss on Mia's forehead, she stood and slipped out of the room.

Daniel leaned against the front porch railing.

"You going to say goodbye to her? It could be a while before we're back." Eva shouldered a padded hiking backpack that was sitting in a rocking chair.

He straightened, muscles rippling beneath the thin t-shirt. "I already did. You all right?"

Eva dragged her eyes away from his chest and cleared her throat. "Yep, fine. Let's go."

She thumped down the wooden porch, not looking back but feeling Daniel's presence clear to her core as his boots thudded behind her. The backpack went into the small trunk of the side-by-side ATV, and she turned one last time to peer up at the house that had become her home—Mia's home.

The now ever-present guard peered out the front window.

Whoever had lived here before had maintained it well. The screened-in wraparound porch and whitewashed walls were still in good shape, the windows intact. It overlooked an old wildlife refuge, the crags and crannies of ancient ice erosion and floods making it look alien and otherworldly.

The screen door hinges squealed, and it clattered shut. Peta, one of the local nurses, waved her hand in farewell. Jack Allen and the woman had started…something—would you even call it dating these days?—and they both agreed to watch Mia while Eva and Daniel were away.

Jack moseyed to the small vehicle. "I still say you two traipsing off into the wilderness right now is beyond stupid. Generals don't do recon."

Daniel quirked an eyebrow and gave the other man a rare half-smile. "Well, then it's good we're not generals. That's your job."

"That makes it worse. No heroics, Daniel. Eva. Get what we need and get back."

Eva nodded. "I've never been one for that, Jack, you know that."

Daniel opened the door to the ATV. "And by the way, if we can, we're pushing on. See what's left of the East Coast."

Jack cursed and kicked the tire. "You stubborn SOB. Seriously? What am I going to tell Mia if you don't come back? Huh?"

Daniel put a hand on Jack's shoulder. "If we don't make it back, all is lost anyway. Do the best you can and follow the plan we laid out."

"God, you sure know how to make an exit." Jack stepped back, dark brows creasing and arms crossed.

"You and Peta take care of her, Jack." Eva's eyes filled up and she blinked the tears away. *Waste of water.*

It was better this way. Yes. The best for everyone. Except Mia.

The little voice that had been nagging her all day since Daniel had decided to join the expedition into Kansas City shouted at her now.

This wasn't right—none of it.

"Eva? Are you going to get in?" Daniel's deep baritone settled into her bones, steady and so, so familiar. Jack walked back to the house, hands in his pocket. He stopped by Peta.

Eva didn't answer, just scooted onto the bench seat of the off-road vehicle and rested her head against the headrest. Closing her eyes, she breathed.

A warm hand startled her. Eva's eyes flew open, and she looked at Daniel in the glow of the yard light. The Shield Serum made it appear as if she viewed him in full daylight, all the fine worry lines etched into his forehead, his skin otherwise smooth and young despite his middle age, and the clear hazel of his eyes. Everything in stark, clear focus. He took his hand off her arm.

"She'll be all right. Jack, Tobias, and Peta will make sure of it. What we're doing, it's more important than all of it. It's more important than you or me. Or her."

"I know. It's just…." Logic told her finding all of the TMRWS scattered like the government's playthings across the country, was their number one priority—if the machines were malfunctioning, they were all dead, with or without Shield. Eva couldn't help feeling that something was off. Wrong. *Are you sure it's just a feeling?* She shivered at the remembered presence inside her, there and gone just as quickly. It was lurking. Waiting. Eva finished weakly, "It's just that I'm going to miss her."

Daniel considered her for a long minute before starting the vehicle. "I will too."

Other words, more important words, lingered in the night air. She closed her eyes again, but the man's presence beside her made it impossible to even think about a quick nap.

This was going to be a long couple of months.

———

Hour after hour passed in grim monotony, marked only by mile markers etched into the concrete pillars of the tunnel and the occasional thud of train wheels rolling across track. Eva leaned her forehead against the cool glass, the dim light reflecting back weary eyes in the passenger seat's window.

Track Three. If the map Daniel had found was correct, it went clear to Virginia, connecting the Eastern and Western United States like an underground trail of old governmental corruption. Paralleling the position of the aboveground cargo railways, these tracks had remained top secret. God, the skeletons they housed, and the ghosts they carried. So many branches and so little time to explore them all. Finding the map to the rest of the TMRWS was imperative or else they could travel these railways for years without much success.

Their final destination of this leg of the trip was the main hub nestled beneath Kansas City. Scouts had sent back word that the track was clear and Territory construction crews were moving on to the next blockage beneath St. Louis. Old rubble from old wars.

The running lights of the train cast shadows against the cement walls of the tunnel. These days, Daniel preferred to sit as far away from her as possible. She couldn't blame him. Not really.

Two other people on their team, Tamara Foster, their mechanical engineer, and Alec Jensen, a biologist, sat in the front two seats murmuring with their heads together. Scheming more like. Both had worked together on the cryo-storage project in the MUC before the Collapse. Both had been thick as thieves for as long as she could remember.

The final member, Chet, operated the manual controls to the train, the automation device broken long before Daniel had found it. A team of guards would meet them all in what was left of Kansas City, guarding the area against possible local hostiles. Huh. Local hostiles, like they were in some old time movie.

She felt him before she saw his reflection in the window. *Speak of the Devil, and he shall appear.*

"When we get there, I want you to stay with the train until we secure the area around the topside entrance." Daniel braced himself against the floor, one hand resting on the seat next to her, swaying with each thunk.

"Not happening." She didn't even turn her head, mental exhaustion weighing her down.

"If there's a meteorite at this site, then we're all at risk. I want to clear the area before bringing you along to sniff one out." Like some sort of dog. Condensation from her breath fogged up the window, then evaporated. All of it fading away. *I know the feeling.*

"I need to see this all the way through. You *were* going to send me on my own; I can't see that anything's changed. I have plenty of baby-sitters."

"You walked out of your house last night. I don't know where you were going, but Hernandez said when he caught up with you, you about took his head off."

The words hung in the air, dense and heavy.

Eva yanked the sleeves of her shirt over the scraped knuckles that hadn't completely healed. Denial had gotten her this far. She finally looked up at him. "You placed a second guard on my house."

Daniel dropped into the seat and gripped her wrist, revealing one of her bruised hands. "Yes."

She re-crossed her arms, brow furrowing. "Maybe I just wanted to be left alone."

"We both know that is not what's going on here."

"Do we?"

A tense minute passed. Tamara and Alec had stopped their conversation and were now looking at them with rapt attention.

"Eva, you're an intelligent woman. It's the first sign that your prefrontal cortex is regressing. We saw it in the lab animals; we saw it in the first test subjects. We both know what triggered it."

The enzymes in the meteorite. Or whatever it was. Did it even come from space? Or someplace else? That remembered trek to the depths of the old government black site buried well beneath the Lower Monumental Dam still made her stomach turn.

"We don't know anything, Daniel. Nothing. Not really. What if you only need one more exposure and you become just as compromised as I am? Have you thought of that?" Eva lifted her chin at a stubborn angle.

Daniel studied her face, the fine lines between his brows furrowed. In concern or just deep thought was anybody's guess. "Fine, but Trae is staying with you the entire time. The first sign of a break, and I'm cuffing you to this damn train."

Sweat dribbled into her eyes, and she wiped it away. "Thank you."

———

Several miles out of Kansas City, enormous piles of slag and rubble filled in the maintenance walkways to either side of the track, and a second switching track appeared, the tunnel widening. The curved ceiling was bare earth and rock from where it had caved in. Metal t-beams scavenged from some aboveground building shored it up along a two-mile stretch until intact tunnel once again bled into concrete and brick. It was a true hub, enormous pillars of reinforced concrete marking different branches. Numbers and letters beside each entrance indicating beginning and endpoint along with a number.

The train engine slowed, wheels squealing to a halt. Air rushed out of the brakes in a puff of expelled energy. Everyone paused a beat, acclimating to the sudden stillness. Daniel was the first one to move.

"All right. The rest of our crew should be in a side branch just up ahead. Reports say the surface is a bombed-out mess, so navigating will be tricky. All the old maps of the area are basically obsolete. The clean-up crew tried to make a rough map of the immediate area around the surface entrance. The area is not nuked, but damn near close enough. We'll split into two teams to cover more ground." Daniel pointed out an area of the map roughly a mile from their location. "Eva and I will take the subterranean sections and the black site. Tamara, you, Chet, and Alec cover the old Federal building. Any sign of Tau-159 and you leave. Immediately. The rest of the maps are our priority. Hopefully there are hard copies. We'll meet back here in twenty-four hours."

He threw them a piece of paper with a rough sketch of the outer limits of Kansas City.

"What if we run into anyone?" Chet concealed numerous weapons, one inside a cracked leather boot, two in a worn belt holster, and one in a shoulder holster. A rifle on a strap completed his lethal outfit.

"Got enough guns?" Eva half-joked. Her daughter would have been proud at the display of so much armament. Her heart squeezed. God, she missed Mia. *This is for her.*

Chet slid a bowie knife into a thigh-sheath. "No."

Eva checked her small caliber gun in its ankle holster, the .45 pistol at her belt, and picked up a rifle. A reasonable number of weapons, in her opinion.

It was amazing Daniel even let her have any. Then again, a guard would stand behind her, gun at the ready. Would he really shoot her if necessary? Shield would do its job but anxiety still knotted her stomach.

"If anybody runs into any hostiles on the surface, take them out quietly, if possible. Hide the bodies. I don't want to stir up problems with local scavenger groups. If they're refugees, avoid them if you can." Daniel shouldered his pack. "Ready?"

The members of the group nodded.

A hundred yards up the track, the glow of an emergency light highlighted a group of men and women in military fatigues. All were milling around, readying gear, or waiting. At the sight of Daniel, they straightened to attention. Some of Daniel's Shielded militia. Most were only teenagers, though life, experience, and the Shield Serum made them a lot more mature —and deadly—than others their age.

They split into their respective teams, a small contingent hanging back to guard the train, the others headed down the track toward one of the few surface entrances in this tunnel section.

It was a true hub. Enormous pillars of reinforced concrete marked different branches. The illumination from the single emergency light lit the area a hundred yards in either direction, though Shield allowed her to see a bit farther. Doors hung open, already searched by their people. Maintenance bays, broken pipes, and conduits lined the base of the curved ceiling. Three tracks ran parallel to each other, a switching station staggered every hundred feet. One section held massive cargo boxes. The piles of rubble ended just inside the cavernous depths. Whoever had bombed the surface had missed the central hub by mere yards.

"Just over here, sir." Trae, one of the Shielded militia kids, pointed down the track to a metal door. An electrical box about the size of a large book dangled from wires. "We had to force it open. It was jammed shut."

"Good work." Daniel crossed the tracks toward the door, but Eva remained where she was. Something was off. She couldn't quite put her finger on it. Maybe the enzyme's unusual influence over her brought out her paranoia. Or maybe it sensed something.

She peered into the darkness of the eastbound tunnel. Nothing stirred the stagnant air. There it was again. A slight movement, barely a flutter of air through matter.

"Daniel."

Something in her voice must have caught his attention because he stopped, his focus on her almost uncomfortable in its intensity.

"Over there." She pointed down the tunnel on the other side

of the tracks and several train car lengths away from their exit point.

His head swiveled, and he zeroed in on the area. "Trae and Aurelia, you're with me."

The lights on the ends of the trio's rifles shone into the dank recesses in front of them. Eva jumped off the walkway onto the tracks and trailed from a distance.

A triangle of light formed around something on the ground.

"You better come see," Daniel called back to her.

On the ground, a dead woman, bullet holes in her chest, lay in a puddle of her own blood. Her clothes were filthy but well-mended, and a pistol was by her side. Also at her side was an enormous German Shepherd dog, hackles raised and teeth bared in a low growl, protecting the dead woman's body.

How the hell had they gotten down here? And past the guards?

"Shh, it's all right. We're not going to hurt you." At least, she hoped not. Eva extended her hand and walked toward the dog. "You're all right."

The dog backed up a step but didn't make any aggressive moves. It was a female, skinny and young. Its eyes flashed with an odd luminescence. She hunkered down. Daniel and the others remained at attention, but none made a move. It wouldn't last long.

Eva riffled in the pocket of her cargo pants and came up with a piece of beef jerky. She threw it to the dog. It stiffened but sniffed the air.

"Go ahead, sweetie. It's not poisoned." Eva took a bite of her own, tuning out the shuffling steps around her. Something about this dog called to her, an energy thrumming in her blood.

The animal picked up the piece of jerky in a quick nip of teeth and retreated.

"Eva."

"Shh, I almost got her."

Eva threw another chunk of jerky to the dog. Those strange

eyes flashed again, and this time the dog picked up the dried hunk of meat quicker, her hackles lowering. She wagged her tail tentatively.

"Step back, everybody, give her some space," Eva called to the others.

Daniel's impatient voice cut through the air. "We don't have time for this."

"The woman has some kind of bag with her. I don't know about you, but I want to see its contents. Without killing the dog." Eva kept her voice calm and low.

After five long minutes, the dog let her near enough to grab the small knapsack. She opened it. Empty vials, a gas mask, and…

A handheld nuclear cryo unit.

CHAPTER 2

MIA

September 2072

Cold air blasted into the small, cramped room where Mia's Aunt Sarah had imprisoned her. Plastic boxes lined one wall, a cot with a bucket beside it was shoved up against another. A single bulb on a wire dangled from the middle of the ceiling. Somehow, this uncharted tunnel and room had power.

Sitting on the cot with her back against the wall, she tore the side of her bra, working the underwire free. Instant lock pick. It's why she wore these kind. She shimmied off the bed and kneeled next to the door.

Over the years, Mia had investigated every square inch of the tunnels beneath the Basin Territory. All the crags and crannies of the original government-built train tunnels, to the new additions used to provide electricity and water clear out to Sector One in the northwest corner and Sector Nine in the northeast beyond the inner, walled territory. The escape from training and duties—and the sometimes dreadful heat—made the solitary excursions some of her favorites from childhood.

It didn't occur to her until she was an adult how strange it was she never had a companion. A friend. Somebody to tell her innermost thoughts to, confide in, get into trouble with. All those things young people apparently did according to the story books. No deep connections to speak of with the exception of her parents and Jack's family.

And maybe Cooper. The fleeting thought perplexed her. Did he even count?

The thin wire slipped from her frozen fingers and clattered to the floor. It was so cold in here. She blew into her cupped hands and picked up the piece of metal, trying again.

The few times as children that they'd interacted, one or the other of them had been in crisis. And it hadn't changed as adults, though she'd not linked the rangy boy with troubled eyes who stole her strawberries and asked her to read him a story to Cooper until yesterday. The boy who'd disappeared shortly after the latter to parts unknown. Mia may have been a loner surrounded by adults as a child, but she remembered him on those rare occasions he made it into the inner territory from Camp Havoc—her father's special training camp. She remembered him well.

That moment in the tunnel earlier played through her head, the touch, the connection, and the knowledge of his every movement for short periods of time making their actions coordinated and quick. It had to be some weird by-product of Shield and her blood. Her mother had said Shield wasn't meant to be used for super-soldiers. Now, Mia wasn't so sure. Something else to add to her growing list of things to investigate.

"For Hell's sake, fit in the lock." She flexed the freezing digits, rubbing them together. The underwire once again ended up on the dusty floor.

Dammit all to hell and back. Didn't they know air-conditioning was a waste of electricity? Unless it was some kind of means to torture. Always a possibility with her aunt.

Think, Mia. She crossed her arms and cradled her hands in

her armpits, closed her eyes, swayed from foot to foot, and forced her brain to work through the problem.

Her enemies didn't want her dead. On the contrary, she was surprised her Aunt Sarah hadn't taken Mia with her after the final bombshell. *Your blood negates Shield. Cure and poison.*

So why hadn't she? What had made her aunt leave her here, weak and alone?

Frustrated, Mia kicked the door, a boot-sized dent chipping the metallic paint. *Not helpful.*

Her parents had kept it from her, the whatever extra it was floating around in her bloodstream. Growling, she picked up the makeshift lockpick, her fingers like fleshy popsicles.

It clattered to the floor yet again.

"Damn it all to hell!" Another boot print joined the one she already made. Stupid lock. Stupid, ineffectual fingers. Stupid large piece of metal. *My parents would have escaped by now.*

She rested her forehead against the door. What else could she use?

Her compass. The needle would be a smaller piece of metal and would fit better.

She patted the cargo pants, and there it was. The etched declination marks stood out against the flowery loops of the gold filigree around the dial, the needle pointing to true north. She ran her finger over the glass face covering, and it bobbed with the motion. The small piece of metal was definitely the right size to fit into the lock. Her head fell back on her shoulders and she looked at the raw boards of the ceiling.

Gifts were a rarity. Gifts from her father even more so. Mia clutched the compass to her chest and closed her eyes. She'd be lying if she said she wasn't more than a little upset by the prospect of destroying one of the few items she'd had her entire life. Even to save herself.

Mia's eyes shot open as something else occurred to her, and she eyed the hinged side of the metal door. Maybe she didn't need to destroy the compass after all.

Whoever had installed the door had done so correctly, with the door opening inwards and the hinges accessible from this side. One thing Mia had already deduced was that this room wasn't originally meant to be a prison cell. The stacks of wooden crates and plastic boxes indicated it was some kind of storage room or maybe a hidey-hole for illicit activities.

Right under Dad's nose. Nothing much escaped her father's notice. That such a massive operation existed beyond his knowledge triggered something deep inside of her. Daniel had saved all the scientists in the Manhattan Underground Complex out at Hanford after they'd been buried alive during the Collapse. He'd helped her mother develop the Shield Serum, which made everyone stronger, more resilient.

And then there was the TMRWS machine—or machines, according to her mother's journals. Pre-Collapse weather-control-system-turned-energy-source that powered all their irrigation and electricity. To Mia, her father was a superhero, somebody whose shoes she could never fill. But these uncharted tunnels and rooms she found herself in…they were an unexpected chink in her father's armor, and it left her feeling…bereft.

The storage containers elicited nothing of use, just scavenged books, roofing tiles, and ceramic flower pots. Nothing she could pry hinges open with.

She placed her ear to the door, listening for any movement outside. Not a peep.

Taking off her shoes, Mia slipped her socks off, put them on her hands like mittens, and replaced her shoes, wrinkling her nose at the smell. Her fingers warmed a bit under the thin fabric. She retrieved the metal underwire from the ground and eyed the bottom bolt. It would just fit under the top. Firmly prying up, she wriggled and jostled.

The bolt shimmied out a few centimeters, and a shot of excitement spurred her on. Soon, she had the bottom hinge loose, the metal plate swinging open.

The top bolt would be the problem. Getting her socked hands

under the bottom of the door, she squatted and heaved, jerking it up and down. In one last jerk, the door hinge gave with a pop and screech of metal, the door tipping against her.

She caught it before it fell to the floor, her heart racing. A rush of warm air flowed into the room.

A distant motor revved and faded. Water rushed through a pipe somewhere in the tunnel nearby. Mia stilled, listening for the sound of footsteps or the timbre of voices. Why hadn't they left a guard?

She stuffed the socks in her back pocket, her hands warmer with the friction of undoing the hinges, and braced the door against the wall. Darkness met her from either side of the tunnel. A lone emergency light and the bulb in her room offered the only illumination. Wooden beams girded the ceiling to the narrow tunnel and a thick layer of caliche rock streaked the wall in front of her.

They had come in from the right. The tire tracks in the dirt didn't help, running in either direction. Sliding a hand along the rough wall she headed right.

Which dead-ended a hundred feet from her makeshift prison. Mia made her way back to the door and took off the other direction.

With the same results.

What the hell?

Returning to the right hand path, she made her way back to the dead end and felt around the end wall. Clumps of dirt and rock clattered to the ground. Dust clogged her nostrils and she sneezed but kept feeling—for what, she didn't exactly know.

The tunnel was about four or five of her strides wide. At the junction of the other wall, she found what she was looking for. A metal control box inset into the earth and the hole covered by a rock, it was about one foot by one foot in width and length. In the center was a lever. She flipped it to the up position. A hum filled the air and the wall in front of her vibrated and rattled, sliding into an inset wooden cavity. It operated much like a pocket door in design, and if she had a light and more time, she would have investigated the wall and the mechanism to open and close it.

Exhaustion hit Mia like a bag of stones. She'd used too much energy throughout the day—including recovery from the two taser blasts and her aunt extracting her blood. Her blood that was apparently some kind of kryptonite to the rest of the Shielded.

Mia wandered through a warren of rough-hewn, unfamiliar tunnels and dead ends, time lost in the dirt and darkness surrounding her. When she'd about given up, light filtered from a side tunnel, casting an elevator lift, cables dangling from the open door above it, in dappled moonlight.

It lifted her to the surface in the middle of a corn field a few miles from Jack Allen's house, the entrance cleverly tucked away, complete with dead husks ready to cover the surface hatch. Had it only been a few hours since the fight at his house? Sector Nine, under her Aunt Sarah's influence, had sent thugs to harass Jack's family for resources they believed he'd hidden. It hadn't worked out in their favor—at least Mia didn't think it had. The first taser blast had left her unconscious and she hadn't seen the finale.

Now to determine her next steps.

Cooper's presence in her head reappeared with a faint whisper. A warm, hazy blip maybe a few miles away? Farther? He was to the north somewhere. Her stomach did a little flip. It would be easy to find him. Finding Cooper wasn't as vital as other things, even if the man's presence was like a shot of adrenaline.

She could go back to Jack's, see the outcome of the fight, find her father and determine next steps in dealing with Sector Nine. The isolationist group's influence was growing and needed to be squashed. But that nagging feeling that her Aunt Sarah had something else planned wouldn't let up. She had killed Jerome— Colville's leader—by accident or to stir up trouble with the outlying settlements was yet to be determined. Her next move would be a lot more targeted. A lot more deadly. No, the most urgent need at the moment was finding her mother. Eva needed to know Sarah had a sample of Mia's blood.

The MUC it was.

Going through the interior entrance to the MUC would raise too many questions, so Mia chose the top emergency entrance that fewer than a handful of people knew about. Outside the wall, it would be an hour drive from her current position, but at least the dark masked her movements.

A sliver of moon shown just on the horizon. Her father's ATV sat parked in the field in a haphazard fashion. That was strange. Where were Jack and her father? Cooper had been with them at Jack's farmhouse the last she knew, but the annoying little ability she'd developed to locate him told her he was at least several miles north. Were the other two men still with Cooper? As if sensing her thoughts, his location stuttered and disappeared. The unnerving ability lasted a little over two hours with proximity.

Indecision gripped her, an unfamiliar sensation. No, getting to her mother was more important than leaving a vehicle for her father.

Mia jumped in and turned the key.

CHAPTER 3
COOPER

September 2072

Wheelbarrow sized rocks and sagebrush surrounded the hatch to the underground tunnel where he'd just deserted two of the people he'd spent half his adult life despising. Jack Allen's muffled cursing below buzzed in Cooper's ears. He chuckled and banged a couple times with his foot on top of the rough metal. God he missed messing with that man. Being gone for fifteen years hadn't changed that.

Cooper hunkered down and listened. Wind filtered through the bushes and the faint click of insects met his ears—with the exception of Jack's bellyaching. A silver half moon hung overhead and the wall around the agricultural interior of the Basin Territory marched along in the distance, a ribbon of metal extending across the desert hills. The Shield Serum enhanced his eyes and they soaked in the dim light, everything standing out in stark relief, as clear as the middle of the day.

He rose and piled a small mound of rocks over the hatch. Whoever had built the tunnel wanted it to be secret, and he would oblige. Besides, he'd rather make it more difficult for

Daniel and Jack to follow. The Seeking with Mia—that connection where he could feel her location in his head—had faded to nothing, more a niggling feeling now somewhere to the south.

The wall loomed in front of him.

This side wasn't as developed as the southern and eastern sections he'd scouted with Jorge. It was wild and primitive, the irradiated desert doing more to keep people from this side of the Basin Territory than anything else. It was good Jorge and his dog Kiva were not with him.

Jorge and Kiva. They should be halfway back to Colville by now. He'd have to stop and retrieve his dog on the way to Montana to rescue his foster daughter, Claire. And thank the young man for caring for her. At least the two of them had gotten away when Cooper was captured.

Cooper estimated he was a couple of miles away from the Northern Gate he'd entered only two days prior. If he tried re-entering the Territory over the wall, there was a high possibility he'd get caught again. This final option of getting into the MUC was like playing Russian-roulette with two bullets instead of one. It was the reason why he'd saved it after exhausting all other options.

Instead of heading east, Cooper veered west towards the emergency exit side of the MUC in the Hanford Reach beneath Rattlesnake Mountain.

The mountain was really an oversized hill, its bald top bristling with old communications antennae bent and broken by wind and war. It dwarfed the bombed out remnants of old government buildings below it. Clumps of sagebrush and Russian Olive—more scraggly brush than actual tree—dotted the landscape. Cooper created a mental map of the largest patches to his destination. If it was even semi-alive, it probably meant the radiation was within tolerable levels for the Shielded.

He took a deep breath and sprinted to the first patch of brush. A red rash, like a severe allergic reaction, crept up his arms and his face felt sunburned. The symptoms didn't worsen thanks to Shield, but if he got too near more severe radiation, it was over.

Cooper held his breath, his cheeks puffing out and he exhaled. He spotted his next destination and sprinted across the desert. Pain sandblasted his skin and nausea roiled in his stomach but he kept going. Both lessened as he neared the clump of brush.

Hands on his knees, he tried not to vomit, his breath escaping in harsh gasps.

God, this was crazy.

Claire is worth the pain.

By the time he reached the perimeter between the desert and the Hanford Reach, he was stumbling, most of his body in agony. Radiation burns splotched his skin, bubbling and ugly. Cooper collapsed at the base of the hill next to an enormous pile of tumbleweeds and a lone, barely alive clump of sage. Tingles of healing coursed through him as Shield worked its magic trying to keep up with the massive amount of damage he'd just inflicted on his body. That bit of fun—sprinting across irradiated desert—was not something he wanted to repeat anytime soon. He had to find another way out.

Mia's presence in his brain had faded completely. He didn't know how to feel about that. The sensation of her—like fresh-baked pie and a warm fire—had awoken a long forgotten feeling: the feeling of home. Not that the woman would like being compared to something so...domestic. Slapping the ground on either side of him, he heaved to standing, the world spinning in slow circles. He shook his head to clear it. Patches of flaky, dead skin fluttered to land on his shirt. He wrinkled his nose and rubbed at his face and arms trying to ease the itching of excess dried skin. He was a damned snake. Time to find the access door he'd helped install sixteen years ago.

The trek across what essentially consisted of a minefield—which gave him pause, a minefield was right up Daniel and Eva's alley—ended in a shadowed escarpment: bushes and tumbleweeds piled deep as far as he could see in either direction at the base of the mountain.

Cooper sighed. What he wouldn't give for a flashlight. Or even a match.

Mia and home. Right before he'd left the Basin as a teenager, he had found her out in the wild reading a book: *A Wrinkle in Time*. Most twelve or thirteen-year-olds would have scoffed but she had read to him. Funny how the most important decisions in life come down to a single moment, a single line in a book. "There will no longer be so many pleasant things to look at if responsible people do not do something about the unpleasant ones."

At the time, he'd come back from Montana with Daniel after they'd raided the mining department at Montana Tech in Butte. The older man—somebody he'd looked up to his entire life to that point—had blown up the settlement, in Cooper's eyes, disregarding any civilians.

It took him years to understand that you couldn't save some without sacrificing others in this brave new world. By that time, it was too late and he was under Sarah's influence, controlled by her through Claire.

There was an old song from before the Collapse, an old singer singing about never being able to go home. Maybe they were right.

God, the last couple of days had made him too nostalgic.

Straightening his spine, he continued to look for the hidden emergency entrance to the MUC buried somewhere in the hillside. He couldn't consider anything else until he'd found what he came here for: a vial of Shield for Claire to permanently cure her from Sarah's poison.

It took him the better part of an hour to uncover the metal door set in the hillside buried beneath camouflage netting and tumbleweeds. At one time it had been the back door to the control room for a Nike air missile site during the first Cold War with Russia. An old guardhouse used to stand next to it but had disintegrated over time, and crushed concrete covered by soil drift was the only sign anything had ever stood there.

Wires dangled from a control panel about the size of an electrical box buried in the hillside. Cooper couldn't tell if they had been recently ripped out or if it had always been that way. He felt around the jam for any kind of trap or trigger.

Nothing.

He took a breath and spun the wheel of the latch and it creaked open, unlocked.

An inky black hole stood before him. Even during the brightest part of the day there wouldn't have been enough light for his enhanced eyesight.

Not an ounce of dust coated the cement floor, and no spiderwebs laced the doorway's steel frame.

Like somebody had just crossed the threshold.

Cooper's lips tilted up. Now he just needed to follow the trail of breadcrumbs down the rabbit hole to his final destination and see who waited for him at the end.

———

The stairwell brightened the farther he descended through the short tunnel. Green emergency lighting coated everything in a ghoulish sheen. The territory was generating electricity somehow. His spies told him there was something out at the dam but none of his people had ever gotten close enough to check it out.

Cement blocks and steel girders held everything in place from what he could see in the dim glow. It ended in a small room with a crooked stairway sign hanging over a handleless metal door.

The room was a little bigger than the average office. Plain white countertops, the empty cabinets above them hanging open, stretched across the far wall. Two doors took up the other walls, the one with the stairway sign to Cooper's left and another to his right. Cooper opened the latter. On the other side was an empty room plunged in darkness, reeking of rodents and stagnant air. He closed the door and searched the rest of the room.

One drawer held a rusted steak knife, forks, and spoons. Scratched, white enamel plates were stacked in the cupboard above it. A breakroom. He grabbed the knife.

The rest of the room elicited nothing. No trip wires, no cameras. Zip, zilch, nada. Only the green emergency exit sign hanging on an electrical wire over the entrance and the cockeyed stairwell placard. If there had been a camera, it was no more.

A tingle of apprehension settled in his gut. He played spy games for a living. Something about this situation didn't sit right. Radiation or not, Cooper couldn't see Daniel leaving this entrance unguarded. Each one of the inner circle followed security procedures to the letter.

Unless…

What if one of poor Danny boy's inner circle was a traitor? It would explain why all of his security measures elsewhere kept getting compromised. That would gut the man. His sense of control breached. Yeah, it would absolutely pile drive him.

The first memory he had of Daniel, he'd been little more than five or six down in the depths of the MUC. Cooper had snuck away from his parents and somehow past the guards into one of the labs. A big chunk of cool black rock in a glass case had caught his attention, and he'd been drawn to it, he'd wanted a closer look. When he'd dragged a chair and climbed on it to press his face against the box, Daniel had rushed in and dragged him by the arm out of the lab, fierce enough that he'd left red marks, reprimanded his parents, and dressed down the guards. It stuck in Cooper's mind even to this day.

Daniel would do worse to a traitor.

The door swung open with ease to the emergency stairs plunging into the darkness of a narrow shaft. Some of the railings had been replaced by wooden beams, and steel plates replaced parts of the wall where it had been blown up once upon a time. It must have taken months or even years to dig out and repair this entrance to the MUC. Scuffs from black heeled shoes marked the cement on the first landing.

Cooper continued his descent down the narrow, closed flight of stairs. He had lost count at around fifteen flights, and he was still descending. The emergency lights in their metal cages above the doors on each landing blurred together, some working and some not. He tried to open each door without success. They were steel doors without windows or locks, the door handles broken off long ago.

In that moment—albeit, begrudgingly—Cooper fully appreciated what Daniel and Eva accomplished tunneling out of the twenty-second sublevel of this place with nothing but their wits and rudimentary mining tools. All while keeping hundreds of people alive, including Cooper.

You were an experiment. He had to keep you alive. The unsettling thought wasn't something Cooper let surface too often. That way lay madness and darkness. His parent's deaths both tied to a corrupt government, with Daniel at the helm of the project. And Eva. Who helped care for him afterwards. Out of obligation? Or because she wanted to? It ate at him when he let it. The fractured part of him that was an orphan—and the reason for it—fighting with the deeply instilled loyalty of being a part of the Shielded Militia as a teenager. So many knots. So many unresolved issues. And at seventeen, angry and volatile, Montana had been the last straw for him.

He rounded the corner on what was maybe the seventeenth or eighteenth landing and one of the doors yawned open, held there by something in the jam towards the top. Cooper slowed and took out the knife.

The faint lighting didn't reach far into the room. He eased back up the stairs and stilled, listening.

A scrape against the floor and a shuffle, like somebody was running their hands against the wall. It faded a bit. Something banged to the floor and the person cursed. Light streamed out of the doorway, shadows dancing. Cooper backed up another step.

The person clomped to the door and reached up to pull out the block that held the door open.

Tobias.

Cooper stood. "Howdy, partner."

Tobias startled, raising his weapon. His eyes were limitless black holes, dilated well beyond what the dark lighting dictated. Was he on something?

"Cooper? Killian Cooper? What are you doin' down here?" Fresh blood was half-congealed on Tobias's face, Shield having healed whatever wound had been there.

"Well, I'm looking for someone. About yay high, hazel eyes, black hair. Somebody took her, and I want her back. You wouldn't know anything about that, would you?" Cooper took a measured step forward, the knife hilt relaxed in his hand. It was better if the man thought Cooper was looking for Mia and not for the real reason, to steal a dose of the liquid gold that was Shield.

Tobias's eyes flicked to the weapon. "What do ya want with her?"

The man slurred his words. Cooper didn't care if it was from the head injury or something else at this point, he just wanted answers.

"I made a promise to help her find Jerome's murderer and I hate breaking my word. What kind of man does that? Betrays loyalty and such." Cooper descended another step. A niggle of guilt worked its way into consciousness. He was going to break his word to Mia. But, he'd made another, more vital promise to another girl. One he had sworn to protect.

Tobias cocked his head to the side and raised the gun. Daniel's oldest comrade in arms. Oldest friend. The man's hand shook with a slight tremor and the tip of the pistol dipped. "I'm no traitor."

"I didn't say you were, Toby. Where'd you get the blood on your face?" Cooper grinned. "Didn't run into a wall, did ya?"

Tobias shook the pistol. "Don't come any closer, or I'll shoot."

Cooper's tone remained friendly, unconcerned. He squared his legs in a fighter's stance. "I just told you, I'm a friend. On your side, looking for one of your people. You don't want to shoot me. Aren't you looking for Mia?"

Tobias brushed a hand over the sweat and blood encrusted on his face. "You're trying to confuse me."

"I'm not trying to do anything. Why don't you put the gun down, Tobes, before you get hurt."

Tobias scrubbed at his face again, the tip of the pistol dipping even lower.

Cooper didn't wait.

He swept his left arm in Tobias's inside guard. The gun went off above Cooper's head, the bullet pinging into the cement stairwell.

Cooper hooked his right foot behind Tobias's left ankle and rammed his shoulder into his gut. The large man landed on his ass but rolled to the side, bringing the gun to bear once again.

In two beats, Cooper stabbed the gun hand in the wrist clear through to the other side, and Tobias dropped the gun. He bellowed, enraged, and charged. Blood splashed, dripping on the cement floor.

Time slowed.

On instinct, Cooper dropped to a knee, braced himself on the floor and kicked Tobias in the gut. All the air left the other man in a gasp of fetid breath, but he kept on charging and knocked Cooper to the ground, landing on top of him.

Oh, shit.

The man was built like a bear.

Cooper attempted to twist his hips out of the way, but the man head-butted him. Stars shone in Cooper's eyes. All the energy faded from his body like air from a balloon. He was still healing from the radiation run topside and Shield was having a difficult time keeping up.

Tobias jerked the knife out of his hand, bringing it to Cooper's throat. He pushed the blade against his carotid. Something wild and feral shone from the other's man's eyes.

Cooper had seen that look on the faces of Cannibals. He'd just seen that look mere days ago at his parent's rundown house out in the middle of nowhere when he went to retrieve his refrigeration device and his father's knife.

His father's knife. It was back in his boot.

A clatter tumbled down the staircase outside the door. Tobias froze, his crazy eyes blinking at the added distraction.

It was now or never.

He reached for his boot.

CHAPTER 4
EVA

August, 2055

The nuclear-powered cooler for delivering bio-agent samples was a black box the size and shape of a brick and had a green light on one end blinking in even intervals.

The German Shepherd eyed the others warily, a strange light luminescing in her eyes, though she'd put her hackles and teeth away. She sat near the head of the woman on the ground, her tail thumping the ground each time Eva looked her way. It moved in a steady, almost liquid manner. *More strange.*

"Cool dog," Tamara murmured. "And I haven't seen one of these devices in years. Where the hell did she get it?"

"Good question." Daniel kneeled, keeping a wary eye on the Shepherd, and flipped the body over. The top of the woman's head was almost completely gone. A logo for "Biological Advancements Center" emblazoned on the front of her worn sweatshirt.

Eva petted the dog softly on the head. Huh. BAC used to be a contractor for the Department of Defense. Had the dead woman stumbled across the device in the old building? Or had she worked for them back in the day?

The dog whined, and Eva fed her another bit of jerky. Tamara grabbed the black box and bent to pick up one of the dead woman's hands. She placed a limp index finger on the biometric scanner. Red light. She tried each finger until it opened with the thumb.

Inside sat a vial of Shield.

Daniel jerked to his feet, eyes narrowed. "Coded to the Virginia facility."

"This is a fresh kill. How did you not hear anything happening?" Eva's question was directed to the Shielded militia behind them.

Trae shrugged. "We were scouting the westbound tunnel and the area around the exit on the surface, sir…ma'am. Somebody must have seen we were gone and somehow gained entry. They could have somehow passed the sentry at the top. Or possibly, there's another entrance nearby we haven't found yet."

"Which means whoever it is probably knows we're here." Daniel cursed, handing the vial back to Eva and striding toward the exit. "We need two more with the train. And change of plan, my team is investigating the BAC. Shoot anybody who comes down those stairs and doesn't give the signal. And get rid of the dog."

Eva rushed to keep up, the German Shepherd following her. "No, Nala's staying with us. She could know something."

Daniel shot her an incredulous look. "Nala? You already named her? We don't have time for this, Eva."

"Have you looked at her closely, Daniel? Something's different about her. I want to keep her nearby, and study her some more. Maybe when we get back, Alec could examine her as well. She could be useful."

"I doubt it. But we don't have time to argue. She's your responsibility. Keep her quiet."

Eva stopped and narrowed her eyes at his retreating back.

"Come on Nala. Let's leave the condescending ass alone." She patted her leg. The dog tilted her head, looked back at the body of her former master, and then continued to trot at Eva's side. Nala looked up at her, that flash of luminescence there and then gone. "You're not what you seem, are you, girl?"

The dog cocked her head.

Guards came to lift the body between them. Daniel led the way back to the exit.

A hellscape met their group on the surface.

"Holy hell. This is worse than back home," Alec gripped Tamara's hand. Chet just stared, his entire body tensed as tight as a mandolin string.

In the distance, mangled skyscrapers sprouted from the earth like the sharp teeth of some demon spawn. A trail of devastation led right to their present location. Craters dotted the landscape, a fishing expedition for what lay beneath. Mounds of twisted cars, concrete slabs, wooden beams, desiccated trees, and downed power poles with wires dangling lay scattered about.

At one time, the entrance to the tunnel had been camouflaged with its surroundings, the dirt over the top making it impossible to see from the air or even from a distance. A metal structure like the cellphone towers from the old days had fallen to its side, a dead animal with its legs dangling in the air.

"It took us two days to dig out around this hatch. Nobody could have come through here until recently, sir. I don't even think a trace was visible from the surface under all this junk." Trae gripped his rifle tighter, the only outward sign he was nervous about Daniel's answer.

"If there's one entrance, there's more. Leave somebody just inside the door. I don't want their presence noted by anybody in the city. Whoever killed that woman is still around, either in the tunnels or on the surface. My bet is on the surface since it was so close to the exit. Let's move out. Everybody has their assignments." He checked his compass and veered off to the right, leaving Tamara, Alec, and Chet to take their assigned team in the other direction toward the Federal building.

Eva touched Tamara's arm. "Be careful. Don't take any chances. Try to find what we need and get back to the train. This place gives me the creeps."

Tamara shivered a little. "Me too. You gonna be okay with grumpy-ass?"

"It's not the first time I've had to deal with his mood swings. I'll be alright."

The other group picked their way to easier walking and didn't look back.

Nala looked up at her.

"Let's catch up."

The dog blinked and took off after Daniel and the others as if she'd understood Eva's words.

Eva jogged after her.

————

Even Shield didn't prevent her from stumbling through the rubble that used to be Kansas City. Shattered glass mixed with crumbling concrete made it next to impossible to move silently. Add in the obstacles of burnt-out vehicles, concrete barriers, and toppled buildings, and it was amazing their group could find a path through any of it.

At least it didn't smell like death and rotting corpses. Animals and time had decomposed or eaten any fleshy remains after the Collapse until nothing but ossified bones remained.

The five of them walked in a single file line, keeping to the shadows as much as possible. The streets were deserted, the lack of anything but this desolate wasteland leaving Eva edgy and irritable. Nala's previous owner's death in the tunnels proved there was at least one other person alive somewhere, so where were they? Eva touched a point on the rough map where he'd marked the black site, and looked around her. "I think we're going the wrong way."

"It's only a slight detour." Daniel inched his way around a pile of rubble. He pointed off in the distance toward where an entire city block's worth of skyscrapers tumbled to the ground. "We'll never get around that before dark."

"Why BAC first? What are you hoping to find?"

Their trio of young guards scanned the debris, guns at the ready.

"That woman had a vial of Shield, Eva. The stable doses of serum we developed during the Year of Hell haven't left the Territory. So how did she get it? It could be fake, but it had our same organizational coding but with the numeral for Virginia. We had some of those doses in the freezer but we're a thousand miles away, so it's not as if I can do inventory."

"You're worried somebody on our side stole it."

Daniel remained silent, a stubborn set to his jaw.

"Do you think I stole it while under the influence?" Eva's own self-doubt and black spots in her memory produced the horrid thought. Had she somehow slipped her guard and stolen a vial of Shield to give to some unknown traitor? It all sounded ridiculous, even to her own addled ears.

Long moments passed. The wind danced through the remnants of the old buildings, weaving its way through the broken remains like the thousands of ghosts that haunted these streets. Nala sniffed here and there but remained content to stay by Eva's side. The three Shielded militia had fallen back even farther, the distance an apt analogy for her and Daniel. He thought her a traitor.

"I don't think you'd do it on purpose," he said, finally.

"Is that supposed to make me feel better?"

An ache she'd never heard before entered Daniel's voice. "Ever since you blew up the meteorite mine, you've been differ-ent. Disconnected somehow. You were sleepwalking the night before we left to come here. You have access to the MUC and to Shield—"

"And so do about a dozen other people. That doesn't prove a thing. There's a guard on me twenty-four seven now. When am I supposed to be doing all this stealing? Tell me that."

Instead of replying, he froze, Nala doing the same, her ears swiveled forward. Daniel cocked his head to the side and held up a fist to stop. They all fell still and silent, copying his movements. A faint sound of voices drifted to them, low and distant but getting closer.

Daniel signaled the others to retreat to a pile of rubble and hold. He grabbed her hand and dragged her into the doorway of a fallen building. Pressed against him, one foot on a pile of stone and one wrapped around Daniel's calf, she held onto him for dear life. Nala hunkered on her haunches, ears forward.

"…no way I'm doing that. He already has enough," a disembodied male voice whined.

"You'll find your head alongside those others if you're not careful. The boss doesn't take too kindly to being told what he can and can't do." This voice was rawer, scratchier.

"One of these days, I'll take one of them for myself and leave this shithole, just watch."

The other guy snorted. "You're a dumbass, you know that?"

Eva lost balance, and her foot scraped against the base of the wall. She caught herself. Daniel gripping her arm so hard that if she weren't Shielded, she'd be bruised.

"You hear that?" The whiny one said.

"Hear what?"

"I thought I heard footsteps."

The voices got closer, stopping just on the other side of the wall.

"You're just hearing things. Who'd come around here these days? Nobody wants to tangle with the boss. He'd eat 'em." Raucous chuckling followed this announcement. Eva's stomach turned. Cannibals.

"Shhh. Stop your blabbering, and let me listen."

Eva held her breath, and Daniel's pulse beat steadily against her hand. Nala's hackles rose, but she didn't make a sound, just waited.

One minute. Two. Seconds ticked by. The two men's ragged breath grated against her sensitive eardrums.

"Huh. I guess you're right. Must just be these old buildings. Let's get going before our rations get eaten up."

The other man harrumphed, and their voices drifted back toward the center of town.

Eva slumped forward, and Daniel wrapped his arms around her. Their hearts synced up, beating as one like before they'd drifted apart. Their connection had always extended beyond love, beyond survival or respect. *Life or death.* Sometimes both. It tugged at them constantly. Even now.

She raised her face to his, their lips only inches away from each other. He blinked and let her loose gently, stepping back, hands clenched at his sides. Now definitely wasn't the time for such a thing. But still…they hadn't been that close since the time on the observation deck above the TMRWS so many months before.

"Too close," he murmured.

She didn't know if he was talking about the two men or the fact they had nearly kissed after almost getting detected. Probably both.

CHAPTER 5

MIA

September, 2072

The path to the top entrance of the MUC was marked if you knew what to look for, a stack of stones here, a patch of planted unique shrub there. There was some minimal radiation along the way, but nothing Shield couldn't handle. And nothing like what one would encounter a hundred yards to either side.

She jogged down the path until she reached the door to the MUC. Tracks led up to it along the base of the hill. Most had been scraped away in a haphazard manner, like someone had tried to cover the path, but Mia's eyesight—and the headlamp adorning her head—was better than most. The gilly-suit-like material on mesh used to conceal the emergency entrance bunched at the corners revealing the cement adit to the stairwell. She pushed it aside.

The faceplate to the biometric scanner hung on a stripped wire, damaged months ago and unable to be repaired. Mia fingered the broken padlock next to it. It dangled from the makeshift eye-ring drilled into the cement.

It wasn't impossible to find the top entrance, just damn near so. Somebody would have to know it was out here, at the very least, and the sporadic radiation in the Reach meant few would try.

She unholstered a pistol she'd scavenged from her father's side-by-side and crept through the suffocatingly narrow tunnel. It opened up into an old empty guard room. Huge metal girders reinforced the ceiling, bowing in from outside pressure. Patched cement splotched the walls in squared away chunks. A door leading to the break room opened to the right. Pistol out in front of her, she entered the room. Drawers and cupboards had been riffled through but nobody remained.

More signs of repair etched themselves on the pockmarked cement and crumbling stairs. The few times she'd been inside this entrance, it amazed her that anybody had survived the bombings of the facility. It had taken years to dig out the topside. The only reason her parents deemed it necessary was to uncover access to some of the other floors for reasons only they knew.

Mia headed down the stairs but froze at a banging sound somewhere below her. It echoed up the shaft with a *bam* and the *zing* of a ricochet.

The noise hadn't been close, but it either indicated there were more than two parties trying to infiltrate the MUC, or somebody was trying to break their way through a door. Either way, her entire body tensed, and she eased down the stairs.

Mia kept her back against the inside wall of the stairwell, using it for cover as she wound her way down. Landings and doors opened leapfrogging every other turn. Her father had them welded shut in recent years, keeping any un-scavenged surviving contents where they belonged: buried in the past.

As she descended, the emergency lights became scarce. Dim shadows pooled around them, casting the empty spaces into gray nothingness.

A scuffle and grunt drifted up to her, closer now. Mia eased around the last corner to sub-level seventeen, her weapon clenched in a tight grip. Two men wrestled on the floor, one spurting blood from his hand, his face turned away from her. He had a knife to the other man's throat.

Cooper.

"Both of you freeze! Or I will shoot." Mia aimed at whoever was on top of Cooper. Until she got this sorted, she didn't trust either one.

The man on top of Cooper turned black, crazy eyes her direction and she stumbled back in shock. Tobias.

Most importantly, who was in the wrong here?

Indecision racked her for a handful of seconds.

Cooper used the distraction to wriggle his arms out of Tobias's full-body hold, getting a lock on either side of the man's shirt with crossed wrists and pulling the fabric in a chokehold across his throat.

"I said freeze, Cooper."

"I can't." He ground out through clenched teeth.

"Tobias, let him up."

The giant man growled low in his throat but didn't seem to hear her.

"See what I mean? He is definitely not in a reasonable frame of mind. You either trust me or you don't." Cooper squeezed harder and Tobias shifted to the side. He took the opening and twisted his hips out from beneath the enraged man, switching into a chokehold from behind. Cooper clung to the other man's back like a spider monkey.

"The thing is, I don't think I really do," Mia kept the gun trained in the general direction of both men.

Tobias flailed, his meaty arms trying to grab the man on his back. He crashed around the room and Mia had to back up not to get taken out by the erratic moves.

"What the hell is wrong with him?"

"How should I know?" Cooper's words were a breathy rasp.

Mia tried again. "Tobias? Are you okay?"

A blank, furious stare met her words.

"A little help? This isn't even slowing him down." Cooper tightened the chokehold without much effect.

On one hand, Tobias had been her father's right-hand-person since before she was born, but on the other, he was acting drugged. Crazed. What the hell could drug a Shielded person? And whether or not she trusted Cooper was irrelevant at this point. If Tobias needed help, he had to be put down to even start.

"Get him turned. A bullet should at least slow him down." The decision made, she aimed the gun with more confidence.

"Uh-huh." Cooper's words were lost as he tried to stay on the other man's back. Tobias thrashed and whipped around, finally reeling back, slamming Cooper into the bricks with a massive thud. The cement wall cracked with the impact and Cooper's hold loosened.

It also gave Mia the perfect shot. For the second time in two days, she aimed and fired at somebody she considered extended family. *Don't think about Chet now.*

The giant man howled as he collapsed to the ground, clawing toward her, teeth bared in a snarl.

She put another bullet into his forehead and the feral lights went out of his eyes.

"Quick, help me get him into the closet." She holstered the weapon and grabbed Tobias's arms.

Cooper sat sprawled against the base of the wall, pain etched into his face. "Give me a sec."

"We may not have a sec. Whatever he is on could make him recover faster. Your chokehold definitely didn't have an effect, and even the Shielded will go down for a few minutes after a chokehold. So, now, Cooper." Mia struggled to drag Tobias across the floor to the emptied supply closet.

"You sure are bossy." Cooper crawled to his feet, closing his eyes as he wobbled in place. He turned to place a hand on the wall. His entire back was splotched with blood where particles of concrete wall had penetrated his skin through the thin fabric of his shirt.

She winced but didn't say anything.

The man was tough, there was no doubt. He pushed off the wall, hunched his shoulders in pain, and picked up Tobias's legs. The two of them wrestled him into the supply closet. Cooper wedged a chair under the doorknob, bending it so it wouldn't turn, and then rested his head on his arms against the wall, closing his eyes.

"Cooper?" Mia hadn't felt his presence in her head on the way down, so whatever it was that made her aware of him had faded. "Where's my Dad? Jack?"

A smile lit his face, a single dimple in his left cheek appearing. "I ditched them a couple of hours ago in some rustic tunnel system they didn't seem to know about. They wouldn't listen to reason."

"How did you know about this entrance? It's classified."

Cooper shook his head. "Your dear ol' dad and his classifications. Doesn't he know the war is over? And the old government?"

"I'm sure he's aware." She deadpanned. "You didn't answer my question."

"Maybe I was just looking for you and stumbled across it." He shrugged.

"Bullshit." Some part of Mia wanted to believe him, but another, more logical side said it was exactly how she named it. Until she figured out what the man was hiding—and she was for damn sure he was hiding something—she couldn't trust him all the way, that nagging familiarity or not.

Cooper turned, a trickle of blood still running down his face from a split lip. It faded to a thin line. He raised his hands like he was surrendering. "Maybe. Maybe not. We should talk to your mom about it, and she's down there." He pointed to the ground before reaching up to wipe away the blood from his face, a quizzical, confused look taking the place of the grin.

Shield should have healed it completely by now.

"Again, how did you know this entrance was here? And did you break the lock?"

He shrugged, meeting her eyes clear and steady. "I was on the crew that started the excavation project back in '53. All newly injected were. It built discipline, and Daniel didn't want any unShielded over this direction for very long. To answer the second question, it was already broken when I got here. Tobias must not have had a key."

Mia regarded him. "Who else helped with the excavation back then?"

He narrowed his eyes. "Think one of them might be your traitor?"

"Just covering all my bases."

"What do I get for the information?"

"It's not like I'm asking you to give up who you're working for, the worker list is information I can get on my own. Now, spill it or you're not coming with me." She narrowed her eyes at him.

"There, see, now I get something out of the deal." Cooper looked at a spot behind her shoulder and squinted his eyes in thought. "Layla—who died in Montana years ago—Spencer, Tobias, Lourdes, Chuck. Oh, and Dr. Badal. He was always pissy about helping out, thought he needed to be doing something more important. Daniel kept him here in case we unearthed anything scientifically relevant. His words, not mine."

Her stomach fell. Only Dr. Badal and Tobias were still around. Amrit. It made a certain kind of sense. According to her mother's journals, he and Sarah had been close in the MUC so many years ago. She heaved a sigh, adding him to her list of possible traitors. "Amrit has access to this entrance. He and Sarah could have drugged Tobias and come down here. She's the one who grabbed me earlier. Don't touch anything."

A flicker of surprise flashed across Cooper's face hidden quickly by his grin. She'd come to realize the man could hide a lot behind a smile.

"No promises." Cooper winked and butterflies fluttered for a split second. Inappropriate butterflies that had no business moving about her stomach. What was it with this man? First the tunnel by her mother's train, and now the wink?

Hardening her heart against the charm, she squished the butterflies. "I'm serious."

"Copy that. Let's get on with it, then."

The duo approached the last landing without further incident.

"Titanium security door, working biometrics. Blood and retinal scanner, huh?" Cooper examined the two different scanners on the wall beside the door.

"Only the best down here."

He quirked an eyebrow. "But not at the top? Interesting priorities."

"The rest of the floors were cleared of valuables a long time ago, Cooper, so don't get any ideas." Mia winced at the finger poke for the blood sample and a beam of infrared light swept over her right eyeball.

Locks clicked inside of the door.

Mia paused, body tense, and drew her weapon. "You trained with my parents and Jack?"

"Is that rhetorical?" Cooper gripped his gun tighter, muscles flexing.

"Before you left, were you ever down here?"

"Not since I was a little boy during the experiment before the Collapse, so essentially, no. Very few were allowed."

Mia nodded. "This door opens into a hallway that branches in three directions after a hundred feet. Right takes you to the secondary labs, straight has a courtyard in a natural cavern with doorways to offices, a kitchen, and bunks. Left is the main lab, and eventually the conference room with the other way out of here. We clear the right, center, left. Got it?"

"Copy that."

Mia narrowed her eyes. That had been way too easy. "So you're just going to follow my lead, no argument?"

"You know more about the layout, I'll provide cover if need be. Why would I argue with logic?"

"I don't know, you have the whole lone wolf thing going for you."

"But that's not where I started. Now, let's get this show on the road."

Mia gave him one last wary look before he swung the six-inch thick metal door open. She stepped over the threshold and he covered her, closing, but not latching, it behind them. Mia raised her eyebrows in question.

Escape route, Cooper mouthed. It only took her a beat to agree. If shit went sideways, precious seconds or minutes counted. There could be either no trouble here or Sarah could have gained access after leaving Mia, and all hell would break loose. Best to have options.

Voices drifted from the right but she couldn't make out the words. If the MUC had been infiltrated, they still needed to check the other passageways and not leave their asses exposed.

Cooper crouched across from her. He eased around the corner to look down the right hand hallway.

He nodded to her and she swept to the left. Cooper followed.

The two of them cleared the first of the secondary labs in record time, their actions coordinated and smooth. As they reached the last room with *Lab Twenty-One* written in block letters over the double doors, something on the other side squeaked, like a wheeled office chair or unoiled hinge.

Without even glancing back, she signaled a retreat back to the last lab—just in case. Lab Twenty-One dead ended this hallway so there was nowhere else to go but back.

She eased the door shut and a gray half-light enveloped her and Cooper. Somebody pushed through the doors.

Who is it? Cooper mouthed.

Mia shrugged and peeked through the small window in the door. A woman, her hair tied in a tight black braid strode down the hall away from them. Sarah. Goosebumps erupted along Mia's arms.

Lab Twenty-One remained locked at all times. Level Four containment freezers and other thermo storage units were secured within its depths. She'd only been allowed into the room once—not that she hadn't tried to snoop since.

Cooper's entire body tensed next to her. His eyes were glued on Sarah's back through the window, narrowed and cold. He straightened, and a resolved look settled over his features.

Mia felt his heart rate pick up and she put her mouth to his ear, so close yet not touching. "What?"

The gloom hid his expression, but he didn't pull away. Instead, he turned to face her. All around, shadows lurked. The outlines of counters and cupboards marched around the room, surrounding them in silence. It created a bubble, a moment in time where everything stood still, like holding your breath before plunging into deep water. The moment lasted less than thirty seconds. Less than fifteen.

It felt like a lifetime.

Cooper framed her face with his hands, and that spark of his lit bright and strong in her mind. *There you are.* Warmth flooded her brain.

For an absurd, wild moment she thought he was going to kiss her. Instead he tilted her head, his lips almost touching the curve of her ear. "Just know, whatever happens next, I genuinely did want to help you. I'm sorry."

Her heart skipped a beat, the words ominous.

Stark determination turned to ice-cold focus on Cooper's face. He shoved her away from him and opened the door, slamming it in her face and bending the metal of the outside handle until the lever couldn't move on her side.

He didn't meet her gaze through the window.

Mia yanked at the door, furious. Instead of following Sarah, Cooper pivoted and shoved through the double doors of Lab Twenty-One.

CHAPTER 6

COOPER

September 2072

An unfamiliar knot twisted in Cooper's gut and he refused to look back at the outline of Mia's angry face framed by the narrow window of the door. Betrayal usually didn't bother him when he felt his cause was righteous.

Somehow, the Seeking burned just a tad brighter in his consciousness as her anger flared. Each flicker of fury cast an ethereal glow that guided his thoughts toward her exact location, riding the turbulent sea of breaking her trust.

He pushed through the doors to Lab Twenty-One. Gun raised, ready to fire at anybody remaining after Sarah left, he moved across the room.

It stank of industrial cleaner and formaldehyde. Stainless steel topped counters lined the wall across from the freezers. Inset lights shone from the cavernous ceiling, the HVAC tubing snaking around the room, dropping exhaust fume hoods next to three workstations like an antique Mario Brothers game. A door at the back opened into a room with long observation windows and a decontamination center with another door and window on the far side.

Sarah. Dammit all to hell, what was she *doing* here? If she saw him working with the Territory…They were supposed to be in recon mode only, him being forced to gather information on the dam on the eastern border and Basin's defenses, and her little minions infiltrating the less stable parts of the Territory to sow discontent. Destabilize by stirring up opposing factions, demoralize by spreading misinformation until nobody knew just quite what to think. End game was overthrowing the established government. Classic. Textbook.

It's what a weaker force had to do in light of a stronger opponent.

If Sarah was here, it could only mean one of two things: either she was escalating the protocols, or she was here without the Western Coalition's knowledge for her own reasons.

Neither of those boded well for his plan to rescue Claire and get as far away from this place as possible. Basin stirred up way too many memories and feelings he'd long since buried. *Are they buried, though?*

Six-foot tall, glass-faced refrigerators and freezers jutted out into the room from one wall forming evenly spaced peninsulas. There were four such rows of three freezers a piece, well-lit, their contents tidy. Like looking at the freezer aisles on old grocery store advertisements.

On silent feet, he swept around each one. No breathing or other signs of life occupied the lab, but he had to be sure. Most people on Shield could hold their breath and control their heart rate long enough to rival even the Shaolin Monks.

It was all clear.

Cooper scanned the contents of the first freezer, looking for small clear tubes that held a numbered, blue liquid in them—Shield. Damn scientists and their coding. He had the one he needed memorized but the organization of the storage container was like a foreign language. He moved onto the next one quickly. That door wouldn't hold Mia forever, and he had a sneaking suspicion she would come for him first. A slight wave of guilt hit him.

You're doing this for Claire. Mia means nothing.

He scoffed at the lie. The…feeling wasn't enough to halt his mission, but there was something, just under the surface. Beyond the childhood memories. Even beyond the spark of connection, or the vibe of attraction. He'd heard once that like called to like more times than not. Was that what it was? Hell, maybe it was just the Seeking. Her presence again, bright and strong like a star.

Why had he re-initiated it? If Cooper was being honest with himself, he hadn't been able to help himself. There was no way he could pursue the pull, the tug, but his hands had found her, sought her out. For all he knew it was just Shield drawing two warriors together.

Each freezer in the first two rows were duds. Odd specimens that looked suspiciously like human fetuses floating in sealed gallon-sized jars took up the third row. At the last one, he came up empty and kicked the damn thing.

Running fingers through his dust-filled hair, he held in a growl of frustration. He wouldn't get another shot at this. Every-thing rode on his ability to find a sample of Shield.

His freedom. His daughter's health.

Fuck it.

Cooper punched the side of the nearest freezer with a resounding thud, leaving a fist-sized dent.

It had to be here. Daniel wouldn't store anything this sensi-tive anywhere else, even if he'd built other labs in the Territory. He breathed in deep and examined the room again. Were they in a different lab? No, it had to be this one.

He walked over to the observation window to the decontami-nation room. Sinks, looped misters, and compartments for hazmat suits occupied the smaller space, nothing out of place. From this angle, the backs of the freezers resembled rectangular black boxes, their cords plugging into outlets inlaid on the floor next to them so as not to trip anybody up.

All except for the last row closest to the back of the room. The cord to the three freezers created a daisy chain, looping into each other until the last one disappeared into a neatly bored hole in the wall.

Cooper tilted his head and peered closer. A thin seam ran along the backside of the freezers on the floor, another seam running parallel in front, the two about five feet apart like rails of a track.

Cooper followed one of the seams until it reached the wall and continued up toward the ceiling. He knocked on the panel beside the last freezer. A slight hollow thud.

He grinned. Leave it to Daniel to hide secrets within secrets.

Going with his gut, Cooper opened the door on the unit. Frigid air blasted his face. He felt around the sides. Nothing. But the top gave him what he wanted. With satisfaction, he pressed the half-dollar sized button, and the freezer started to hum. Cooper took a step back.

The entire section of wall and the peninsula of freezers glided across the room, revealing another lab the size of a large dining hall. A dozen morgue freezers lined the far wall, and two more Level Fours stood guard at the far end. A single stainless steel counter with an exhaust hood above it abutted the wall next to the door panel.

Cooper took a step toward the medical freezers. He really needed to hurry. Mia was on the move.

Too late. A pistol cocked behind him and he froze, his feet lead weights. He was close. So damn close. *Joke's on me.*

"You know you don't have to cock a semi-automatic, right?" He tried for his usual cocky smartassery but it came out stilted and a little desperate.

Mia wasn't having it, anyway. "It has a more dramatic effect when I do. How did you know this was here?"

"I didn't. I do have some rather fine-tuned powers of observation, though."

Mia snorted. "You betrayed me."

"Did I? I thought I just locked you in a room."

"Turn around, Cooper, so I can see your lying face."

He pivoted to face her. Hurt and rage twisted her lips and made her eyes blaze in a glorious dark hazel storm.

Cooper sobered. "Can I explain?"

"No. I might just lock you in here until whatever is going on down the hall is sorted. You know Sarah."

"Yes." He drew in a breath. Either he had to trust her, or they would fight and somebody would get shot. Too much lay on the line for him to allow that to happen. "Sarah's people are holding my daughter hostage in return for my cooperation. They know my connection to Daniel and the experiments because Sarah told them."

Mia's hands tightened on the gun, confusion added to the other emotions. She didn't really have a good poker face; everything ran right on the surface with Mia. Just like her mother.

"Daughter?"

"Foster daughter."

"Damn it, Cooper. You've been working for Sarah all along."

He took a step forward, hands out as if to calm her. She leaned into her stance with the pistol and glared. If it went off, they were both toast.

"No, I'm trying to fix it—to get me and Claire out of this mess for good. That's why I need what's in that freezer. Sarah's not supposed to be here. Something else is going on I don't know about. I swear I'll tell you everything I do know, just let me get a dose of Shield." God, he was almost there.

Mia's entire body tensed. "I don't understand."

"If Claire doesn't get a dose of Shield, she'll die. The people I work for used one of the old biowarfare agents, like what was used on Jerome. She needs a maintenance dose of their cure every day or she dies. Shield will cure her forever, not just on a daily basis."

"Okay. But then what? I can't just let you walk out of here after this."

"Please, Mia. I never beg, but I am begging you now. I am telling you the complete truth. I swear it on my parent's graves. They're buried right outside the Territory on the old family farm."

Mia examined the room, her eyes pausing on the morgue freezers. She shook her head and Cooper's heart tightened in his chest. He'd have to take her out. He'd do anything, even this, for Claire. Forgo home and finding the answers to why his parents would sacrifice everything to be a part of some human experiment. Forgo pursuit of whatever connection lay between him and this woman.

"Trust is something earned. Built over time and experience. My father hid this room from me all these years. I always wondered where he kept Shield." Her eyebrows drew together. "Everybody must think me incompetent and stupid if they're not giving me all the information. Go get your damn sample, Cooper. It needs to be refrigerated, so won't last very long anyway."

Pain joined the maelstrom of emotion on her face. She didn't lower the weapon all the way but the tip dipped to aim at the floor instead of his face.

He dug in his pocket for the device he'd grabbed at his parent's house—was it only three days ago? The compact rectangular box was a little bigger than the old-fashioned cell phones before the war. He flipped the switch. The small nuclear-powered battery clicked on, the light turning green. Mia shifted behind him to get a better look.

"What is that?"

"Nuclear-powered portable freezer." He placed it on the counter and opened one of the medical freezers. Bingo. An entire shelf of vials, all with the organization code for Shield, glowing turquoise in the light. Insulated padding surrounded a vial-sized depression in the device. He placed in the dose of Shield and closed it, initializing the fingerprint scanner on the side of his pinkie.

"It still works? That's impossible."

"Tell that to the scientists who invented it." He stuffed it back into the pocket of his cargo pants and buttoned it shut. "Where to next?"

"Just like that?" Incredulity creased Mia's face.

"If Sarah's here, it means she's not with my kid. I'd like to keep it that way until I can make it back to Montana where she's being held."

"Hopefully your little side trip didn't cost lives." Mia said sourly. She glared at him and tilted her head, contemplating something. Maybe what she wanted to do to his face.

He shifted uncomfortably.

"Don't you dare. You need my help, especially if Sarah's here. You don't know what she's capable of." Cooper glanced at his watch. Only fifteen minutes had passed since he and Mia had walked through the door of the MUC.

"How do you know what I was thinking?" Mia lowered the gun.

"You looked like you wanted to wallop me over the head with your pistol and dump my body somewhere deep and dark. I know the look." Cooper walked to the double doors. "Let's go see why Sarah's here. If we can stop her here, then I have more time to get back to Montana."

Mia hesitated, indecision playing across her eyes and tensing her body. "Cooper, stop."

He met her eyes. The storm had simmered but not by much. Every muscle wanted to run, to take his chances across the MUC to the emergency door, through the irradiated desert, and across hundreds of miles of drought-plagued land to get to his daughter. Something in her voice though…so, he waited.

Steel laced her words and entered the set of her mouth. "At

the first sign of treachery, I take you out. Sarah could be on my ass, about to kill me, but I'll make sure you're going down too. Do you understand?"

He liked this Mia. Fiery. A definite mix of her parents; in that moment, all of Eva's intelligence and Daniel's backbone.

"I got what I came for. My only goal is to save my little girl. The only reason I did anything for Sarah is because I was forced to. If I have to help you first, so be it. No more lying."

"Prove it."

He smirked. The world was lighter with Shield in his pocket. "Yes, ma'am."

———

Loud voices echoed along the hall. Mia let him keep his gun. Her presence lurked behind him like a hurt, dark cloud. He didn't blame her. She'd been betrayed a lot in the last couple of days by people closer and more important to her than him.

Two bodies, a man and a woman, lay on the ground outside the main lab. He and Mia weren't the first ones here, then.

After the intersection, the words became more distinct.

"The past is never dead, dear sister," Sarah's hard voice, cold and calculating. "It haunts us for the rest of our lives. I'm taking what I need and blowing this shithole to hell. Finishing what the Eastern Bloc started almost thirty years ago."

"Stop, please. You're sick, Sarah, let me help you. I know what's making you sick." Eva pleaded.

"Press self-destruct, Amrit. We just need Shield, the samples, and the hard drive, then we can go. Tobias should have our transport ready," Sarah said.

"Yes, ma'am." Amrit responded.

Cooper frowned. How had Tobias been supposed to arrange transport five levels above their head?

He waved his hand. Mia focused her attention on him, a cold, hard look, so much like Daniel's it gave Cooper pause. She was beyond pissed. Good. She would need it.

He signaled that they needed to enter, now. Mia nodded.

Cooper veered to the left of the doorway, his back to the wall. Mia went right. Her every move imprinted on his brain.

"I see we're late to the party." Cooper scanned the room. Eva pointed a pistol at Sarah, who had Rani tied to a chair. She lay against the workstation island, blood spreading like a Rorschach inkblot in deep, rich red. Amrit, the sour bastard, stood at the computer, a finger hovering over the keyboard.

Everyone's eyes swiveled to them.

CHAPTER 7
EVA

August, 2055

As buildings went in post-Collapse Kansas City, the Biological Advancements Center had fared better than most. The skyscrapers surrounding it took the brunt of the bombings in downtown, their broken backs and stubby remnants little more than rubble. Empty window frames peered out of the remaining five stories of the institute like vacant eyes.

The once tall tower—ten-stories or more—was a mutilated creature, with its upper concrete flanks shattered and entire upper floors ripped away to expose the steel bones beneath. A musty decay lingered, a reminder of all the death congregated in such a relatively small area. Where glass doors used to stand, only the metal frames remained.

"We'll start at the lowest level and work our way up." Daniel's voice was just above a whisper but carried to them all due to Shield.

Eva picked her way through the doorway and into the dim, cool shade of the building's interior. "What if they have an underground facility? It won't be easy to find."

"They don't. At least they didn't a year and a half before the

Collapse." He ducked through the door and duck-walked toward the large reception desk, half-buried by a t-beam and concrete. They had to tread carefully, not only because of the unstable conditions but because if the mystery woman had been here, there could be more people.

The trio of Shielded militia followed, moving quickly to flank her and Daniel. She craned her head, trying to pick up the slightest noise. Nothing. Not even the creak of an old building settling.

Daniel signaled for them to move out, rifles ready and covering all angles. Nala trotted beside Eva, ears perked up. Since they'd entered the building, the dog had become more animated, hopping from paw to paw in a silly dance.

An elevator bay, doors cracked open, was off to the right, a once-plush waiting room to the left.

"Stairwell." Daniel indicated with a nod of his head.

Nala already waited by the unhinged door. It yawned open to an emergency staircase, a set of stairs descending to a sub-level, the other ascending into gloom. The dog looked at them and then took the stairs going down.

Eva shrugged in Daniel's direction. He just shook his head and followed Nala into the darkness below. The ambient light from above shone enough to light their way down.

So, he had decided to follow the dog?

Ha. And he thought her a nuisance.

They passed one door, locked and intact. The click of the German Shepherd's claws echoed against the concrete stairwell, descending further into the bowels of the building.

On the next sub-level flight, she was assaulted with a tsunami of sensations, leaving her battered and overwhelmed. She collapsed to her knees, hands clawing the sides of her head at the rush of erratic anger and fear, helplessness and grief.

A hand from behind caught her before she toppled down the stairs. *Trae,* some dim part of her brain, acknowledged as if through the hollow sound of a conch shell. Was it her own voice or somebody—some*thing*—else's?

"Sir!" He hissed into the darkness. Eva barely caught the word, so entrenched in the violent thoughts and pinpricks of a presence just out of her reach.

A whimper lodged in her throat, each wave more intense than the next. All external feelings disappeared as images flooded her mind, the colors wild and inverted. She panted, trying to control whatever was happening in her head.

And just as suddenly as it had begun, it stopped. She fell limp against something warm and solid.

Eva flickered open heavy eyelids, and Daniel's face materialized above her. She tried to sit up, but he pushed her back down, her head cradled in his lap, his back against the stairwell wall. "Shh, take it easy."

At some point, Trae had turned on the light at the end of his rifle, and everything had a harsh, clear quality, a sharp contrast to what had just happened in her mind's eye.

Worry lines etched Daniel's face, and his entire body felt as tense as a coiled spring. His hazel eyes regarded her, their depths a dark moss green in the shadow created by the stairwell overhang.

She drew in a long breath, taking stock of her body and mind. No aches or pains. No headache. Just a heavy weakness that weighed down her limbs. Shield would take care of it, she had no doubt. *But what if the enzyme* in *Shield is part of the cause? The enzyme we got from the meteorite…*

Like calling to like.

Was it that easy? Could it be that the enzymes just wanted to reunite with the whole? Were they sentient, or had they just become so because of their human hosts?

It all felt too fictional. Too…insane. She thought back to each time she'd had a reaction. How Daniel hadn't been affected at all by the meteorite at the black site, except to almost be attacked by them. What if they had been attacking an enemy enzyme?

There had to be more than one of the larger meteorites. It still didn't explain why Daniel hadn't reacted like her. Their doses of Shield had come from the same Tau-159 sample—hadn't they?

Eva closed her eyes, not letting him see the dawning realization sweep across her features. Had he known? There were two different codings on their supply of Shield after all.

Daniel had skirted around it, but his need to make all the TMRWS operational overrode all else, his focus consumed by a project he'd worked on for decades, long before he'd met her. If Shield was her baby, the TMRWS was his.

He placed a hand on her forehead. "I'm sending you back to the train with Trae."

"No." She batted the hand away and struggled to sit up. With a frustrated sigh, her head landed back on his lap.

"You can't even sit up, and we can't afford another episode like this. What happened?" He didn't touch her again, his arms to either side of him on the cold concrete. Only his now inscrutable gaze showed itself.

"Nothing, just a headache. It's gone now. Shield must have taken care of it. Let me up, we need to catch up with Nala."

"The dog is fine. You are not. Has this happened before?"

"Nothing like this, no. I'm completely in control. See," she moved her hands up and down, wiggling her fingers, "not an involuntary tendency in sight. Just give me a minute to catch my breath."

She dropped her hands to her chest, heart pounding beneath her palm.

"I can force you."

Eva squeezed her eyes shut and expelled a breath. "You could. But Trae's young and relatively inexperienced. Who's to say what would happen once we got back to the train?"

Trae shifted uncomfortably next to them.

"Don't test my patience, Eva."

"And don't test mine, Daniel. We each have our specialties.

What if you miss something because I'm not here? I'm coming. End of argument."

He narrowed his eyes, lips pursed. Nobody talked to him that way—and got away with it—except for her and Jack.

"Please," she said softly. "We're close to something. I can feel it."

Whatever he saw on her face softened his mouth. "You're not to leave my sight."

She struggled to sit, the world spinning. This time she stayed upright. "Even when I'm walking behind you?"

"Don't be a smartass." A muscle in his jaw twitched.

"Yessir."

———

Two sublevels later, they reached Nala, sitting patiently by the landing door. She tilted her head, tail thumping a couple of times on the floor, and perked her ears as if to say, "took you long enough."

Daniel stared at the dog, and the dog stared back.

The man blinked first.

"Huh. That was strange," Daniel said.

"Told you." Eva put her hand on the door handle. "Ready?"

He gave the dog one more considering glance and nodded, readying his pistol. Eva opened the door so that she was behind it and Daniel and the others could enter, checking the interior with lights on. This far below ground, any gunfire would be masked, so they didn't try to hide their presence. Besides, the place just felt empty, and wouldn't Nala alert them to anybody else?

Maybe she was giving the dog too much credit.

Eva entered last, pistol in front of her, ready to fire just in case.

At one time, the Biological Advancement Center had been one of the foremost private research labs in neuroscience. Piggybacking off of NYU's cognitive and behavioral health programs, they studied the physiology of human neurodivergence. An area of focus Eva delved into after early prototype Shield survivors showed extreme changes in personality and physical development. It was a long way from her specialty in plant genetics, but where one path led, she followed.

A wide hallway opened up beyond the door. Office desks lined the cracked gray drywall. On the other side, three glass-enclosed cubicles housed individual spaces. Old computer monitors topped the desks, and even a few virtual reality headsets lay on their sides. Broken fluorescent light bars and metal piping lined the ceiling. At the end of the hall stood two metal doors, side by side, their small rectangular windows dark. The space reminded her of a cookie-cutter government building. This hallway could have been one of hundreds spread out over the country at one time.

Nala trotted to the far left-hand door at the end of the hall and stopped, one paw scratching at the surface. She glanced back at Eva and gave a low woof.

Daniel and the team entered the right-hand door first, ensuring nobody lurked in its depths. Eva could see row upon row of filing cabinets lining the walls. Interesting. Pre-Collapse, people rarely kept hard copies of anything, choosing to store documents with their AIs.

The dog pawed at the other door impatiently.

Eva opened it, bringing the pistol up just in case, though, from the dog's reactions, they all would have known if there had been anybody behind it.

The room had been turned into a small living space.

"Daniel. Come see this."

He appeared in the doorway. The rest of the team remained in the file room, opening drawer after drawer in search of anything important.

A single cot was pushed up against the far wall of the tiny office-turned-apartment. On the other was a row of office desks with various paraphernalia: a camping stove and several propane bottles. A pile of scientific journals and books mixed with a few fiction paperbacks covered the top of another one. A third had a stack of wire-bound notebooks and handwritten slips of paper. Cans of food, including dog food, two five-gallon containers of water like the kind used in old water dispensers, and a manual microscope that looked like it came from a museum sat on the last desk. A generator with a detachable solar panel and battery was jerry-rigged atop a gray filing cabinet, a single extension cord running from it to a lamp by the cot. A set of dog food and water bowls were in front of it, an empty bucket beside it all.

Everything was neat and tidy, like the person who lived here cared about the place. *Like it was home.*

"Wonder how she ended up in the tunnels?" Eva flipped through the notebooks. They were journals. Eva ran a finger over the rows of neat cursive. She opened the desk drawers. Pencils, old pens, torn notes, binder clips, paperclips, used index cards, and various other office supplies filled the top two drawers. When she opened the bottom drawer, she froze, fingers tingling in reaction.

"It looks like she was an employee, a researcher here at the Institute. She was out of town when Kansas City was bombed. Her name was Hope." Daniel flipped through one of the journals.

"Daniel." She pushed his name past her lips, panting.

Wait. That wasn't right. He wasn't Daniel. Specks of something dark speckled his skin, turning his eyes black. No, not Daniel at all.

A sensation like a warm trickle spiraled up her arm from her grip on the hard plastic box, a chunk of black rock rattling inside. She pocketed it and opened the top drawer.

Letter openers came in various styles and strengths, with many sporting elaborate and ornate handles. What was left of the government letter openers were utilitarian and sharp at the tip, with a simple wooden handle for the grip, nothing so finely made as those in the late nineteenth century.

Eva always wondered what one would do to the carotid, or better yet, the jugular. She couldn't remember which one held more blood volume from her anatomy classes. How would she measure that down here in this place? Maybe after she got not-Daniel to the ground, she could empty one of the cans of food and track the volume that way? Yes, that was what she would do. This perfect specimen needed to die anyway.

All she had to do was stab.

CHAPTER 8
MIA

September, 2072

Mia aimed her gun at Amrit, and Cooper did the same with Sarah, his stance predatory. Focused.

Tension hung thick in the air, so heavy you could reach out and grab it. Ugliness etched itself into Amrit's face, the unfamiliar sneer startling, and eyes so dark, any white was lost to memory.

"This goes only one way, Sarah." Cooper glared at the woman.

"Your daughter's life is forfeit, stupid man. There's nothing I can do to help you now."

His lips twisted, all his usual humor gone. "You mean, like how you helped inject her with a daily dose of misery every day. That poison will eventually kill her, regardless of the small amounts of antidote you control her with."

Sarah shrugged, a nonchalant raise and dip of shoulder. "She is alive, isn't she? I can only control so much, Killian."

Mia stepped closer. "You've got to be kidding me. You're saying you helped his daughter? What, just like you helped Jerome?"

"I told you girl, that solution was meant for Jack. It wouldn't have killed him like it did the old man…just incapacitated him. These two old fools lied to you about what he ingested." An evil grin tipped her lips. "Dear old sis, still working toward a corrupt government's goals by keeping state secrets. Haven't you learned better by now?"

"Shut your lying mouth, Sarah." Eva's pale face whitened further and Mia glanced down at the ever-widening puddle of blood. Panic tinged the borders of her concentration. Why wasn't her mother healing?

"You mean, not tell her that the solution Jerome ingested could manipulate a Shielded's brain chemistry so much, you could control them? That precious Mommy Dearest was doing much more than saving the world? You should ask her, Mia, what really happened during the Year of Hell."

The bullet from Eva's gun spun Sarah around, her shoulder blooming a bright red.

"That's enough," Eva's arm dropped like a limp sail. "We have more to worry about than the past. If you destroy the TMRWS, then all the water is lost, stored and unable to return to its natural cycle. I told you, we can fix it. I don't want to kill you, but the next bullet will take you right between the eyes, sister or not."

"You're outgunned and outmanned." Mia eased around the island to the right of Eva.

Soft steps and the light in her head told her Cooper moved as well, forming an angled attack vector.

Rani crammed herself down in the chair as far as possible.

"Ah, dear. Do you even know what your parents have been doing all this time?" Sarah tapped Rani on the head between the eyes. "These people need to learn to share."

"It doesn't matter. At least they're not eating other humans." Doubt crept on silent feet through her mind. Her parent's weren't telling her everything. Sweat slicked the hand clenching her gun.

"Ha. Yet. You should ask them why that's happening. Amrit, time to go."

"I couldn't agree more. I've had enough of pretending to care about any of this." Amrit pushed a button on Rani's keyboard. An alarm klaxon screeched throughout the facility. The lights dimmed and red strobes flashed down the hallway and through the lab.

Shit.

The entire room filled with gunfire.

Mia's bullet grazed Sarah's head, Eva's took her in the other shoulder. Cooper fired at Amrit and the man stumbled, collapsing to his knees. A bloody hole created a third eye in his forehead.

Rani jerked the chair over on top of her like a turtle, working the gag out of her mouth and trying to loosen the bonds.

A bullet hit Mia in the side, and she yelped, ducking below the island for cover.

Sarah sprinted for the back wall and the old broken elevator shaft that hadn't worked since before the Collapse.

The lights flashed across Mia's retinas in an insistent pulse, both the strobe and the alarm bright and nauseating. Her side burned where the bullet had entered.

Cooper was on the move, his position in her mind careening toward Sarah.

She had to kill the self-destruct or they were all dead.

Out of her peripheral, Rani worked her hands free and crawled to Eva's side, the latter moaning in pain on the ground. Mia's heart pounded in her chest.

No time to think. She just needed to react.

Solve the problem first, emote later. Her father's voice drilled into her head from childhood.

Side blazing, Mia stood, sighting down the barrel of her pistol, she fired again at Sarah's retreating back.

And missed.

Her heart sank.

The other woman jumped into the shaft, grabbing a rope and slamming the doors together in Cooper's face. He clawed at the seam. They didn't budge.

Rani left Eva's side and rushed to the computer, fingers flying over the keyboard.

Mia joined Cooper to work at prying the doors, side burning from the bullet graze. The edges bent, the shriek of metal joining the cacophony of sound throughout the MUC hammering her ear drums. Something jammed them from the other side.

"What's on the seventeenth sub-level? Where we left Tobias?" Cooper shouted, his mouth so near her ear his breath brushed her cheek.

She squinted, the klaxon hammering her every thought. "The closed off shaft to the mainline that runs from here to Lower Monumental Dam. Dad's had it secured for years."

Cooper shook his head. "You sure about that? Bet seventeen is where she's going. I think she's doing this on her own dime without prior approval from the Western Coalition."

The Western Coalition? Secrets surrounded her from all corners, dark and hurtful. She was beginning to realize how painfully naive she'd been. So innocent to think honesty could rebuild the world.

She put her mouth by his ear once more. "I'm not sure about anything anymore, Cooper. You go! I'll join you after I help turn off the self-destruct."

If she could. They had ten minutes. At best.

He nodded and disappeared out the door toward the emergency stairwell. Would she see him again? Or would he betray her? *No time to worry about that.*

She didn't look at her mom on the floor. Could barely think with the scream of the alarm and pulses of light. She leaned to look over Rani's shoulder.

Amrit surged from his place on the floor, blood spraying out in droplets from his head. He rammed Rani's side and the woman toppled into Mia.

Mia turned in a smooth motion and jumped onto *his* back. The man stumbled to the floor on his side. She didn't let go, just rode him to the ground, smashing his head into the concrete floor, letting all her frustration and rage out in each smooth motion. Swinging her leg up and over Amrit's head, she jerked back on the other man's arm. It snapped with a crack.

The man flopped around. Mia put another bullet in his head.

Heal that, *you sonofabitch.*

One bullet to the head could sometimes be survived. Never two within minutes.

Later, she would feel guilt. But not right now. Not with the alarms blaring and her mother dying before her eyes.

"Mia." A rattling cough followed the barely perceptible word.

And that's when she saw it, hidden beneath her mother where her back met the counter.

A needle lay on the ground at Eva's side. Sarah's doing, no doubt. It must be why Shield had failed.

Mia knelt, clutching her mother's hand.

"In case I don't make it, you need to fix the last TMRWS. Everything you need is in the rest of my journals, and your father…tell him…"

"Shh, Mom, no." Tears pooled in her eyes.

Desperation battled the rage within Mia.

Rani had gone to the computer and furiously typed, her eyes alight with fury and panic. Her chest heaved and bloody hands trembled.

Mia covered her ears. It was all so much.The sound of the alarm piercing her every thought and her mother semi-conscious on the ground.

"I need your father's code!" Rani screamed, jerking Mia back to the present.

"What?"

"Tell me your father's code or we're all trapped down here when it self-destructs."

Mia froze. Her father's code? But he wasn't here… She didn't know. Her heart beat a rapid drumbeat.

The spark of light indicating Cooper's position flared above her and to the east, moving quickly. Had he made it to the seventeenth sub-level so quickly? Was he after Sarah?

"Mia! Your father's code, get it from your mom!" Rani snapped, the whites of her eyes showing in panic.

Pull it together.

Mia settled her mom's head on her lap, tapping the older woman's face."Mom, I need you."

Eva groaned, lids fluttering.

"Poison…"

"I don't understand. I need Dad's code. Please, stay with me." Mia placed her ear close so she could hear. Wet raspy sounds rattled from her mom's throat. Black ink swirled in her eyeballs, breath a fetid stink.

"Journal…"

"What? No, I need Daniel's code. You've got to know it." Dread shot through her. Her mother was so out of it, fading fast.

Eva's eyes rolled back in her head and a seizure gripped her body, arms flailing and body trembling in rapid jerks and starts.

"Shit!" She rolled Eva to her side. "Stay with me Mom."

The bloody wound in her mother's gut started to leak again.

"No, no, no." Mia put pressure on the gunshot. "Rani! She's out!"

The alarm wailed faster, the pitch higher. Like a countdown.

"I need the damn password! I have mine, and I'm trying to backdoor his, but it isn't working."

A cool hand covered hers. Startled, she looked down. Her mother somehow resurfaced again. Dark circles ringed her haggard eyes. "Numbers…journal."

Realization shocked Mia into action.

"Rani try my birthday combined with Eva's." She shouted it, her throat raw with the effort.

The older woman didn't look up from the keyboard or computer screen as her hands moved like the wind.

Blessed silence fell throughout the facility.

Mia covered her mother's hands. Eva's eyes rolled back in their sockets and she was out once more.

Rani slumped in the swivel chair and turned to face them. "Too close. Too damn close. Self-destruct is off."

"Something's wrong with her, Rani. Help me." Mia brushed her mother's chilled face with the tips of her fingers.

"She was poisoned."

"That's what she said. Can you do anything?" She wiped the tears from her cheeks.

Rani rested a hand on her shoulder. "I'll try. Go. Get that bitch."

Mia laid her mother's hand gently on the floor and checked the clip in her pistol. "I need more ammo."

Rani's eyes widened. "Some in the armory."

"Copy that." She stopped, remembering her original purpose for coming out here. "And Rani, Sarah has samples of my blood. Tell my mom if she wakes up."

Rani's eyes widened and her mouth formed an *O* of horror. She'd left the woman speechless.

Later. Always later. Cooper's presence sparked in her mind, a flurry of movement that caused a moment of anxiety. Was he in a fight?

Before she could leave the lab, her father and Jack burst through the door, both men's bodies coiled for a fight. "What the hell is going on?"

CHAPTER 9
COOPER

September, 2072

Cooper careened up the stairs, panic propelling his burning thighs to the limit. Sarah knew how and where to hit. And she hit hard.

The utility room door where they'd stuffed Tobias earlier gaped open, and he cursed. He should have taken care of the man in a more permanent fashion regardless of Mia's protestations.

A small foyer opened in front of the emergency stairwell, a hallway led into darkness branching off to the right. Next to it, the crushed elevator doors revealed an empty shaft and a chain dangling from a dented ceiling. This elevator must have stopped here back in the day.

Another exit sign, its ghoulish green glow the only illumination, flickered above a half open door on the other side of the room.

Cooper skirted the horseshoe desk to get to it, a two-foot-tall "17" set against the cement block wall. Somebody had slashed through the number with a dark red X. A bloody wound foreshadowing whatever lay beyond it.

He put his back to the wall, pistol at the ready and eased the door open the rest of the way even though every muscle screamed for him to hurry. Even though his heart clattered inside his chest at what might happen to Claire. He had to do this by the book. Rushing got you killed.

Another long hallway stretched out before him. Somebody had assembled an emergency lighting stand, a single bulb sitting atop a battery-operated generator.

The hall was empty.

Cooper padded along, checking the few small empty and dark rooms along his path.

The end revealed an enormous maintenance room, with lockers and various tables, chairs, and workbenches lining the walls beneath an observation window. On the other side lay a railroad tunnel.

Holy crap.

He recognized that tunnel. Like some bloody playback on the wayback machine. This was the tunnel Daniel and the rest of the surviving people of the MUC had escaped through—had burrowed through five stories of earth with their blood, sweat, and sanity—after being buried alive for a year in the complex. This was the tunnel that crept into his nightmares, even as an adult.

The entrance from this level was at the far end of the long room. Cooper swung around the door. Empty.

The tunnel, like most government funded projects back in the day, was brick and steel, curved to accommodate a full-sized locomotive. At some point this branch ascended to Track Three in a gradual angling toward the surface. If he remembered right. He had been six years old after all.

Faded red paint marked the dead-end on this section of wall. Sarah and Tobias's only option was to head east into the darkness of the track. Two against one—two *Shielded* against his already overworked serum would make it trickier.

He cursed.

Another emergency light atop a battery glowed in a cocoon of light a hundred feet away.

Cooper crouched around the door, softly closing it behind him. The walkway or the track?

Always take the higher ground. Daniel's words, burned into his memory, came to him. Because of where he was? Or because it was sound advice? He couldn't tell. He could repeat so many of the man's sayings with perfect recollection.

Pistol leading the way, he tracked along the rough cement access, head on a swivel.

Crack.

He froze, all attention focused on whatever loomed ahead of him.

A skittering and then silence.

Cooper padded forward, slower this time. Each breath, each step purposeful.

A shadow disengaged from the wall in front of him.

"You should have killed me."

Tobias.

Cooper obliged and tried to shoot the other man in between the eyes.

Tobias moved too quickly, running and leaping to bring the knife down where Cooper had stood just a moment before.

He ducked and shot the man as he twisted his body around. The bullet grazed Tobias's cheek.

The other man shot forward, slashing down with his knife and knocking the gun away. It slipped from Cooper's grip.

Both men slashed and punched, only connecting glancing blows as Shield enhanced their movements.

Cooper dropped to the ground, kicking his legs out to where he anticipated Tobias.

And connected.

Tobias flew across the tracks, and Cooper followed, pushing his enhanced self to meet the other man when he landed.

He picked up Tobias's knife, flipping the blade over in his hand.

As he reached the groaning man on the ground, he plunged the knife into the back of his neck.

Tobias went limp, his eyes rolling in their sockets.

"Where is she?" Gravel coated Cooper's throat.

The other man gurgled. "Go to hell."

"How could you help her? You've been loyal to Daniel for… since I've known you."

"You don't know everything, traitor." Tobias spat, the words harsh and strained against the impediment narrowly missing his vocal chords.

"I know you and Amrit were his lapdogs for far too long to turn against him. Where is Sarah? Tell me now, or I will make it permanent." He shoved the knife deeper until the clink of metal against cement told him he couldn't go any farther.

Tobias's entire body jerked like a puppet on strings.

"That's enough, Coop."

Jack. Where the hell had he come from?

Cooper never looked away from Tobias. "He's working with Sarah. He knows where she went. They have my daughter, Jack, I can't just let it go."

"You dumped me in a tunnel and now expect me to trust you?"

A barrel met his temple.

"What happened to trust but verify?" Cooper took his hand off the knife in the back of Tobias's neck.

Jack snorted. "Mia said you're working for the WC. Have you lost your ever-loving mind?"

"Like I said, they have my daughter."

"*You* have a kid?"

Cooper clenched his fists. Every bit of time arguing with Jack was one more minute Sarah was getting closer to Claire. "Foster. I saved her. I didn't want another person to be abandoned. Orphaned and left out in the cold."

The gun disappeared. "You left *us*, kid."

"Seriously? After Montana? Now let me get answers from this asshole and find Sarah."

Jack kicked the limp body. "I think he's out. He turned on us, huh?"

"Can I get up?" Cooper craned his neck to look back at Jack.

The other man gestured with his pistol to rise. "I should. But I'm not. Mia said not to yet, anyway. Daughter, huh? You better not be b.s.ing me."

Relief flooded through Cooper. "Sarah is down here somewhere."

No more emergency lights lit the dark.

"You sure? Track's blocked about a half-mile down."

A quiet dread filled him. Could he have been so stupid? So short-sighted? Could she have gone out the top? Into the irradiated desert?

No, he would have heard her ascending the stairs.

Cooper started to curse. "We need to split up. I'll take the topside if you take the track."

"Hold up—"

"I can't hold up! She's going to kill my little girl, don't you get it?" Cooper shoved Jack aside and stumbled over Tobias's body.

"Seriously, when did you start taking care of a kid?"

"I don't have time for this."

Jack grabbed his arm. Tight. "Make time. She won't get far."

Cooper glared. "Fine. After I left, after Daniel abandoned those people in Montana, I wandered for a few years."

More than wandered. He'd been looking for…something. Home? Probably. A sense of purpose? Most definitely. A purpose beyond just doing Daniel's bidding. Living for the protection of the MUC and Basin. A place where he could finally come to terms with how his parents had died and what had happened to him afterward.

"Daniel didn't abandon them, we left them because none of

us would have made it back with that many civilians." Jack widened his stance. Did he think Cooper was going to strike out?

He ignored Jack's same old excuse for Daniel's actions.

"I helped settlements relocate, built wells, built walls, tried to fight off the bigger bastards when they came. Claire was orphaned down in Oklahoma. I couldn't leave her there to… well, let's just say orphans are usually fodder for the sex trade. Ended up back in Montana for a job a few years ago, Sarah grabbed Claire on one of her raids. I surrendered to save my daughter's life. You see, Sarah recognized me from our trip to Montana Tech, and that's that. She works with the WC, finding weapons and drugs and whatever else for them, and in return they leave her alone." He didn't tell Jack that the reason why he'd been in Montana to begin with was because he was heading home. He may not have agreed with how things were run, but at least Claire would have been safe within the Territory's boundaries. The irony wasn't lost on him that he still considered the Basin Territory his home.

"Why can't you just leave? Take Claire and get the hell out of Dodge?"

Cooper snorted. "Right. Sarah's given certain family members of the militia a poison called Oblivion. If they don't get an injection of the antidote every couple of days, they're dead. I needed Shield to save her. Plus, if they all escaped, who would take in that many? I heard Daniel's closed the borders."

"How is she getting all these fancy poisons? The WC?"

"Hell if I know."

"She needs to be taken out." Jack's voice was flat.

"Not going to argue." He gestured down the tunnel. "Can we now proceed with doing just that?"

A loud metallic screech echoed through the tunnel from the darkness in front of them. The last light shone like a beacon next to them. Maybe she hadn't gone out the top. Maybe she had come right through this tunnel somehow, regardless of whether it was blocked.

Footsteps clipped along at a rapid rate. Many footsteps.

"How many?" Cooper had been wrong. She had more help than just Amrit or Tobias within the Territory.

Jack cocked his head to the side, listening. "Six? Maybe seven."

He touched Jack's arm, a speck of light indicating his location clear as a bell now in his head. The Seeking. Whereas Mia's presence ignited a bright spark of light in his head, Jack was a plain white dot, utilitarian in nature like most of the people he could sense. Further contemplation of that would have to wait until later.

If Jack knew what Cooper had done, he didn't say.

"Sarah's going off the books. One last thing, Jack, your Sector Nine folks are planning a rebellion fueled by Sarah and the WC. I think they want your resources and the MUC." Cooper disappeared into the shadows on the other side of the track, like he hadn't just thrown a monkey wrench into the entire Territory operation. Let the bastard suck on that for a while.

The group of fighters hadn't bothered masking their sound. Either overconfident, or stupid. Or both.

He softened his step and walked closer to the tunnel wall.

It wasn't villagers with torches and pitchforks but damn sure close.

"We have come for the Infected. To destroy this shithole and everything in it."

Cooper shook his head, sticking to the darkness. God, they even had a name for the Shielded. Sarah sure knew how to incite riots and subversion

Jack stepped in the middle of the track, the lone light shining on him. What the hell was he doing? "It's just me down here, Gustav. You know I wouldn't put any of our people in harm's way."

"That's what you told us thirty years ago, but now we have people starving out in the settlements while Daniel and the other abominations remain unchanged, forever young.Their serum is antithesis to nature. He has food stores stacked high down here, enough to feed everyone comfortably for decades, and he's just sitting on them. People are dying, Jack. We aren't getting what we deserve." Six other people fanned out behind the older man, their headlamps bobbing in the dark like discombobulated buoys.

"That's all b.s. This can go one of two ways. First, you all can go back to your Sector. Then, step down from the council, Gustav, let Carmen lead Sector Nine, and be lucky you're not thrown out of this territory. Or we can do this now and I'll drill a bullet through that thick head of yours. Your choice." Jack widened his stance and stepped away from the direct light.

"You're lying! They've Infected you too!"

"There's no food under here, Gus. Just old government files and medicines that need protection. You know when little Mika needed antibiotics, and there were none topside? They came from the stores down here. And you want to listen to some stranger's propaganda and destroy that?"

It wasn't enough. It was never enough.

Cooper popped up behind the group and signaled the go ahead.

One of the women in the crew fired.

Distraction and infiltration. A tactic often used to disrupt the structure and power base of the settlements. Cooper had been dealing with it for years—on the wrong side of the struggle due to Claire.

Had Sarah allowed her greed—or other desires—to outweigh the Western Coalition's plan to infiltrate the Territory? She must be after something major if she was willing to risk pissing off the WC and moving against Daniel and Eva so soon.

Sarah played a dangerous game.

Cooper shot the largest person in the crew in both legs before he could even turn. In this day and age, traitors needed to be taken care of, but a bunch of Sector Nine folks ending up dead would destabilize the Territory more than it already had.

A dark-haired woman in jeans and a t-shirt dropped to a knee and aimed. Cooper was too fast. He swerved, and came at her from the side. She fired, eyes wide. Cooper pistol-whipped her, knocking her out.

Jack finally got Gus in a combination arm and head lock between his powerful arms and legs. He squeezed, simultaneously distending the elbow until it popped with a crunch and choking him with the other arm. The bigger, unShielded man passed out, face red.

Cooper knocked out two more with ease and the last two, a young man and woman with fear shining in their eyes, held up their hands in surrender.

Footsteps clattered along the gravel between the track, and Sarah strolled toward them, a large tranquilizer gun in hand. "This is the end of the road, Cooper."

Cooper didn't miss a beat. He dipped into his dwindling energy stores to zigzag down the walkway and leap an almost impossible distance to land on the track beside her. If he didn't take Sarah out, it was over. Sarah swung the tranq rifle around to clip him, but he spun with the momentum of the gun.

Sarah refused to release the rifle and they wrestled in a tug of war of wills. Sarah twisted to elbow him in the face and break free, then took aim with the rifle once again.

And came face to face with Daniel and his pistol, Mia behind him.

"This is the end of the line, Sarah. I should've taken you out a long time ago." Daniel's voice was icy and even.

Sarah fired. Daniel fell, his mouth open in shock.

Cooper knocked the rifle away, took out a very long blade from a sheath in his boot, and held it to her neck all in one quick, smooth motion. "You know, beheading is a very effective way to kill one of us."

"Cooper," Mia interjected.

"This bitch and her people have my daughter in a cage, Mia." All other distractions faded away, he could only see Sarah's slim neck and pulse beating a rapid tempo. "They have monsters who feed on humans. She's not worth your words."

"Her dart got my dad." Mia kneeled, at Daniel's side, a hand at his neck. "Tell us what was in that thing, Sarah, or I will let Cooper kill you."

Sarah just laughed.

Every muscle in his arm tensed with the strain of not sliding that blade across the woman's neck.

Jack cleared his throat, gun still pointed at the two Sector Nine folks. Eyes flicking back and forth between them and Daniel's prone body lying on the track. "Mia, I need to secure this entrance before any more yay-hoos get in. You got this?"

She hunched her shoulders but nodded. "Go. Cooper and I will take care of Sarah."

Jack turned back to address his hostages. "Show us how you got down here. Now." The two from Sector Nine stumbled to their feet, hands still clasped behind their heads. They glanced at Jack nervously, and led him into the inky black, their headlamps casting a thin beam ahead of them.

Sarah piped up once they were gone. "You chose, Cooper, how does it feel to sign Claire's death sentence? If I don't send a runner to Montana within the next couple of days, your daughter is dead within the week."

Did the woman have a death wish?

The blade his father had given him warmed his hand. It seemed fitting he'd use it to deliver justice to the one person who had caused so much suffering. Hands shaking, he started the cut.

And Sarah stabbed him in the leg with her own knife. Pain sizzled into his thigh.

Mia fired, the bullet hitting the other woman in the leg, but

Sarah was quick, quicker than she should be, even Shielded. In one blink, Cooper's knife was digging into her throat, the next, it was simply dripping blood into empty air. Sarah bounded away into the dark toward where Jack had disappeared.

Cooper dropped to his knees, leg numb, and toppled sideways.

CHAPTER 10

EVA

August 2055

The specimen that wasn't Daniel wouldn't stop dodging. Eva cocked her head to the side. This might be more difficult than she thought. She swiped the letter opener. He grabbed her wrist and tried to pry it from her fingers. Eva tightened her grip, slamming an elbow into his side. Air escaped his lips.

So it did breathe. Curious.

The other creature on four legs growled, the fur on its back standing up, its teeth showing. Dog. That's what it was called. It lunged, and she punched it in the side, knocking it against the wall. It yipped but didn't stay down. Even more curious. It should have.

Other people came into the room, shouting at her. This wouldn't do at all. She would never get to finish her experiment with all these people. They had to be contained. Then, if the first test-run failed, she would have other arteries to drain.

"Don't hurt her!" The thing that was not Daniel shouted.

She kicked at one of the smaller people, swung around, and hammered the female in the face. Both motions took several seconds, her grip on the letter opener slowing her down some. Eva couldn't lose grip on it. The experiment was imperative.

Hands gripped her from behind. She slammed her head back and something crunched. She smiled in satisfaction. The other two smaller people rushed her. The letter opener slashed in front of her—and, oh, a gun. That's right, she did have one of those. Eva aimed and fired. It hit the wall. Waste of ammo.

Now, where was her primary specimen? She couldn't lose him. He was impersonating Daniel.

The dog rushed her again, nipping her leg and jumping away before she could kick it. Nasty thing. Blood seeped from the wound. She aimed the pistol once again and fired, but it skittered away faster than a dog had any right to move.

Damn it, Eva just wanted to finish her experiment. Why wouldn't they let her? She fired the gun again at the four insignificant humans attempting to slow her down. Somehow she didn't hit a thing, though one of them looked like a bullet had grazed her. The gun clicked on empty. Useless thing anyway. She threw it across the room, and it thunked off of a cot.

Strong arms wrapped around her upper body. No. This couldn't happen.

"Get the damn thing out of her pocket before she kills somebody."

The specimen didn't need to shout. And they wanted to take the treasure from her pocket? No, that wouldn't do.

Eva bucked and writhed, trying to escape the muscular frame of the person holding her. They tumbled to the floor. His grip tightened until she couldn't breathe. Pants of air escaped her lips. They couldn't…She wouldn't let…

"No, no, no!" They had to understand. The experiment was imperative.

Long legs wrapped around hers from behind until her entire body was taught and bowed like a willow branch.

Hands from the other people raided her pockets, and she tried to bite at the arm holding her but couldn't get her head low enough. Maybe if she forced her arm out of its socket? Shield would numb the pain.

The female whom she had clipped with the bullet yanked the box with the black rock out of her pants, and Eva gagged, spikes of pain knifing through her head.

Daniel's arms and legs didn't loosen from around her. It was too much. Everything in the room spun the world out of control. Whorls of light and sound intermingled inside of her mind, pummeling the fragile edges of her consciousness.

Eva screamed.

Her throat was raw, the coppery taste of blood thick on her tongue from either it or her throat. Shield healed the damage, and her body went limp.

Daniel's heartbeat thumped quick and loud against her back, his breath heaving in uneven rasps. Long scratch marks where she'd gouged him healed, leaving behind the remnants of blood to drip on the ragged carpet below them.

"Daniel?" Her voice was rough. Her arms loosened and she rolled off of him to land on her side. Daniel remained flat on the floor. The others were leaning against walls, eyes wide and wary, guns at the ready. Nala sat panting by the doorway, froth at her mouth. "What…why, oh God, Daniel. Oh, God. I don't…"

Eva covered her face with her hands, sobs and tears streaming out of her in an uncontrolled flood. Daniel's arms wrapped around her, gentle this time. Nothing felt safer. He still hadn't said a word, but she didn't care.

"Trae, I want you to find a glass container and put that box in it. Hell, find two, just in case. Then, I want you to bury it in a pack and take it back to the train. Hide it somewhere in the tunnel. I don't care where, but I don't want to know where it is until we've completed the mission. You understand?"

Trae's deep voice, so grown-up sounding it made Eva's heart ache worse, answered in the affirmative. "Can I take Jess with me, leave you with Coy? I need to get the bullet out of her arm before it closes up all the way, and don't have the supplies here."

"That'll work. Gather up as many supplies from down here as you can and take them back with you as well. Coy, go help them. Give us a minute."

Faint footsteps faded away, and Daniel shifted. "Sit up, please. I need to make sure I didn't hurt you."

"I'm Shielded, remember?" The tears wouldn't stop flowing but she did as he asked.

He swiped a thumb under her eye, wiping the moisture from her face. "Are you okay?"

Eva turned away so she couldn't see the concern shining in his eyes. Her entire body shook. "No."

Strong arms encompassed her. Daniel rested his chin atop her head. "Was it like that when you blew up the mine? Or the night before we left? Crap, and even in the stairwell earlier?"

Eva frowned, forcing her scattered thoughts to coalesce. "I don't remember the night before we left. The stairwell…I could remember everything. I wasn't myself, but it was like the mine. What just happened, it was like most of what made me Eva just wasn't there anymore. I'm so sorry, Daniel. I shot Jess. God, I could've killed her if I got her in the head."

"We'll get it figured out, but we're all returning to the train. If this mystery woman had a chunk of the meteorite, I want to read what's in those journals. Maybe there's something in there that can help you. And from here on out, you're not leaving that engine."

"But—"

"You almost took out four Shielded, Eva, and a dog that seems to have superpowers. We can't risk another episode, not if we want to find this information and get out of here."

She regarded her folded hands, the bruises from where she'd hit Nala healing in a slow pattern, the purple turning yellow right before her eyes like one of those hyper-color shirts from her childhood. She'd hurt them all.

No, not her.

The enzyme.

Eva covered the bruises, hiding them from sight. "Fine. But I'm reading her journals too."

"I wouldn't have it any other way."

———

Coy, Jess, and Trae kept their distance, eying her warily. Nala too. It hurt, but not as much as knowing she could have killed one if not all of them.

Everybody had remained silent as they filled their packs with the canned food, Nala's dishes, and all of Hope's journals. Hope. An ironic name these days.

Daniel rested a hand on her shoulder. "Here, drink some water. You haven't had any all day."

Not that she needed much, but the fight and subsequent tears had taken it out of her. She gripped the canteen and murmured her thanks. The water was cool and sweet on her tongue. It chilled her half-healed throat, and she moaned in pleasure.

When she turned to hand the canteen back, Daniel was watching her, his eyes focused on her face, a mixture of worry and something else. She gave him a tentative smile, and his usual mask replaced any emotion.

"Let's move out."

They took up the same positions they had on the way here. Nala whined, sitting by the door to her old home.

"Come on, girl. Hope's not here anymore, you're coming with us."

She thumped her tail on the floor and trotted to the group. This time she stayed just out of Eva's reach.

At the front entrance to the building, the group halted, perusing the route through the rubble.

"Eva and I will go first. Trae, Jess, and Coy, you bring up the tail end. Any sign of trouble, you hightail it south back to the train by any route possible. You copy?"

"Copy that, sir," they chorused.

Daniel nodded and took off for the wall of rubble where they'd almost met the two men from the cannibal settlement somewhere nearby.

Eva followed, head like a swivel, senses on high alert after the last episode. If a small chunk of unprotected meteorite could take her out like that, what would a bigger chunk do? *Didn't you find that out back at the mine?*

She and Daniel reached the wall of the crumbled building, its ceiling open to the air and the walls shattered around them. She turned. Trae, Coy, and Jess, Nala at their side, almost stepped out of their covering positions from the doorway of the BAC when a gravelly voice from the shadows grabbed their full attention.

"I knew I heard footsteps."

CHAPTER 11

MIA

September, 2072

Men and women from Sector Nine lay sprawled on the ground, none conscious. None of them were Shielded, which would make the road to recovery much more complicated. They wouldn't fare well out at the prison beneath the dam.

Mia dropped to her knees beside Cooper, inspecting the knife buried to the hilt in his leg. Her eyes darted between him and her father lying unconscious on the ground, one leg dangling over a railroad track.

"It hit a nerve." Cooper managed through clenched teeth. "Yank it out."

"What?" Her thoughts were still on her father and whatever the hell had been in that dart. "But—"

Cooper's hand trembled but he wrapped it around the hilt.

Mia batted it away and jerked up in one smooth motion with a sense of perverse satisfaction. *That's for locking me in the lab.*

Cooper grunted in pain. He rolled until he sat with his back against the cement wall leading up to the walkway.

"There. I was going to say, what if it's poisoned with whatever's incapacitating everyone?"

"Still needed to come out. Hand me that gun and go help Jack. I'll watch over your father." Cooper caught her wary look and grinned. "I won't shoot him while he's down. Not a fair fight."

"I'm going to hold you to that."

"I'm sure you will."

Mia shook her head in disgust, with herself or him she couldn't tell. Probably both. Her pistol had a full clip, but she collected extras from her father's belt and a headlamp from one of the downed Sector Nine people, then jogged into the dark after Jack and Sarah.

Too many enemies. Cooper wasn't exactly trustworthy but he also wasn't trying to kill any of her people at the moment. The Territory was his best chance at retrieving his daughter.

Gray outlined the curvature of ceiling and walkway, the glow from the last emergency lamp providing just enough light for Mia's enhanced vision.

Up ahead, enormous blocks of concrete reinforced by rebar, the kind used along old highways as sound barriers, blocked the track right before the junction of the Mainline and Track Three.

On the other side, the two tracks paralleled each other miles apart until a branch connected them at Lower Monumental Dam once again. Track Three continued on toward the other side of the country while other tracks had been built off the Territory Mainline to supply the Basin with underground electricity and water.

For all intents and purposes, this part of the track that used to connect the MUC to the wider world of top-secret government ops didn't exist anymore. It was unusable and impassable. No doors lined this section, no banks of elevators; there was nothing but blocked tunnel and railroad track. So where did Jack, Sarah, and the others go?

Mia jogged along the walkway on the other side of the track.

There had to be another secret door of some kind like where she'd been held.

A scuffling sound drifted to her and she froze to listen, closing her eyes and tilting her head. It happened again, muffled and low.

She hopped onto the track bed. There it was, where the enormous blocks of cement met the corner of the walkway and rail bed. She turned on the headlamp to get a closer look. A rough door outlined the coarse surface.

Mia patted all around, finally finding a rope looped through a hole. She backed off to the side, pistol ready and yanked the rope. A mechanism clicked and a false wall gave way, opening into a narrow, dusty passageway through the barrier.

They had all grown so complacent over the years. New tunnels being built, skimming the edges of their territory, secret doors and supply caches, enemy infiltration. Basin Territory sprawled across the desert, but it wasn't so large in the greater scheme of things that operations like these would be overlooked.

Jack shot her a startled, relieved look from the other side. The two Sector Nine folks lay subdued on the ground. "I was trying to open the damn thing. She locked it from the other side. Dark as sin in here.

"Bloody hell."

"You can say that again." He shoved the two prisoners out onto the track.

Mia closed the passage through the barrier and cut the rope. She'd go secure the other side later, but it begged the question, just how many new tunnels and passageways infiltrated the Territory's borders?

Her heart sank. As head of security, she should have caught that, should have taken Sector Nine more seriously.

Between her and Jack, they got the other two Sector Nine people back down the tunnel and dropped them next to the others. Arms and legs of their prisoners secured, she and Jack moved to help Daniel and Cooper.

"Why didn't you go after her?" Cooper demanded.

"Down which tunnel? She was able to get through all of us, had a head start, and you want me to try and track her on my own? We'll do it a different way after I check on my parents."

Jack hauled Daniel into a fireman's carry, mouthing the words "good luck," before heading down to the Project Shield labs on the twenty-first sub-level.

Cooper worried about his foster daughter; it was etched in the deep lines of his face and along every tense muscle of his body. She couldn't blame him but she also had a Territory full of people to take care of. And if they knew both her parents were incapacitated, all hell would break loose.

"Jack would've helped you." His lips compressed into a thin line.

"And left the prisoners? Cooper, we'll find her. We'll make her pay. I know you're worried about Claire—"

"You have no idea, Mia, no idea at all just how sadistic these people can be. The only thing keeping her safe is my cooperation and knowledge. Without it..." He limped toward the double doors leading back into the facility, a fire in each hitching step.

Mia shook her head and locked the doors behind her. She'd have to send somebody to retrieve the people on the track but for now, the space was as effective as a prison.

"Cooper, wait." It didn't take long to catch up. She very carefully avoided touching him, even though he dragged his leg with every angry step and she could've helped. The—bond? Connection?—simmered on the edges of her consciousness.

He moved toward the emergency exit.

"I have the sample of Shield, I need to get back to Montana before Sarah if I have any chance of saving Claire."

"Will you hold on for just a second and listen to me?"

Cooper trudged to a stop, entire body vibrating with impatience. He whipped around. "I don't have time for this, Mia."

"I will lend you a side-by-side and some supplies, but you need to listen."

His brows drew together as he met her eyes, completely focused now.

She continued, "If you're truly against Sarah, then we have a common enemy. Be careful. I think she's got her hands on some kind of mind control serum from the old days. It's why Tobias and Amrit went crazy. You can't help anybody if you get injected."

"Your concern is touching. Why hasn't she used it on me before this?"

Mia shrugged. "Limited supply? I read about it in my mother's journals, but it took me a while to put it together. Bring Claire back here, Cooper, after you rescue her. You'll both be safer for it. It used to be your home after all."

And why had she said that? He had betrayed her, lied to her. *But he also helped.* There was something about the man that drew her to him. Beyond the few childhood memories, beyond any attraction. She *knew* he was telling the truth somehow. Blood called to blood. Or maybe it was just all her imagination, maybe it was all Shield.

Cooper studied her face. "We'll see. I really am sorry about locking you in that room."

"We'll work on building back that trust later. Now, go save your kid." She dangled the ATV key in front of him. "It's parked at the end of the wall. Follow the stones and clumps of native grass to the east to get through the irradiated zone. When I get downstairs, I'll call the guards. Tell them not to shoot you."

A faint grin lit his face. "Why are you doing this?"

"No little girl should have to live through what you've described. Now go. I'll deal with Jack." And an entire territory of people who would fall apart without her parents—regardless of the council.

Cooper grabbed her hand and swept in to plant a kiss on her cheek. "Thank you."

Mia flushed, the spark that told her his location flaring up brighter than before.

He pulled away before she could react and limp-jogged to the stairwell without looking back. Her hand covered the spot where lips had met flesh.

———

"Have you lost your damned mind? He knows about us, Mia, and the resources we have." Jack's hands gesticulated in the air in a wild whirl.

Mia glared. "They already know about the resources, Jack. They've apparently dug tunnels everywhere, right under our noses. Cooper is saving his daughter. Let him."

"Are you sure he's telling the truth? Your father's going to kill us both, you know that?"

"If he survives. And yeah, something tells me Cooper's not lying about that part." Even if he lied about the rest.

A lump formed in Mia's throat. Her father wasn't doing well. At first, she thought he just needed time. Time for Shield to do its thing. But now, both her parents lay side by side atop matching hospital beds. Rani swept in, injected Eva with something and checked Daniel's pulse with a frown.

"We need to find Sarah, before she can leave our territory."

"I already sent teams to check the tunnels but nothing yet. We need to shore up the Inner Territory walls. If she's here there's possibly more coming. We also need to get a team together, Jack, and go confront those Sector Nine bastards. Even if we find her, who's to say we won't get attacked by our own people?" Something told her Sarah was long gone. Mia'd lose precious time searching for a ghost when the most pressing need was quelling an uprising from Sector Nine and protecting the rest of the people of this territory.

Jack considered her. He finally nodded. "Fine. We'll start with the ones we have locked in the tunnel upstairs."

Mia paced back and forth at the end of her parent's beds. The clean white linens, faded and thin from time, contrasted with the dirt and filth covering her parent's clothes, hands, and face. When was the last time they'd showered? Taken a break? She stopped in the space between the two beds. "They never slow down."

Jack shook his head. "Not since I've known them. A lot of guilt inside those two."

Rani walked in.

"Both of you go. I got this. Fretting won't make them better." She pried Eva's eyes open and gave a satisfied hum. "Eva will recover. Shield's just having a difficult time repairing the damage from the neurotoxin she was injected with."

"What about my father?"

"I don't know what was in that dart. I'm still running more tests."

"Come on kid, let's go get those assholes." Jack reached a hand out. "And have a discussion about your taste in men on the way."

———

Mia had been a stubborn child. Obstinate. Not that much had changed. As an adult she could look back and tie it all back to genetics on both sides. She hoped both her parents fought like hell, dug down deep, and used it to survive.

Icy fingers of doubt gripped her. Could she do what they did on a daily basis? All the lies, all the hidden secrets nibbled away at her confidence. Before the last few days, she would have said without a doubt that she was confident and strong. But if that were true her parents would have told her about their past, about her role in it.

What did they see that she didn't?

Jack called topside to add guards to the station above the conference room exit. He said nothing about Sector Nine and nothing out of the norm had been reported from other sectors.

The incident on the sub-level seventeen track had been isolated. For now.

"Time to go rattle some cages." Jack led the charge up the stairwell to sub level seventeen. She let him. He did have more military experience than her. It had nothing to do with her flagging confidence. Nothing at all.

"Shouldn't we get a few more people?"

There had been seven of the bastards in all in the tunnel.

"We're meeting Talia and Eric on the landing."

Mia snorted. "That's still four against seven."

"Nah. Even if they get untied, they're not going to be moving very quickly."

He skipped stairs and Mia had to speed up.

On the landing of the seventeenth sub-level, Talia waited with another young guard, also with enough weapons to sink a barge. She'd tried to tell the young woman that three or four weapons were plenty, but Talia always insisted on more.

"We want to question them, not kill them," Mia said.

Talia grinned. "It's just a little incentive. And it's good to see you alive."

God, the girl was bloodthirsty. Mia just shook her head and tried not to smile.

Eric, the other guard, nodded at her. "Boss."

"It's good to have you both here. Here's what we got." And she related the most pertinent events to this point. They didn't need to know about Daniel or Eva. Or Cooper, for that matter. She told them about Sector Nine and an outsider stirring up problems. The rest needed to be kept quiet. Hell, maybe her father had rubbed off on her. "You have anything to add, Jack?"

He had checked the offices and rooms while she'd debriefed their back-up. Now he stopped and shook his head. "Nope, let's go talk to them."

———

Eric dragged an emergency light stand to the door leading onto the walkway for the portion of blocked-off track where the prisoners were held. An inky gloom met them through the observation window, no people in sight.

Back against the wall, Talia at her side, she readied the baton and nodded for Jack to open the door. Fighting she could do. Something she was very good at.

A rock flew through the entrance, landing near the stand. So they *had* gotten free. She ducked and cut diagonally across the entrance at a crouch, moving quickly and taking out the person standing there. Talia followed going the other direction. Jack went down the center.

"Pull it in, turn it on, and lock the door." She ordered. More rocks flew where she'd just been. Mia continued forward. A shadow stirred in front of her and she struck out with the baton, as quick as an adder. The person went down and a nasty grin slashed across her face.

Grunts, groans and a few more thuds emanated from the shadows.

Suddenly, the tunnel was lit up like an old football stadium on Friday night. Four men still sat against the walkway, nursing their wounds. The other three were in various stages of getting their asses kicked. Again.

Gustav lay in front of her, folded over.

"I would think you would have learned your lesson earlier," Mia told him. He flipped her a vulgar jester, gasping for air. At the sight of their boss on the ground, the other two surrendered, blood dripping from various cuts and scrapes.

She pulled her pistol, Jack and Talia following suit. "Now, go back and sit against the wall."

"Water."

"Not happening until you give us answers." Was he kidding her? Mia shook her head. "And anyway, I'm Infected, remember? You'd take water from me?"

"Go to hell."

"Speak nice to her, Gustav, or I'll make sure you dehydrate. Now get your ass to the wall." Jack took a step closer.

Big bad Jack to save the day. She hid her grimace. Gustav stumbled to the wall and collapsed next to his people on the ground. Talia trained one of her pistols at no particular person in the group but kept it ready. Smart girl. If they didn't know who she was pointing at, it could be any one of them if they got out of line.

"Now, we'll give you food and water if you tell us what we want to know."

The goons all remained grim-faced and silent. One of the women spat to the side and glared. Great.

"Who else from the sector are working with you?" Jack bent down and filtered his fingers through the minute pieces of gravel between the tracks. He fisted some in his hands and stood. "I can't figure Carmen for wanting to stir things up. She likes her rations too much."

Carmen, the second-in-command for Sector Nine on the Council, was an older woman and liked the status quo. Gustav was the one usually railing against the machine. His words. An old phrase. Some people just did not like order or being told what to do. She kept her eyes on the man. Somewhere in his mid-fifties, he had been young—but not too young—during the collapse. He and Jack had known each other a long time.

Due to Shield, Jack still looked like he was in his late thirties. Must be difficult to see. *Why didn't my parents consider the ramifications of slower aging?*

Infected. It wasn't too far off the mark, actually.

"I get it." Mia holstered her pistol. All eyes turned toward her and she ignored them, walking in front of the group of people from Sector Nine. Jack looked taken aback. Good. "I do. It has to be hell. Watching your sons, daughters, friends and family all grow old. Die. Yet, here are these survivors from some top-secret facility who just stay the same due to a limited super-medicine. Must be infuriating. Even some of the council have been given this gift, but not you, the common population. Hell, a few years ago it was barely noticeable, but now, yeah, now, it's very obvious that something is going on and you want in. Am I getting close?"

Several of the people shifted uncomfortably not meeting her gaze. Except for Gustav. His eyes blazed with fury. "I won't become Infected, bitch."

"Uh-huh. But you will kill your fellow citizens even though they help keep you fed. Watered. Keep your people healthy? Seems like a fucked up situation to me."

"You give me your medicine and I'll tell you everything," said a voice from the end. Karen. That was her name.

"You want to become like us?" Mia didn't use the word.

"Yeah, I want Shield."

So, they did know the name of her mother's super-drug. Wonderful.

"Mia," Jack warned. She ignored him.

"How many are rebelling in Sector Nine?"

"Shut your dirty mouth, whore!" Gustav made as if to stand, but Talia stepped forward. He glared at the young woman, his eyes darting back and forth between her and Karen.

Karen didn't appear phased. "Don't know. We meet with our group and aren't told the rest. There are six in my group plus Gustav. He joined us today."

"How long ago did Sarah join you?"

"Who?"

"The woman from Montana."

"Oh, her. Don't know. She's been coming in every couple months I guess with bullets and stuff. Maybe a year? Maybe less?"

Gustav's face turned a bright red. If Mia's crew wanted to keep Karen alive after this, they'd have to take her with them. He looked fit to kill.

"What does she want in return?" Jack this time.

"All I know is she has asked us to search for a special cavern near the dam, but that place is so guarded it's been difficult."

"You stupid bitch, you really think they're going to Infect you? Like them? I will kill you before that happens." Gustav growled and tried to stand up. Jack stepped forward this time. Karen finally looked a little uneasy.

"How are they getting in undetected?" Mia asked.

Karen looked between her and Gustav. "You going to give me Shield, aren't ya?"

"Answer the question."

"You answer that and—"

Talia lunged forward, pistol-whipping Gustav across the face. The man slumped forward, cursing and holding his nose. She raised her arm again.

Mia stopped her. "Karen?"

"You know my name?" The woman side-eyed the man now lying on the ground. The other members of the group were either still too out of it, angry, or too intimidated to say anything.

Mia just raised her eyebrows. Waiting.

The woman shrank in on herself, shoulders hunching, eyes darting from the ground to Mia's. "There're tunnels. In the north. Now where's my medicine?"

"Take her to the dam." Mia ordered Talia. The younger woman went and grabbed Karen by the arm, jerking her up and cuffing her. "We don't give traitors Shield."

Venom flooded the woman's eyes.

Mia whistled to Eric still standing by the light stand and the door. He threw down a backpack and she set it on the tracks. "Food and water. We'll check in soon."

Jack backed up the stairs to the walkway in front of the observation window and Mia followed suit. Talia had already taken Karen into the sub-level.

"You could have left her," Jack murmured.

Mia flicked a glance his way. "They would have torn her apart. I love and admire my father, but I'm not him."

And maybe that was the problem.

CHAPTER 12
COOPER

September, 2072

Cooper read extensively when time allowed. Biographies, science-fiction, murder mysteries, the classics. History. Sometimes he needed the escapism of a good fiction book, but at other times he had a drive to learn about the past, to figure out when everything in the old world started to go wrong—this time. What led to the eventual Collapse. Some thought it was the COVID outbreak in 2020, others, the peace talks with Russia in 2032 that fell apart.

But Cooper had a different theory.

On September 11, 2001, the first direct attack on United States soil since World War II occurred. God, it had been decades since that historic event, but he truly believed that was the beginning of the end. A lot of other countries would call it American arrogance thinking they were the lynch-pin for so much. But he didn't see it that way. When a large portion of the world's market ran through one place, it was bound to affect everyone when that place fell apart. Like the Roman Empire. All empires fell eventually and when this one did, so did the world.

Nine Eleven. Seventy-one years ago. It showed that even the

most powerful could be bloodied. And like sharks, other places took advantage of that in subtle and not so subtle ways. Old enemies and new.

The side-by-side bumped over a pothole in the cracked and broken highway. Around him fallow fields and hills rolled out to the horizon for as far as the eye could see. It was early evening and he was approaching the old interstate.

In the years following the Collapse, Daniel would send patrols out this direction to either recruit or kill the scavengers preying on refugees from the western side of the Cascade Mountains. Cooper had spent his fair share of time out this direction helping people. Killing some when necessary. All as a teenager in Daniel's militia.

A line of dust in the distance caught his eye and he slowed the machine. Not many people north of the Territory. Colville, Jerome and Jorge's settlement, was still two day's ride North by cart, maybe half a day in the ATV barring having to stop to recharge the secondary solar battery.

Jerome. His death had wound Cooper up in Territory business faster than a bobbin on a sewing machine. What would have happened if he and his dog Kiva hadn't hitched a ride with the grandfather and grandson duo? Where would he be now?

Oh, Kiva. He missed his dog. *She'll have to wait.*

Screw it. Cooper needed to stay on course and get ahead of Sarah, not get mixed up in anybody's else's business. Even if that dust cloud indicated Sarah's whereabouts, he was in recovery mode—and he wasn't confident enough he could stop her by himself. Cooper patted the box in his cargo pants, reassuring himself that the dose of Shield was still there.

Nope. The trail of dust was not his problem. He'd turn off at the next road, or even go cross-country and avoid whoever approached from the northeast.

The drive smoothed out, the road less worn and crumbled, only sporadic sand and soil drifts covering the surface. Brittle sage dotted the landscape, very few of the bushes alive this far from the Basin Territory and its massive stores of underground water.

Something Jack said stuck in Cooper's brain like a splinter. You *have a kid*. Like just because he was a single guy he wasn't fit to care for anything let alone another human. Which gave rise to another thought. Why *had* he bonded with Claire out of all the other little orphans along his solitary path? He'd never given it much consideration…

———

"…and when the rabbit steps into the snare, it can't move. Are you even listening, Claire? This is important." Exasperation filled Cooper's voice.

The seven-year-old girl wove the rough strands of bunchgrass into little knots, making a tiny necklace for her ragdoll.

The Nebraska prairie stretched out all around them except for this little oasis in the middle of nowhere. The gulley led to a small settlement with the only deep well still working for a hundred miles in any direction. He had traded his help during planting season for room and board as they worked their way north and west.

She blinked up at him, her luminous eyes refocusing on his face, her tiny lips pursed in a stubborn set. "I was listening, Cooper, but I hate rabbit, it tastes disgusting."

"Well, when you're starving to death, you might change your mind and be glad to know what to do to feed yourself." He untangled the string for the snare and threw it in his pack. She obviously wasn't in the mood to learn anything today. "Grab your pack, we'll head back to town."

Like a zoo gazelle let loose back in the wild, Claire bounded across the clearing to grab a faded fuzzy backpack with a unicorn horn sticking out the top. He sighed. She needed a proper pack. Something a bit more utilitarian and not so…girly.

Cooper picked up his walking stick. Claire joined him, skipping back and forth in front of him, picking more grass and pocketing bits of stone. Those would be fun to find later on when he washed clothes.

The sun set in a deep vermillion, and for a rare moment, he was content.

That is, before Claire disappeared with a sharp screech of pain amidst the large clumps of bunchgrass.

Panic spurred him forward as he dropped his stick and sprinted to where she had been. And almost tripped over the same rock she must have in his rush.

"Daddy, it hurts." She held her ankle, tears wetting her lashes, chest heaving from the sobs.

Even though he had a hurt, crying little girl on his hands, that one word speared his heart and wouldn't let go. Daddy.

———

Several hours later, the motor started sputtering and Cooper hit the steering wheel. The batteries needed to be switched over or he wasn't going anywhere.

He guided the side-by-side next to a large white barn, its sides peeling and revealing the gray, weathered board underneath. The entire shape was curved and old-fashioned, built in the early 1900's and restored at some point pre-Collapse.

Cooper guzzled water from his canteen and switched the cables, hooking the solar panel line to the dead battery. The sun had started its downward turn toward sunset. He'd have to stop for some rest before too long—his body was able to withstand a lot with the Shield Serum, but even he needed a few hours of sleep after such a long night.

Sandy soil, tired and used up, surrounded the barn. He could almost picture it in the old days, with fields of golden wheat surrounding a picturesque building, tractors and farm animals dashing hither and yon. It looked like it hadn't been scavenged yet. A minor miracle.

Something scraped on the other side of the barn.

Cooper drew his pistol and crouched behind the ATV.

A rifle ratcheted a round into a chamber.

"I heard that, idiot. Now I have your position." Cooper shouted. Whoever it was already knew his position. He scanned the area on his exposed side. Not even a dust devil. So just the north side. A scout from a settlement? A little west for that, but it was possible.

Utter silence.

A breeze wafted by, smelling of death and rotten food. Squatters in the barn, then? Very real possibility, especially if there was water nearby.

"I'm just passing thr—" A shot whistled by, clanging off the roll bar of the side-by-side. A dog started barking from somewhere inside the barn.

A familiar bark…

"We want your vehicle. Too nice of a ride for a dumbass. How'd you even get one that runs without gas?" said a man's voice.

It came from the east side; the man was using the barn for cover. Cooper had twelve rounds in his pistol, and Daniel had stocked a box in a compartment in the bottom of the cab. He could afford one round as a warning shot.

Cooper tilted his head and attuned his hearing for breath sounds. Whoever was over there must have had bad allergies. His shot whacked the side of the barn and he crouched back down.

Cursing followed. Heh. Got some wood shrapnel.

"Tickles, doesn't it? Just let me drive on out of here, and I'll leave you all alone." He'd sensed and heard movement on the west side of the barn. Cooper walked at a crouch to the other end of the ATV and peaked around. Two more shadows.

"We'll let you walk out of here. Leave the keys." This was a different voice, harder.

"The way I see it, you're a day from Daniel Burgess's territory. You are either stupid, or suspicious. I just came from there and trust me, the hornet's nest has been stirred. Actually, several hornet's nests and a few viper's thrown in the mix for fun. Just let me be on my way."

Gunfire met his words.

Cooper cursed as bullets pinged around him. He didn't return fire. Let them waste their ammo.

A lull, and he pushed off from his haunches and sighted in on an arm. *Bang.*

A cursing scream followed the shot. Somebody got their gun reloaded and returned fire. He scooted to the front of the ATV. The man he'd shot was gripping his arm and sitting on the ground.

Another beat. The barking inside the barn yipped to a stop.

Bastards. They better not have hurt Kiva.

Ten seconds, fifteen tops to get to the corner of the barn.

He ran, faster than they could aim due to Shield. Gunfire whistled by.

Cooper reached the corner and pistol whipped the bleeding, pale man, his shock of brown hair standing out in ratty strands. The guy slumped forward. Cursing met his ears from the other side of the barn.

"Seriously, you have about two minutes before I come over there and beat your asses. I mean, how much ammo can you guys have left?"

He peeked in the hazy, warped glass of the window. Two long tables, the old folding ones with fake wood tops and metal legs, ran down the center of the main part of the barn. Guns, reloading equipment to make bullets and a few buckets worth of brass, sat in the middle. A tall metal toolbox on wheels sat next to a small door on the other side, other smaller boxes and paraphernalia scattered like islands in the rest of the room. A far corner held cages.

Well, crap. Where the hell were they getting the gunpowder?

He sidled along the length of the barn until he reached the back corner. Shuffling and wheezing, the bang of a door, and somebody trying to start the ATV. It didn't turn over. He snickered to himself, patting the cable in his pocket.

Cooper whipped around the end of the barn. Nobody was there. He repeated the move around the other corner on the side where the other two people hid.

A tall, broad-shouldered woman met his gaze. They both fired at the same time. Cooper threw himself to the side, aimed and nailed her right in the shoulder. She went down with a cry. Her bullet went wide, whizzing past his ear. God, he needed to slow down, do this right. His worry for his daughter was driving him past the point where he'd take care, and he couldn't let that happen.

A side door at the far end where the woman had fallen was closed. The other man was inside. He tried to look through the window but something was obscuring it.

There were two options: go in the door into the barn, or go around out front by his ATV. They had tried to start the ATV but could have gone in through the big double doors out front. Hmmm. Either would be covered so it wouldn't really matter.

"He's not going to let you live, you know," said the woman at his feet, face twisted in pain.

"No time for a chat. Night-night now." And he knocked her out.

Cooper kept his body and pistol pointing toward the door as he put his back to the wall. He reached across, opened it while remaining in place. It swung open and a bullet splintered the wall next to him. He shoved the metal toolbox, pushing it and using it for cover.

The other man hunkered behind a box at the other side of the room.

"So, you *are* stupid. Man, what're you planning? Taking on the Basin Territory? See, just plain stupid."

"You're just guessing. Who are you? One of the Infected for

sure, moving that fast. A plague on this earth. Our people will take care of that, with or without me."

The man took another potshot. It pinged against the side of the toolbox. One more should do it.

"Infected? You mean people with the Shield Serum? Hell, that stuff can save your life. Make you need less food and water, make you stronger. I'd call it a blessing, not an infection." Maybe a curse too, but he wouldn't say that nugget out loud, not in this company.

The other man didn't answer. Cooper was ready when he lifted up to take another shot and got him right between the eyes. He crashed to the floor.

Cooper closed his eyes, listening for any other sign of movement. The barn creaked as wind whistled through the cracks. Nothing else stirred besides whatever was in the cages partially hidden on the other side of the room. *Secure the scene and then get the dog.*

He'd need to tie up the other two he hadn't killed.

He stood and went to examine what he'd found.

The ammo reloading station was front and center. Dried food filled one of the wooden crates, plastic jugs of water filled another. This was a long-term operation, then. Did Daniel and Jack's scouts not venture out this far anymore? Cooper riffled through various tools and other odds and ends. Another crate held two large drums of gunpowder.

He made his way to the man he'd killed. The body lay at an odd angle, arms and legs splayed around the torso in a halo of blood. Silver threaded the man's dark hair, his clothes threadbare and patched. A silver chain with the small corner of a pendant peeked out of the top of his t-shirt.

Curious, Cooper yanked it out. A metallic ouroboros the size of a half-dollar, its neck snapped and reattached in a ragged, bloody wound lay against the dirty gray shirt. The ouroboros was the symbol for the Western Coalition but this…

That can't be good. That can't be good at all.

"Cooper?" A raw, husky voice said from one of the cages.

There, stuffed inside two oversized dog kennels were Jorge and Kiva.

CHAPTER 13
EVA

August, 2055

The relics of a bygone era punctuated the jagged concrete protrusions littering the street. Broken cars, buses, and bikes twisted along a narrow passage where two of their assailants had appeared. Trae, Coy, and Jess scattered, finding cover behind various rusted vehicles.

Adrenaline coursed through Eva's veins, and she shot her pistol. The man was fast and seemed to anticipate the move, rolling away and ending across from her.

Daniel leaped, changing direction in mid-air, and fired at their opponent. It winged the other man as he straightened from the ground.

But he kept coming.

Shouts from Trae, Jess, and Coy and barking from Nala alerted her to more fighting outside. She couldn't focus on that. Another person, a woman this time, entered over a broken wall and took aim at Eva with a riot gun. A hard rubber ball narrowly missed Eva's leg.

The woman fired again in rapid succession, one of the rounds catching Eva in the arm, numbing it. She ducked down behind a pile of rubble, and at the first chance she got, whipped around and shot at the woman. Bullseye. The woman went down, a bullet in her head.

There were three more rounds in her pistol. Eight in the gun at her ankle and five in the cartridge for her rifle. She should've taken a page out of Chet's book and packed more firepower so she didn't have to reload.

Daniel wasn't faring better. The man he faced had a baseball bat and some kind of modified rifle shooting odd-looking projectiles. Were those rocks? They were. Whatever he used for propellant was effective. A hard rubber ball bounced off the wall behind her and rammed her in the back on rebound.

Eva cursed, peeked around the broken cement, and fired a shot at a filthy man holding one of the strange projectile weapons. Her round took him in the gut but it didn't slow him down. A cold frisson of shock wormed its way through her. These people acted like they were Shielded.

Their opponents kept streaming into the surrounding cavernous remains of old office buildings and leftover humanity like a relentless tide. Three more voices? No, four. *Dammit*. She raced to another pile.

Trae, Coy, and Jess needed help.

Barking, a nasty yip, and then silence from Nala. Her heart plummeted. *Not the dog.*

The three teenage soldiers were trapped by advancing hostiles in rags, their hair in ratty knots—more projectile weapons with no normal gun in sight.

They wanted to capture them all alive.

Eva's heart stuttered. If they were captured, it meant…God, it meant so much.

"Headshots only, everyone, they're Shielded!" Daniel yelled from back where she started, confirming what she'd already figured out. A grunt, groan, and crash as somebody went down. Daniel, or one of the hostiles? *Not now, just move forward.*

She sprinted to the next pile of rubble, making her way

towards the teenagers. They were well-armed and well-trained, but this was their first actual all-out fight, and somebody needed to back them up. She almost wished for the super-strength from the meteorite, except without the psychopathic rage.

The sounds of battle raged around her. Guns fired, chunks of rock and hard rubber balls thunked against concrete and bodies. Grunts, groans, and swearing accompanied the noise. She finally reached the backside of the decimated building as near to the front of the BAC as she could get without exposure.

Three bodies of their attackers lay on the ground. Trae fought another while a second harried him from behind. She aimed at the person's head and fired. A red hole appeared in between their eyes, and they collapsed to the ground.

Jess was cornered by the door to the BAC, her shots going wide. With a click, the rifle was empty. She charged the man shooting at her and used the gun like a bat. It clipped him in the shoulder, but he turned into it, bringing the butt of his own gun down on the young woman's back. Jess screamed in agony.

Another woman in rags appeared from the shadows, hollering a war cry. Coy came around a pile of rubble, blood dripping from a sharp cut along his hairline. It must have been deep for it not to have healed yet. He shot the woman in the head and rounded on the man who'd shot Jess. It missed.

Eva took aim. The shot went wide, the man moving too fast.

One more round in her pistol.

Nala whimpered near the door to BAC but remained crumpled on the ground. At least she was alive. Thank God.

An arm snaked around her throat and squeezed.

"No more games! I've captured one of your people, stranger. Come out, or I'll put a bullet in 'er skull."

Rotten breath made Eva gag. She lifted her foot and slammed it into a kneecap with a hard downward thrust.

The man yelled in pain but grabbed her windpipe harder with his greasy fingers. Eva choked, black spots forming in her eyes. *Not like this*, Dios mio, *not like this.* It was half-prayer, half supplication.

Daniel walked out of the building, eyes on fire. He aimed his rifle at the man behind her, and she squeezed her eyes shut, frozen, ready for him to take the shot.

The rifle clicked empty. Eva's eyes swiveled in their sockets. All their people were down. There had just been too many opponents in the end, skittering from the rubble like Shielded rats.

"Gather 'em up," said Greasy Fingers. "We're bringing 'em back to the boss."

———

Chains ringed Eva's wrists behind her back. The others fared the same. Her captor kept a tight grip on the chain, giving it a good yank down every few feet, opening the fresh abrasions Shield tried to heal. After Daniel had attempted to talk to her, his mouth had been gagged, and she could sense his presence like a coiled lion stalking the man behind her.

Why hadn't he left her there? Left the others and escaped back to the train? Then he could've rallied the troops and got them out of this mess.

If she could get their captors talking…

"Where are we going?" She said through swollen lips.

A closed fist shot out and slammed into her mouth. "No words, gussie."

She moaned and spat out a glob of blood. Shield healed the wound but it still stung. Daniel grunted in pain her, and a rattle of chains thunked against the cracked asphalt. The militia members walked in front of her, heads on swivels.

As they neared the town center, the piles of rubble took on a more uniform structure, neat pyramids of cement and brick. Cleared pathways to some of the more intact buildings gave way to a tarp city which opened onto an enormous wall leading up to the World War I monument.

In front of it was some sort of—*Dios*, was that a throne? It was. Two slabs of rubble had been formed into the large chair, and it was embedded with glass-encased marble-sized pieces of black stone, each one like miniature ships in a bottle atop a dais. Below, a large flat horizontal slab of rock, black with blood, was surrounded by a large group of people, men and women but no children.

An enormous man, muscle plaited on muscle, sat on the throne. There really was no other word for it.

"Bring the trespassers forward. Let me look at them." The man's arms rippled as he leaned forward.

"Yes, Mr. Hensley."

Oh. Oh, shit. The monster of the Midwest in person. She'd only ever heard rumors from the few refugees who had escaped and made it to the Northwest.

Daniel moved up beside her. Wild fury darkened his features, scary in its ferocity. Usually, he contained it, hid it so that very few saw the true depth of his emotions. But not now.

The only time Eva had ever seen him let loose was during the battle with Sarah. But…she'd heard the stories from the early days of the Resource Wars. Daniel had earned his reputation—and medals—in the military.

Whispers of sound coalesced deep inside her, the words unclear but trying to push their way out, to strike out at the hulking male on the throne. A din of something…other.

She clamped down on the foreignness of the sensation, the chaos that came with it. That way lay dragons, uncontrolled ones with rows of sharp teeth. Eva clenched her jaw and focused on her breath.

Hensley cocked his head, eyes narrowing on Daniel. "Who are you? Why are you in my city?"

The gag was jerked out of Daniel's mouth. "Let us go, and I'll tell you."

A booming chuckle emitted from the big man's chest. "You

think you have power here? No, you invaded my territory and were caught in my lands. This goes only one way."

"Okay. My name's Jack."

"And why don't I believe you?

"Jack Allen, second Ranger battalion. Would you like my rank?"

"Okay, Jack. We searched you, but you don't have any of the black rock on you. How did you fight for so long? You and your people took out five of mine, and those good men and women carried the rock."

Daniel clamped his lips together. A rifle butt swung, taking him right in the exposed gut through his tattered shirt. He doubled over, his breath expelling in a pained grunt. Another swing took him in the back of the neck, bones crunching, and he fell to his knees.

Eva winced but kept her eyes pointed to the ground.

"Well, Jacko, or whoever you are, let's see if this will get you to talk." Hensley gestured for them to bring Jess to the dais. The teenager tripped forward, glaring at the man in front of her, mouth still gagged.

"Put a bullet in her."

Eva couldn't contain herself. She raised her eyes, locking them with Hensley. The cold presence in her blood coalesced with the emotion, her and her creature as one. "Only monsters kill children."

An evil grin lit the man's face. "Ah, so we have a player in this group. And who are you, gussie? His whore? Or something more?"

Hensley gestured with his hand like he was shooting a gun, never taking his eyes from Eva's. One of his men did as Hensely said and shot Jess in the back of the head.

All of the emotion froze inside her like superheated sand turned to glass.

Coy and Trae roared, pulling against their chains. This time, the guards shot them with tasers, pumping volts of electricity through their young bodies. The two collapsed to the ground, twitching among moans of pain.

"Two more to go, grown-ups. Never bring kids to a gun show. It never ends well." The tone was almost lilting. He was enjoying this.

Bile crept up Eva's esophagus, the cold inside her turned to molten lava. *Focus. You lose focus, and we all die.*

Eva's smile was brittle. A rictus of lip and teeth. "I'm trying to decide if this is all due to mommy issues or if you're just that insecure with your manhood."

"Eva, enough," Daniel croaked.

"Brave words from a whore. Tie her to the altar. Jacko, here, is about to get a little demo of our God's desires."

A ragged cheer, half undulating moan, rose from the crowd. Eva blinked, wanting to struggle but knowing it would do no good. Two sets of rough hands thrust her forward toward the blood-encrusted stone in front of Hensley. She fell to her knees, ripping a hole in her jeans.

The two men slammed her onto the rock, and the turquoise blue of the sky came into focus. Her thoughts scrambled to catch up to what was happening. A rank rag was shoved into her mouth, and she tried to spit it out. Filthy fists tied a rope around her head and feet to keep them in place.

Panic and the edges of the claustrophobia she'd controlled for over a decade now resided in her chest, squeezing until she couldn't breathe.

"Leave her alone!" Daniel growled. She rolled her eyes to look at him and saw fear, even desperation in the lines of his face.

No. He couldn't give them away. There was still a chance Mia could survive, that their territory could survive if Tamara, Chet, and the others made it back home. They could still figure out how to fix the TMRWS machines with Rani and Amrit's help. Figure out how the meteorite played into all of it.

"Then tell me your real name, Jacko and what you're doing

here." Hensley bent and in one fell swoop, licked her cheek clear to the temple.

She shook her head, pleading with Daniel, trying to get him to be his cold, logical self. Except, Daniel had never been cold and logical when it came to her.

Her throat burned where words tried to escape around the nasty cloth in her mouth. That presence inside of her squirmed, causing small halos of light to spot her vision.

Daniel wouldn't look at her; he had eyes only for the man on the throne. "Get her off there, and I'll answer your questions."

Hensley smiled his little smile and flicked his finger at her hulking guard. The guy took out a twelve-inch blade, serrated on one side.

"Do it."

And the knife plunged into Eva's abdomen clear to the stone beneath her.

Fire raged along every sinew of contact with the blade. She bucked against the restraints, trying to ease the agony spearing through her innards. Coppery blood coated her raw throat, her jaw clamping the repulsive fabric to fight against the nausea.

The knife disappeared, and Shield rushed to fix the damage like ants crawling along the searing wound.

Her surroundings and mind snapped back in place. Daniel lay on the ground, lacerated along every inch of exposed skin, one arm dangling from its socket.

His eyes found hers; pain and fury, love and torment reflected in their depths.

Eva shook her head again. He couldn't tell them. They both knew how this went. Damned if you do, damned if you don't.

The knife slammed down into her gut once again. And again.

Unconsciousness wouldn't come, Shield keeping her from sweet oblivion. Soon, the pain turned to numbness, her consciousness leaving her body with each thrust of the bowie knife.

"I'm Dr. Daniel Burgess of the Basin Territory. Now, stop!" His voice was so raw.

"Ah, now we're getting somewhere. The famous Commander Burgess, Defender of Diomede. Alaska never had it so good. War hero at my doorstep, folks. What're you doing here, war hero? Tell me, or she gets another five."

"Just scavenging. We made our way cross country, trying to find the WC." Each word was punctuated by a gasp.

"Western Coalition, huh? You think me a fool? Knife her!" Hensley's voice bellowed this time, impatience and anger infusing each word. *Volatile,* some logical part of her brain processed.

"No! Fine, I'll tell you. Just leave her alone."

"You lie to me, war hero, and I will chop off her head. No coming back from that."

"We're looking for a black rock. We heard you had some. Came to steal it." Daniel panted the words, blood leaking from the lacerations on his face. Some were half healed, others still bleeding as Shield tried to keep up with the damage being rained upon him.

Eva's heart skipped a beat. Daniel met her eyes one last time before her eyes drifted closed.

His final words faded as her world turned to gray. "My life for theirs. They were just following orders."

CHAPTER 14

MIA

September, 2072

The underground could hide so much. Life, death, sorrow. Horror. All buried in the bowels of the earth like ancient curses forever entombed in the darkness, waiting for unsuspecting passersby.

How had the old government kept such a long train tunnel hidden for so long? Hell, Mia's parents hadn't even known the full extent until they'd found some maps back in '55 and discovered an entire infrastructure writhing in the underbelly of old world America. Snaking more like. And apparently expanding long after the Collapse.

Fix the last TMRWS her mother had said back at the MUC. That would have to wait. Right now, they needed to secure their borders before chaos took over.

And gain time for Rani to fix her parents.

"Where do you think it ends?" Her words were muffled amidst the dirt and timbers around them.

Mia and Jack had been walking for an hour, working their way through the rough hewn tunnels near where she'd been held. They extended farther north and east than she'd originally thought.

He'd grown grimmer and grimmer the longer they'd ventured into the system. "I don't know."

Mia checked her compass, the flashlight beam reflecting off the glass case. "Still northeast."

"Yep."

She rolled her eyes. No more than one to three word answers had left his lips since she'd shown him the false wall and storage room where she'd been, well, stored. He blamed himself.

"It happened right under my parent's noses as well, Jack. And mine. And the entire rest of the council for that matter. We have a lot of ground to cover and make-up for."

Jack halted abruptly and Mia almost ran into his back. "We should have taken Sector Nine more seriously, should've worked harder at dispelling their concerns in the council meeting. Instead, we made the power move."

She snorted. "My father knows a different move to make?"

He glared at her. "Your father is the greatest strategist I've ever known. And that's saying a lot. I was a Ranger pre-Collapse and worked with many, many..." He hit the side of the tunnel. "Dammit. We got complacent."

"So you've said." Many times. "But I don't think it's only complacency. Where did they take all the dirt? I mean, our scouts would've noticed large quantities of dirt being removed to the surface, so where did it all go?"

Her words were met with silence.

The two of them wound through the tunnel system, ending up at the hatch in the roof where Cooper had dumped Jack the day before. Somebody had cleared the rocks and it now stood open to the sunlight, a guard above them.

Jack marked something on his map. "It's still our responsibility to know what's happening in our territory, Mia, regardless. We should have been taking the unrest more seriously, realizing there was more to it than people blowing off steam in a stressful situation. The signs were all there but we were too focused on Eva's mission to fix all of the TMRWS and finding an answer to the drought. The council and I should have at least dug into it more, let Daniel and Eva worry about the rest."

"You mean I should have. As head of security." Bitterness coated her tongue.

Dust motes filtered through the sunlight, tiny specks of earth clogging the air. Jack regarded her. "But I've been the one training you. You've only had the job for two years." He swept his arm toward the tunnel. "This has obviously been going on far longer than that."

"Hindsight and blame are getting us nowhere. We need to find where all of this started." She walked to the dead end wall and started feeling around for a false wall or mechanism like the one near her prison.

After a moment, Jack followed suit.

Finding nothing, the two of them backtracked down the tunnel and took a different branch. At each dead end wall, they looked for a hidden door or anything to indicate that particular tunnel's purpose.

"Tunnels to nowhere, That makes no sense," Mia said after a while. "It's like they were searching for something."

Jack's brows drew together. He just shook his head, marked his map, and continued on, head lamp bobbing.

All righty, then, back to grunts and monosyllabic caveman speak.

At the next junction, a large X was marked on the wall next to a backwards D.

"This is where your father stopped when we were down here looking for you." He flicked away at the rocks and compact dirt to get rid of it. No sign that anybody had been this way remained, except their shoe prints behind them, which could have been anybody's.

The intersecting tunnel veered off to the left and right. Mia checked her compass. The left hand tunnel was pointing more north, right hand tunnel more southeast.

Jack and Mia both looked at each other and without saying a word, both turned north, their headlamps barely cutting through the inkiness in front of them.

The black swallowed her, long and viscous gulps of time and distance. Each step taking her closer and closer to an answer she didn't know the question to. Her parents knew, maybe even Jack.

And Cooper.

Somehow he was tied up in this tighter than a sailor's knot. *Troubled brown eyes regarding her solemnly as she read to him.* The shard of memory was there and gone. He'd always been a part of it, just absent for a long time. Maybe that's why she felt an instinctual need to trust him even though he'd betrayed her in the MUC. Childhood connections could bind people together tighter than even some family bonds.

She clenched the compass in her pocket, its familiar weight and grooves comforting.

It could've been a mile, it could've been ten, but the tunnel took on the gray glow indicating some type of light source ahead.

She and Jack turned off their headlamps almost in tandem and slowed their pace. He waited for her to step up beside him, her other shoulder brushing the side of the tunnel.

Jack dipped his head to talk in her ear. "If I've marked the map correctly, we should be somewhere roughly beneath the old highway 395."

She nodded her understanding. Sector Nine's northern most border would only be a few miles south of here.

Mia drew her pistol, only a little behind Jack. Where there was light, there could be people. The tunnel straightened and widened, brightening until the outlines of the rough-hewn beams and craggy walls became clearer and more distinct.

Jack froze, throwing an arm out to stop Mia from proceeding

any further. Up ahead, in the center of a natural basalt cavern, an emergency light shone atop a solar-charged battery like the ones they had on the outskirts of the Territory. Crates and barrels were stacked off to the side. Two more tunnels branched off about the size of the one where they resided. Two people, a man and a woman, were loading a large wheeled cart like the kind that could be hooked to a four-wheeler.

Sector Nine?

Jack flashed her a hand signal, *take them alive,* and she nodded and holstered her pistol. She'd engage the woman.

They both flew at the two in the cavern, Shield taking over their movements with brutal efficiency.

The woman lifted startled eyes, body tensing. Mia slammed her fist into the woman's face, a quick jab. Blood gushed from her broken nose. She grabbed something from her waist and hurled it at Mia, stumbling behind one of the crates.

The knife sliced across Mia's arm and made an irritating gash. She didn't slow down.

Mia grabbed the woman's vest and turned her hips to throw her to the ground. She was blocked.

Crap. This person knows Judo.

Jack had lost his edge from the surprise attack as well, the two men fighting in earnest. Jabs and full out punches and kicks snapped through the air in rapid-fire succession. Jack had the upper hand but barely.

Nobody had drawn a gun. Either Mia and Jack were the only ones who had them, or their opponents also had orders to take anybody coming through the tunnels alive.

Mia used one of the crates as a springboard, the woman already sprinting for the tunnel farthest away. Were there more people that direction? If so, they must be at some distance because neither person had shouted for help.

The jump took her to within feet of the other woman. Mia landed and pushed her body to overtake the running figure. She didn't want her reaching that tunnel.

With one last rush, Mia tackled the woman's legs and they both went down with a grunt. She wrapped her arms around her throat in a chokehold, thighs clamping onto her middle. The woman gurgled and ripped at Mia's arms. Long scratches marred her skin. She gasped but maintained the squeeze, her chest heaving at the exertion.

A thud and a grunt from across the room told her somebody had gone down. Mia couldn't see who but nobody came to help the woman, so she assumed it wasn't Jack. The body beneath her slackened, going limp. She kept the hold for another couple of beats to make sure she was out, then released her arms, rolling away.

Jack was tying up the man with some chain he'd found in one of the crates. He threw her a section and clamped the woman's hands behind her, dragging her by their other prisoner.

"Let's see what else is in these crates." Jack pried one open and swore. "Rifles."

Mia pried a lid off another barrel. Shell casings.

Another held dehydrated food. From Basin Territory's stores.

"Do you recognize those two?" Mia asked. She tossed a packet back in the crate in disgust. Their accountants kept careful records of how much they produced and what got distributed. More traitors. She'd have to get somebody down here to collect all of it.

Jack studied the two on the ground, frowning. "Neither of them look familiar."

Her stomach clenched into a hard knot.

If these two weren't from Sector Nine, who were they? Time to see where the other tunnels led.

CHAPTER 15

COOPER

September, 2072

Sunset cast the deteriorating barn in the rich hues of a pink so deep it bled. Dirt filled the air from a dust storm, coating Cooper's hair and creeping its way beneath his clothes. Even though he could drive through it, Jorge and Kiva weren't equipped. He itched to get moving but figured no one was moving very fast in the low visibility, and unless Sarah had an ATV, he still had the edge. What worried him was the thought she had a different mode of transport, one faster than his.

One hour. He could spare one hour to get the two sprawled on the floor in shape enough to jump in the side-by-side. His planned route took him to within a half-day's hike from Colville. Jorge could ride along until that point.

"What happened? I thought you well on your way home." Cooper smoothed his hand over Kiva's jutting rib cage. He'd dribbled water in a bowl, only letting her lap up a tiny bit at a time. The dog had been tough—unusually so—since he'd found her in the tunnels of Virginia, but even she still required some food and water on a regular basis.

"We got waylaid by these jackasses on the east road. Drove the dog wild, she almost took one of their faces off. I'm not in too great of shape so it didn't take them long to put me down. Been in that cage for two days. Took them a bit longer to capture Kiva, even though she could have escaped easily enough. Loyal dog." Jorge swigged another mouthful of water and chewed on a jerky stick. Both of them stunk to high heavens like they'd been living in their own waste. Probably had.

"Find a change of clothes, rest up. We leave in an hour. I'll drop you to within a half-day's hike from home, probably send Kiva with you, and then be on my way."

The lines between Jorge's brow deepened. "What about my grandfather? I still need to find his killer."

Cooper blinked. The kid hadn't been around the last few days and so wouldn't know. How much to tell him, though? What would whet his appetite? "Territory knows who killed your grandfather, and it's pretty complicated."

Jorge shot to his feet, wobbling on unsteady legs. "What? Who? Where are they? I want to see them."

"Slow down, kid. When I say it's complicated, it's not a lie. Your grandfather was just a victim of circumstance."

The young man tilted his chin at a stubborn angle. "Not good enough. I'm heading back there, right now and—"

"And what? Demand they tell you what's going on? Basin Territory has hidden their secrets for a long damn time. Some settlement kid isn't going to get them to give them up, no matter if you're taking over for your grandfather." What Cooper said was true; he'd seen first hand what happened when Daniel and Eva closed ranks—what happened when orders weren't followed, no matter how heinous. Kiva bumped his hand with her head as if she could read his thoughts. He stroked her soft fur. "Look, I'm going after one of the folks responsible right now if it makes you feel better. I'll stop off at Colville on my way back, let you know how things went."

Jorge took a step forward. "Don't call me a kid and I'm coming with you."

"Oh, no, no, no. Not happening. They have—they have somebody I care about. I need to sneak in, secure that person, and get out." Hopefully killing Sarah in the confusion and gathering intel for Mia. Proof that he could be trusted. "I do not need to babysit somebody else."

"But I could help. Just tell me what to do and I'll do it. No questions."

Cooper's stomach knotted. "Have you fought before? I didn't think so. Between Basin Territory's shadow, your grandfather's long leadership, and your settlement's isolated location, your settlement hasn't had to deal with much in the way of the wider world in recent years."

"That's not true, we've dealt with our fair share of scavvies and thieves."

"Those are different than the groups out there in the major population areas, Jorge. Very different. I don't want to get you hurt, your people need you."

"What they need is a leader unafraid to protect them."

Cooper shook his head. The kid—the young man—was brave. A naive fool but brave. "Tell you what. We'll talk about it more on the way. I need to get going, not let her get ahead of me or it might be a moot point. Help me load the gunpowder, go get yourself cleaned up so I don't have to smell you, and we'll get out of here."

Jorge looked like he was going to argue further but set his lips in a thin line and nodded once.

Cooper pulled the side-by-side into the shelter of the barn and they loaded the barrels and whatever supplies were laying around. Kiva settled herself on the floorboards, resting her head on her paws and regarding him with wide, soulful eyes. He stroked her matted fur. At the first chance, he'd have to give her a bath.

He found a plastic face shield in the piles of junk lining the walls, threw a handkerchief and sunglasses to Jorge, donning his own, and they were off. If he stuck to the road, they wouldn't get turned around in the roiling clouds of dirt permeating the air.

Cooper hoped—no, needed—Sarah to be bogged down by the storm, unable to move very far. If there were more underground tunnels leading out of the Territory, then both him and Claire were screwed.

The wind abated just north of the Palouse, those rolling hills of once fertile farmland in southeastern Washington.

Him and Jorge bumped and jostled over an old cracked highway, silent. Cooper, for his part, was stuck on how he was going to infiltrate the Butte, Montana compound where Claire was being held. God, he should've just avoided any settlements in Montana two years ago. Where would they be now?

The day was so clear, so cool. It was a small settlement of eighty people in Western Montana, all huddled around a well, two large solar generators, a windmill keeping the flood irrigation going, and a lot of faith. He had agreed to dig out another deep well in return for room and board. Him and Claire had been traveling for months, moving from isolated town to isolated town, making their slow and steady way north and west. Now it would just be west. At least when he figured out how to avoid the center of the state.

Hot sun beat down and he shoveled around the shaft where a large pipe bit into the dirt. The old well had dried up long ago, along with the machinery to make this job easier. Dirt steps, planks of wood covering them, led down into the narrow pit. He and the others took turns digging it out, taking buckets of dirt up the steps, and repeating the process.

Cooper had to be careful. With Shield, he could work all day under these conditions and then some. But these simple folk had no clue what he had running through his veins. As the years passed post-Collapse, old fears and superstitions returned. He didn't want to fuel that fire, both him and his eight-year-old daughter needed a rest before making the last leg home. Home. He hadn't been back to the Basin Territory in a very long time.

He swigged from a canteen and brushed a hand over his sweaty forehead. The long pipe, still half buried in the hillside to give it stability, rose about him. Forty feet? Taller? He couldn't tell, he was never good with measuring, learning how to shoot guns having taken up most of his childhood.

They still had a ways to go but it was hard work—beneficial work that soothed some part of him that wanted more than just the death and destruction since the Collapse. Not that he had known much different. Not that Claire would know much different. Hopefully, taking her back to the Territory would at least give her some stability. She definitely wouldn't get it out here. If he had to, he'd beg Daniel to let him back in. Do anything. Be anything.

Capping the canteen, he thrust the shovel back into the earth, digging faster and faster to dispel the lingering anger at that particular thought. Begging Daniel left a sour taste in his mouth.

"Whoa, Coop, slow down, you're going to dig yourself right to China and then keel over." Nick, one of the pseudo-leaders of this little burgh outside of Billings, had stopped digging and regarded him with wide eyes.

Shit. Get a hold of yourself, Coop.

Cooper grinned, dropping the shovel and shaking his arms out like the muscles were burning. "Nah, I'd croak long before China. Just trying to burn off a little pent up...frustration."

There, that little piece of nonsense should keep the other man distracted. It was no secret that a few of the townswomen had been after Cooper, seeing him as some kind of saint for taking care of Claire. He'd taken it in stride, keeping them at arm's length. There was no way he was going to get entangled with one of the settlement women.

It worked. The man shook his head, a smile tipping his broad mouth. "Either Josie or Luann would make a fine mother for Claire. I don't know why you haven't done anything about that yet."

"I told ya, I'm heading home and my people might not take too

kindly to an outsider." He shrugged his shoulders and picked up the shovel once again.

The conversation was interrupted by a teenage girl, gasping for each breath. She peered over the edge of the hole. "Come quick. There are people here from Butte."

All of the air went out of Cooper's lungs. Claire. Not giving a shit what Nick thought, he scrambled up the stairs, taking them three or four at a time. A razor wire fence, reinforced with metal siding, surrounded the occupied houses and wells.

The gate stood wide open, two big men and a woman with dark, dark hair in a braid down her back standing just inside the entrance. They were all armed to the teeth. One of the men held Luann by the hair and shoved the tip of a gun into her temple. Townspeople hid behind houses, a few of the guards stood in a half circle, hands in the air surrendering.

The big man fired the gun. Luann sprawled in the dust, blood pooling beneath her. The people shrank back, some weeping, others screaming. Cooper ducked behind a house, ghosting along. There may have only been three of them, but he could guarantee more laid in wait down the road. They always moved in groups of ten.

"I said, twenty gallons of water from your stores and enough food to get me and my people back to Butte."

"Our…our water stores are low, ma'am, we're having to dig a new well. If we give you our supply…" Nick's voice wavered.

Cooper opened the back door to the tiny house he and Claire shared with another family. She wasn't there. Shit. He grabbed the gun from his pack and checked the clip. Eight rounds. It would have to be enough.

He slid out back and around the side of the house.

"I could give a shit about this measly encampment. Give me what I need or more of your people will die. Look at it as a win-win. Fewer mouths to feed."

That voice. So familiar.

Cooper stooped over and slunk along the fence line. He had to get around to their flank, catch them off guard. Nice and easy, Coop. Daniel's voice this time, imprinted onto his brain from so long ago.

A fourth man from Butte had rounded up two more of the towns-folk. Nick stood, his hands in front of him in supplication. There was no give from the woman.

He straightened, his back to a dead tree next to the fence.

In one smooth motion, he whipped around the tree, sighted, and shot the man closest to him. The bullet took him in the head. He streaked across the space, sighting on the other man, taking him right between the eyes.

The woman whipped around, as fast as Cooper. He tried to aim but she side-stepped, dropping below his sights. He picked up speed, zigging until she appeared in front of him. She punched the air, a glancing blow. Cooper dodged, kicked out at her leg. Direct hit. It didn't slow her down.

She was Shielded. Had to be.

No time to shoot. It would be a waste of ammo. They flew around each other, arms punching, legs jabbing.

He was able to twist her into a throw, getting her down to the ground and both of his knees on either arm, the tip of the pistol beneath her chin. "Let those people go, or I'll pull the trigger. Twice to be sure."

The woman gave a raw chuckle. "Who are you?"

"The one who's going to kill you." So cliche, but God, the woman stood between him and keeping his daughter safe. These people *safe.*

"Many have tried. You really think those guys holding your towns-people care if I die? They'll pick their teeth with my bones."

He lowered his face until they looked each other directly in the eye, only inches apart. "You're Shielded. I think they care."

A piercing whistle split the air from the gate.

She chuckled, a harsh, grating sound. "Just who has the upper hand? Me or you?"

Seven more soldiers filed into the compound. Rifles pointed into the settlement.

"Daddy! Daddy, help!"

Claire. He didn't react, though the woman below him must have seen something. A slow, sly smirk turned up the corners of her mouth.

"One of two things is going to happen. You kill me, they kill them.

Or, I find that sweet, sweet voice, gather her up, and you both come with me. I'll take what I need from these townsfolk, leaving them alone to live out what miserable lives they have left. Which one is more appealing?"

Put Claire in danger or get dozens of people killed? He was ashamed to admit he considered the latter for a moment. The townspeople huddled in small groups, clinging to each other. Nick regarded him with fear and horror. He was close enough to hear the woman's words.

The woman, who he finally recognized.

And immediately, he knew there was nothing else he could do. He lowered his gaze back to hers, knowing without a doubt who this was. "How you and Eva could've come from the same people is the greatest mystery of our time."

Cooper threw the gun to the side, jumping back in one smooth motion, raising his arms to either side of his head. A rifle butt took him in the back and he fell back to his knees.

I'm sorry, Claire.

CHAPTER 16

COOPER

September, 2072

Dozens of tiny ghost towns dotted the border between the Columbia Basin and the rocky hills and canyons of the foothills to the Rocky Mountains. At one such town, at the point where Cooper would boot Jorge out to keep heading north while he continued due east, he stopped for a break.

The young man and the dog lolled, dozing in the seat and floor of the ATV. Cooper was a bit jealous. Memories and flashbacks had dogged him since they'd left the barn. Hell, since he'd crossed into the Territory's borders—was it only days ago? Mia's location in his head had faded hours ago, leaving him alone with himself. What was she doing now? Probably shoring up the walls of her parent's territory, preparing for a fight. He gripped the steering wheel tighter. Gah, he must be tired if his thoughts drifted there.

Lack of sleep, expending too much energy, and not taking the time to eat or drink had finally caught up with him. Shield needed time to get him operating at full. He still had at least a day in the side-by-side before he reached Butte. If Sarah was on foot, she was somewhere behind him. Maybe.

He needed a couple hours of sleep or he'd be worthless to Claire.

A rusty, dented green sign with the words St. John, hung at an angle on a metal post, half folded in on itself. Tumbleweeds drifted across the street of the boarded up town. Nothing moved but the wind.

Find a public building. Hole up. Cooper hated squatting in houses. Ghosts lived there, he was sure. Flitting around pissed at how their world had been upended.

A mechanic's shop appeared to his right. Perfect.

He left the side-by-side to idle and hopped out. The bay doors were closed. He checked one. Locked. The other opened on a smooth glide, amazing for its age. Cooper scanned the interior, satisfied that it would serve his purposes for what little time they'd be here. The ATV fit like a glove inside the bay. He let Kiva sniff around and do her business before calling her back in and shutting the bay door, locking it behind him.

"Where are we?" Jorge's voice was rough from sleep.

"Ghost town. St. John. I'm going to get a couple of hours of sleep, then get you outfitted for home. You have watch."

"About that…" Jorge straightened in his seat, more alert. "I'm going with you. If you leave me, I'll just follow."

Cooper ran a hand through his hair. "Dammit, kid, I don't have time for this. I won't put my daughter at further risk, not again. You being there is a liability."

"Daughter? You have a daughter?" Incredulity filled the young man's voice and Cooper narrowed his eyes. Jorge continued. "Whatever. I may not be as fast or as strong as you, but I am smart and I have just as much of a stake in this as you. These people killed my grandfather, whether they meant to or not, they murdered him in cold blood. I'm a part of this now. I'm going."

Cooper's tired brain couldn't keep up with all the reasons why that was a bad idea. "Let me take a nap and then we'll discuss some more, but Jorge, you don't know what you're asking. You've only had to deal with a few scavvies at a time, these Montana people, they'll literally eat you for breakfast. And they're not even the worst ones out there. Remind me to tell you about Kansas City sometime."

"I won't change my mind."

"We'll see about that." Cooper closed his eyes and crossed his arms, resting his head against the seat. Kiva sniffed around the garage, poking into the nooks and crannies.

"I'm going to go snoop around, see if I can find anything useful."

"Don't disturb the ghosts." Cooper settled further into the seat "And take the dog with you."

Poke, poke.

"Five more minutes."

Poke.

Cooper swatted at the hand jabbing him in the shoulder. But it wasn't a hand. He awakened in a jerk, taking hold of the rifle barrel and pushing it toward the ceiling. "What the hell?"

A tiny, old lady, her steel gray hair sheared off, and ice blue eyes regarding him with a gimlet stare, just shook her head. "Took you long enough. Sleep like that can get you killed."

He blinked. God, he must have been more tired than he'd thought. "Who are you?"

"Dana. Found your friends here foraging in my cache. They were lucky I didn't take them out."

Jorge and Kiva were by the door, relaxed and smiling. Well, as much as a dog can smile. Enjoying the show, the bastards.

"You're living in a ghost town?" He lowered the barrel and Dana pulled it back.

"Me and a few others. Got pushed west by that horde of mongrels in Montana. Figured we'd be safer the closer we got to

Basin. Didn't want to live by their rules either. Not that the asshole running the place would let us in anyway." She poked around in the back of the side-by-side. "This thing come from there? I hear they still have such things."

Cooper cleared his throat, trying to catch his scattered thoughts. "Mongrel horde? Pushing you west? You mean Butte's moving west?"

"That's what I said, wasn't it? Nasty bunch of people. Don't want to get caught in whatever they have planned. What do you got in the barrels?"

"Water," he lied, "Where are the others in your group?" He cocked his head to the side, trying to hear beyond the doors. Nothing. He eased out of the side-by-side.

"Here and there. Wanted to make sure you weren't going to kill us and eat us. The boy assured me not, but you never know these days. Dog's real nice. She convinced more than the human. Those folks in Butte would have had her kind ate long ago." Dana lifted his pack and pawed through the rations.

"Leave those alone." He itched to swat her hand. She'd probably shoot him.

"Your kid ate some of our rations. We don't have much left from the move, just trying to replace 'em."

Jorge shrugged. "Figured it was some traveler's cache. Sorry."

Cooper rubbed the bridge of his nose. "Take what you need. On one condition."

"I'm the one holding the rifle, boy." She snorted.

"That you are but there are some unhappy folks behind me heading home to Montana that would kill you as soon as they see you are breathing. Head to the Basin Territory, ask for a woman named Mia. She'll let you and your people in. Tell her Cooper sent you and tell her exactly what you told me. Also tell her there's gophers digging in a barn a day's ride north."

Dana's eyebrows shot to the rafters. "You ordering me around?"

"No, ma'am but I have enough death on my conscience. I can't force you to go, but I definitely wouldn't stick around here."

"Ma'am." Dana snorted again. "Haven't been called ma'am in donkey's years. This Mia will let us in, huh? What makes you think these bad folks are coming up right behind you?"

Cooper's lips twitched. "Yes ma'am, she'll let you in. And I know those people will be pretty anxious to get to Butte and this is the clearest path. Tell Mia a *Wrinkle in Time* is still my favorite story. That should let her know you're telling the truth."

She considered him for a long moment, then stuffed nearly half of the packets of jerked meat and fruit into her rucksack. "Interesting."

"Copy that." Now he'd have to gather more food along the way. Or make Jorge do it.

Dana patted Kiva's head on the way with a "good doggie" and shut the door behind her.

As soon as she left, he turned to Jorge. "Traveler's cache? Seriously?"

Jorge shrugged again. "Didn't figure to look for any actual people this far out."

"About you coming with me—" Cooper started.

Jorge interrupted him. "Look, I can help hunt and scavenge, I'll stay hidden once we're there. I *want* to come, I *need* to come."

Cooper had already decided that he wasn't leaving him here, not with the "mongrel horde" on the move. Who's to say scouts hadn't already been sent as far north as Colville? He didn't let the young man off the hook, though. "These people use other people, Jorge. You're either one of them, livestock, used for entertainment, or a breeder. Something has so twisted them since the Collapse, some of them have all but lost their humanity. There's piles of bones around the compound. Piles."

Jorge gulped, then straightened. "I...I understand."

"No, you don't. But you will."

"Please, Cooper, I—wait, what? I will? You mean, you'll bring me with you?" A fierce light danced in Jorge's eyes.

Cooper closed his own for a beat to shut out what he saw there. The damn kid was excited. He'd learn. The new ones always did. "God help me, yes. But like before, I say jump, you jump, I say hightail it, you take the dog and get yourself out of dodge. Only this time, you head for Mia and Jack, you got it? Tell them anything you've seen. This isn't going to be pretty. This is going to be rough, and dirty, and horrible but I need to do it to save my daughter."

"I still can't believe you have a daughter. How old is she? What's her name?"

"Claire." Cooper took out the folded polaroid picture, a line down the middle and the colors faded from rubbing against the inside of his pocket. He handed it to Jorge. Her black curls and kind, dark eyes, kinder than she had any right to be. "Her name is Claire. She's ten-years-old. She's my foster daughter. I'm the only person in the world that she has."

Jorge looked from it to Cooper and back. "You know, now I can't ever hate you."

"Don't worry, Jorge, I'm sure you could."

Cooper whistled for Kiva.

They left St. John and a small line of people snaking their way west, children of all sizes in the middle.

Good luck.

CHAPTER 17
EVA

August, 2055

A cool hand rested atop Eva's head, and she jerked back to consciousness. The hand disappeared, its owner skittering back.

Somewhere between Hensley declaring she would fit right in at the breeder's house, and ordering Daniel, Trae, and Coy to be thrown into the pit to feed the hogs, Shield had shut her body down to continue its repairs of the massive damage from the stabbings.

The girl attached to the hand couldn't have been much older than sixteen or seventeen. Clumps of dirty-blond hair stuck out at odd angles as if sheared by a knife. Liquid blue eyes peered from beneath long lashes. Dark circles rimmed the undersides in half-moons. She cradled a large pregnant belly, crouching, and her spindly bare legs poked out of a filthy mumu with worn tube socks on her feet. There had been no kids outside by the throne but there was definitely some inside.

Eva's abdomen burned. She lifted the tattered, bloody t-shirt. Her skin puckered in over a dozen half-healed slits the width of a knife blade. She cradled the wounds, weakness weighing her limbs and body down. Shield had never been tested to this extent before. Eva closed her eyes and expelled a slow breath.

"How you heal so fast without the God's gift?" The pregnant girl crept closer, head tilted, examining her as if she were an interesting bug.

"Excuse me?"

"Only the God's Chosen can heal thyself. I checked. You don't have the God's gift, so how come you can heal quick?"

Eva's brow furrowed. *God's Chosen?* "What does the God's gift look like?"

The girl's face screwed into a frown. "I'm not s'posed to talk 'bout it."

Eva sat up, and the room spun, the back of her shirt, half-dried with blood, stuck to the wooden planks of the floor. She crawled the few feet to a wall and let it prop her up. No driving rage filled her veins, no thoughts that weren't her own pulsed in her brain. Her blood volume must not have replaced itself yet, the enzyme and Shield at their limits.

God, she needed water and something to eat. *Who knows what they would feed you?* Bile rose at the thought of the type of flesh they consumed here in Hensley's territory. She swallowed, her throat dry. Shield reduced the need for food and water at normal function. This definitely wasn't normal.

"My name is Eva. What's yours?" Too late now to give an alias.

The girl's eyes widened. "Names are power. Why you give me yours? You don't know me. I could put the voodoo on you now."

Oh, my. "Then, what do they call you?"

This appeased the girl. "They call me Kel, though that isn't my name. I'm nice and don't do the voodoo but others aren't so nice, so don't just be giving your name like that if you want to live."

Eva nodded her head solemnly, like she understood the gibberish coming from Kel's mouth. "Where are we, Kel?"

The room was little more than the size of an office. A pile of neatly folded rags, a blanket atop it, sat against one wall. A bucket, the stench of urine and feces emanating from its depths, was tucked in a corner. A metal framed outdoor chair and a small table with a candle took up another. Gray paint peeled away in chunks from the walls, and any carpeting had been removed at some point.

"My room. Since I is almost done with the breeding, I get my own room. They put you here with me cuz the others are busy." Kel stood and waddled to the chair, sighing as she sat, her big belly humped up under the thin fabric. She picked up a basket of knitting next to her. "This baby's coming any day now. Thank the God."

At this pronouncement, Kel's belly rolled and lumped up on one side as the little life inside moved around. Eva winced in remembered sympathy.

"Tell me about your God."

"Are you stupid or something?" Kel's brow wrinkled in confusion. "The God knows all and sees all. He empowers the Chosen and protects the weak. We sacrifice our lives, and he gives us food and water."

Eva took another tact. "I'm just a wanderer, looking for salvation."

"Sal-what?"

"Protection. For me and the people I came here with."

"That's not what Vic said. He said you were trying to steal from the God and had to stay here until your Conversion. Vic said you wouldn't hurt me because I is breeding." The girl cocked her head to the side and crossed her arms, eyes narrowed in suspicion.

"Vic's right about one thing, I won't hurt you, breeding or not. And we weren't here trying to steal from your God. We were looking for protection, uh, against another God. Will your leader help us?"

The woman glared at her. "Now, you think I'm stupid. I

might not know those bigger words, but I'm not stupid. Mother says I'm the smartest of all the breeders, and that's why I'm carrying Mr. Hensley's baby. He's not just our leader; he speaks for our God. What he says goes. So no more tricky words, Eva, or I *will* perform the voodoo."

Eva's shoulders slumped forward, and she laced her fingers together in her lap. Such thorough brainwashing would take too long to override, and she didn't have the time for this—Daniel and the others didn't have time for this, and she was too weak to storm the door. Time for a different plan. "You have any water?"

"Yes. But I'm only permitted to give you a small cup once. You sure you want it now? It'll be a whole day before the Conversion ceremony."

There was that word again. Conversion. "I'll take it now, Kel, and then get some rest."

The girl pushed up from the chair and went to the door, knocking in three sharp bursts and two long. A guard stood outside, a black rock hanging on a thin piece of leather around her neck, hair cut to ragged strands, like Kel's. "The thief wants her water ration."

Empty eyes glanced at her and then nodded, gesturing to someone outside Eva's line of sight.

A thick glass jar, half full of water, was passed through the door to Kel. "She know she only get one?"

"Yep."

"All right, then." The guard shrugged and closed the door.

Kel handed her the glass, almost tipping it over. Eva caught it quickly, her reflexes at least coming back to her.

The girl's eyes widened once again. "You move too fast for not being Chosen."

"A natural talent," Eva sipped the water. Every cell of her body told her to chug it, but she couldn't afford to vomit it back up. She needed to escape, find Tamara and the others, and save Daniel and the boys. Jess. Oh, poor Jess. Eva hadn't allowed herself to go there since coming to, but it was like the water to her lips opened the floodgates.

If they didn't get out of here, *Dios*, the world really was done for. Questions tumbled, one after the other inside her head. Were the black rocks the guards wore part of the meteorite? That must be how these brainwashed psychopaths had Shield abilities. Or had they found a version of Shield stashed away somewhere? Earlier versions had been transferred to Virginia. Maybe they hadn't actually made it past Kansas City.

Eva finished the water, her body becoming stronger as Shield converted it to blood volume. The other thing inside of her stirred, a slow languishing sensation along her nerve-endings. It wasn't enough for full strength but would have to do.

"Kel, what's the Conversion ritual?"

The girl shook her head as if Eva was the stupidest person on earth and continued to knit the thin yarn into some kind of small blanket. Probably for the baby. "Only the highest sacrifice and honor. Your body will be given to Mr. Hensley, and then each part of you will be portioned so that the Chosen can consume your strength. I don't see how you earned it, being a thief and all, but Mr. Hensley knows what's best, and it's not my place to question."

Consume your strength. A cold suspicion sunk into Eva's bones.

"Do the Chosen have the black rocks around their necks?"

"Well, yeah. Anybody who touches them and is not Chosen gets fed to the hogs." Knitting needles click-clacked together in a consistent rhythm.

For the first time in a long time, Eva paused and took note of the world she found herself in. Here was a teenager talking matter-of-factly about feeding people to pigs and consuming human flesh like it was a normal day-to-day occurrence. Pre-Collapse, teenagers would be worrying about what college they were going to or whether somebody had a crush on them or not —not birthing a child for a psychopath in some kind of demented cult. The more disturbing thought, though, the one that squeezed her heart and wouldn't let go: were she and Daniel any better?

They injected teenagers with Shield and taught them to be soldiers, killing and protecting their Territory and secrets. Human flesh may not be consumed, but the world had so changed, so regressed, that this generation of humans was rapidly becoming hard survivors, their childhoods consumed by her own generation.

If she ever made it out of here, she was for damn sure that the Basin Territory's kids and teenagers would at least get something back of the old days, even if she had to fight Daniel tooth and nail for it.

"Mr. Hensley says crying's for the young ones, and if he catches us biggers with tears, we get ten lashes. Water's expensive, you better dry them up, or I'll get the guard."

Eva blinked away the moisture before it fell. She had mere hours to formulate a plan to get her, and then Daniel and the others out of this.

Hopelessness filled Eva and a single, unavoidable tear fell to the hand on her lap. She put it to her lips and sucked it away, a bit of salt on her tongue.

That little voice in the back of her head told her there was no getting out of this one.

CHAPTER 18

MIA

September, 2072

The radios didn't work this far underground—and from this distance. She and Jack couldn't call for back-up. With two other tunnels to search, they would have to split up so as not to leave their asses exposed—and lose the two prisoners and all the stolen resources.

Jack unholstered his pistol. "You find anybody you don't recognize, take them out. I have a feeling your tunnel is going to end somewhere in Sector Nine. Cut it off somehow if you can, so they can't use it."

It was the most he'd said since his speech earlier. She answered by drawing her own gun. "Yours might go farther. No heroics, Jack. We need information, and with my parents incapacitated at the moment, we need you alive."

"You're just as bossy as them."

"At least I come by it naturally." She turned and started to jog down the tunnel. Each step a reminder that her parents were laying in twin hospital beds fighting for their lives. Each step kicking up dust that blurred her eyes and burned her lungs.

Whatever she found at the other end of this tunnel, she hoped it somehow gave her some of the answers she was searching for.

"Follow your own advice, kid," drifted behind her.

Right. No heroics.

The tunnel curved south. Unlike the other one they used to get to the cavern, this one had no branches, nothing of interest. A well-used path cut through the dusty floor. Already on high alert, Mia's muscles bunched and tensed the closer she came to whatever waited for her at the end. The anticipation of a fight.

Jack was right. They had gotten complacent in their relative place of power. Basin Territory had the resources, the old tech, and electricity. The region relied on them but as was human nature, they railed against the strict control her father employed —contrarian and independent. The Territory had been reactive instead of proactive, her parents too focused on the fate of the TMRWS and Shield.

Frustration joined the anticipation of a probable fight, her parent's secrets weighing heavy on her.

After what she assumed was a mile, a string of old twinkle lights looped near the top of the ceiling, an orange extension cord tacked next to it. They marched along the tunnel into the distance. Some of the lights were cracked and broken but enough worked that it kept the tunnel bright enough to see.

Mia slowed.

There was no cover.

She slunk into one of the shadows and crouched down, cocking her head to the side.

Faint scuffs and murmurs reached her ears. Still far away but near enough for the adrenaline to spurt into her veins. She couldn't wait for them to come to her. She had to take this slow.

Slinking from shadow to shadow, unplugging the twinkle lights as she went, she soft-stepped forward. The sounds became more distinct. Voices, the clack of things moving against each other, and shuffling steps all mingled together. They didn't sound urgent, just pissed.

She crept closer, leaving the last string of lights in place before another large cavern.

"…all of them. Every single one. Tanner hasn't heard a word." A rough female voice.

"They're Infected. It makes them stronger. We should have just blown the whole thing." Male this time.

They were talking about the fight near the MUC. And the way they said *Infected*, it was like they were being accused of something.

The woman grunted. "Then we wouldn't be able to get to the stockpiles. Plus, that Montana woman, Sarah, will give us more bullets if we keep the girl alive."

Mia blinked. Were they talking about her? She tried not to cringe. She hadn't been a girl in over a decade. She recognized the voices but couldn't place them. Since she stuck to the shadows down the tunnel she couldn't see their faces but bet these two were from Sector Nine, unlike the other two back in the cavern behind her. They sounded familiar. Yeah, but who? And why?

"Those Montana goons get that cave cleared and we'll blow the tunnels to keep those Infected assholes from finding the passage here. They have enough to worry about topside to come exploring yet."

She slunk against the wall opposite of the lights. Fortunately, more were broken on this end and only a dim glow lit the compacted dirt wall and rough-hewn wooden beams.

This cavern was larger and taller than the other, like a vast underground amphitheater. The emergency lights on solar battery operated generators dotted the entire room, skimming the lines of crates and shelving in harsh light. No other tunnels branched off from what Mia could see but a wooden door on the opposite wall hung open, the base of a staircase barely visible.

Stacks of crates, plastic boxes, shelves of every shape and size packed with dried goods, building materials, desks, metal filing cabinets, barrels—both metal and wooden, all crammed into the space within. If somebody were on the other side, hiding behind something, she'd never see them. They must have been stockpiling for years.

Her heart sank.

It wasn't just *part* of Sector Nine running this operation. It had to be most if not the entire sector to accumulate and keep quiet about what was going on.

Mia could kill the owners of those voices and follow Jack's orders. Or, she could do something else.

A wicked grin lit her face. This would require stealth.

She waited. *Patience is like a fine wine*, her father would say. Not that he would ever let her partake back in the day when he was telling her that.

The two voices drifted farther into the cave away from her, stacking things and clearing aisles. Making room.

Mia drew in a breath and sprinted between the long line of crates along the back wall in neat rows. She froze and listened. Nobody came ripping around the boxes toward the tunnel, the two voices still muffled on the other side of the cavern.

She hunched and used the veritable hills of supplies as cover as she worked her way toward the wooden crates and barrels. Unless they were going on their own scavenging trips, they must be hoarding a great many of the resources the council allotted them instead of rationing it out to their residents. No wonder they had asked for more resources at the council meeting. That or some third party, Sarah or the WC, was giving them handouts. Or both.

She didn't let herself think about what it would mean if somebody on the council knew. The older woman who was one of Sector Nine's representatives, Carmen, was mild-mannered and seemed more concerned about their cattle and hay than politics. Mia would have sworn on her grandmother's grave and the old world that the woman couldn't be a traitor at that level— hiding and stealing resources, colluding with outsiders.

Mia neared a path through the piles, shelves on either side

stacked high. She peered around, a slow, steady bob of her head and back. Jerky movements drew the eye.

She scooted around, heart beating fast, and padded towards the center. The two voices had disappeared and she couldn't see the door anymore. The final few feet to the crates would leave her exposed. Vulnerable.

No heroics.

Imploding the tunnel was something her parents would do though, regardless of the risk or waste. It would keep Sector Nine from accessing the secret tunnels from this end and prevent them from moving any more supplies. And if she could keep the damage to this side, they could always access this storage cavern from the Sector's entrance.

Mia crouched back down and listened. The lights clicked and her pulse pounded in her ears.

Now or never. She walked across the open space, sliding against the wall of ammo boxes, crates, and barrels similar to what held the shell casings in the other cavern.

A box with the letters PETN caught her attention. *Pentaerythritol tetranitrate.* Perfect. It was what they used to use to create a fireline around wildland fires back before the Collapse. Now, nobody tried to put them out anymore unless they threatened a water source near the settlements. Not enough people to manage the forests these days. Somebody must have found this box in an old Forest Service warehouse.

Several feet of the stuff should do it. She found a blasting cap from another box nearby and retraced her steps.

"What do we have here?"

Her heart thudded hard and she took off, sprinting toward the tunnel.

A gun fired and she zig-zagged down the path between the tall shelves, pushing her legs to move faster. Heavy steps thudded behind her.

She careened around the line of crates, the tunnel right in

front of her. The woman who owned the earlier voice stepped into view.

Her eyes widened when she caught a glimpse of Mia's face, then tilted her chin determinedly and pointed a gun toward Mia's legs.

Mia dropped the explosives and slammed the other woman back against the cavern wall just as she fired. She'd have to deal with these two before securing the tunnel.

Ida—she recognized the woman—aimed her gun again. Mia drew in one smooth motion and shot her in the shoulder. She went down with a grunt. One smooth kick sent the woman's gun skittering.

The man's name was Quentin, a bitter a-hole who had been at every one of the protests in recent months.

She shot him as he stopped in a pool of light to do the same to her.

"Infected, bitch." He spat. She kicked his gun away in one smooth snap of her leg, faster than the man was prepared to dodge. A neat round hole oozed blood in his gut.

"Get up."

"The guards topside will hear the shots and be down here quick. Better run back to Daddy," the man said.

Mia didn't let the rage show. Oh, how she wanted to. "Get the hell up now. Both of you."

Ida writhed on the floor, moaning.

"Go to hell," she spat.

Mia shot the crate next to Quentin. "Next one's going in your head. Get Ida, and get the hell up."

The man glared at her but stumbled to his feet and limped to Ida on the floor. He looped an arm beneath her shoulder.

"Good, now get up those stairs. I shoot whoever comes back down."

Moaning and whimpering, the two Sector Nine fools limped to the door across the cavern. Mia made sure they made it up the long wooden staircase ascending into the dark before curving back around toward what she assumed was another floor. The depth of the cavern was anybody's guess.

As soon as they disappeared from sight, she closed the door and found a crate to block it off. It wouldn't hold but she didn't need it to for very long.

Running to the PETN crate, she grabbed a long line of the det cord, placing it in front of the door and along the wall to the head of the tunnel. Screw them and their stolen hordes of supplies. She'd end access to it all. It could just stay down here until the council sent somebody to dig out the resources.

Mia ran out a length of line and the blasting cap, just enough to cave-in the resources but not enough to collapse the cavern. She got far enough down the tunnel and set the whole thing off.

Rock and rubble filled in the space behind her as she ran back toward the smaller cave.

The rumbling faded behind Mia and she kept one hand on the left wall, trailing her fingers along the cool, coarse sediment. Roiling dust billowed in the air and she covered her nose and mouth with her t-shirt.

She should have grabbed one of the gas masks on the shelves.

Coughing and hacking, she made her way back into the smaller cavern that seemed to act like a hub of sorts.

The two prisoners were gone. Jack hadn't returned.

She lowered the shirt and ducked back into the tunnel, crouching. It could mean one of two things. Either somebody had come and untied them, or they'd broken their bonds.

Nothing moved in the space. None of the boxes had been moved. Somebody could have lurked in the opening of the cave leading back to the Territory where she and Jack had started but it *felt* empty.

Mia cocked her head and focused on listening. Air sifted

through the tunnels, a soft sigh murmuring across earth and timber. Any other time a soothing sound, familiar and aching of home. Now it just brought stress and unease. No other sign of occupation drifted on the breeze.

Mia checked the clip in her gun. Six rounds left and a clip at her belt. Unless she wanted to take the time to rifle through the crates for the correct ammo.

No time. Move.

Urgency spurred her on and she moved to the tunnel Jack had gone down. Unlike the one she'd just come from, this entrance was lit with the emergency lights on their stands. Tracks from the cart and many, many footprints dug into the dirt. Mia readied her pistol.

Strands of her hair stuck to her sweaty face, the headlamp around her neck like a noose. Everything itched where the dirt clung, her pants and shirt filthy and reeking of body odor. When was the last time she'd changed? Slept? She really couldn't remember. Shield had kept her going in more ways than one.

Just as the glow began to fade from the last light, the tunnel branched off. Her heart raced, indecision like a stone in her chest.

She'd have to chance the headlamp.

Taking it from around her neck, she secured and turned it on. Sparse tracks crisscrossed the dust, hinting at recent traffic. Jack? Or somebody else? The left hand wall bore a mark, an upside-down J scraped into the wood like some kind of demented candy cane.

Bingo. Left hand tunnel it was.

Mia's clammy fingers gripped the pistol tighter. The tunnel continued for another five hundred feet before she slowed at a clattering noise from somewhere up ahead.

Crap. She jerked off the headlamp and shut it off.

Mia crouched. A man stood below a ladder, a hatch open above him.

The male prisoner from the tunnel.

Sporadic, angry words drifted through the hatch ten feet above, the metal rungs of a ladder marching their way up the wall. One of the voices was Jack's, another a woman's familiar, abrasive tones. Sarah.

A maelstrom of voices wove together into shrieks and screams and were cut off by a gunshot.

What the heck?

Not taking any more time to consider, she fired a single bullet at the guard, center mass. Surprise etched across his face as he fell to his knees on the ground.

"You…"

Mia kicked the gun from his limp hand into the depths of the tunnel in one smooth motion.

"Me." Mia struck the side of the pistol alongside his temple and he fell. *My father would have shot him in the head.* But the world he lived through had created this one. She had to be different.

The voices above stopped screaming. She didn't waste any time. Rung after rung and the hatch was at her head. Mia's head popped out like a gopher in a hole long enough to get the lay of the land.

A group of people—fifteen or twenty—were huddled next to an old boarded up shack maybe a hundred feet from the hatch. Jack stood in front of them, blood running down his head, a hole in his shoulder.

Mia popped back down mere seconds later.

Sarah along with the woman Mia had choked out earlier were pointing their guns at the group.

"Best come out, niece, or I'll start shooting hostages."

All the stories about this woman flowed through Mia's head. Her erratic behavior in the MUC during the Year of Hell, her descent further into the abyss after she'd escaped and ended up in Montana. According to her mother's journals, it had started with being held against her will by the old government but something else had propelled her aunt toward the events and acts she had committed against innocents. A domino effect of massive proportions leading to this place.

Relying on Shield, she braced her feet on the last rung, launched herself into the open and fired four shots in quick succession.

Two took her aunt in the gut, the other two took the other woman in the chest.

Jack charged forward, the people around him screaming and curling around themselves on the ground. He kicked one of the guns from Sarah's grasp, punching her in the face. She head-butted him and more blood sprouted from his nose. Fists and legs flew, faster with each hit.

Legs aching, Mia sprinted and clotheslined the woman from the cavern across the throat before she could turn from terrorizing the group of people huddled near the shack. She went down with a gurgled gasp.

Both women lay still beneath the tireless sun. Not dead, but knocked out for the time being.

Breath left her lungs in a ragged exhalation. "We need to secure them all."

Jack retrieved a pack from near the group of civilians. He took out three pairs of handcuffs.

"Where did you find those?" Exasperation filled her voice.

Jack shrugged. "In the crates. Thought we might need them."

"What happened?"

He studied her from head to toe. "I could say the same."

"You first. You're with the extra people."

"They came from the town of St. John about a half-day's hike from here. A woman by the name of Dana said Cooper sent her group our way. They were stopping for water. Total fluke I popped out of the hatch about an hour after they arrived. Sarah came along not soon after. The other end of that tunnel descends to a train track. Found it before I backtracked here to the hatch."

"You sure they came from Cooper?" Mia nodded toward the group.

"Don't know but we can sure ask." Jack grimaced as he stretched his injured shoulder. "And you? Why are you so filthy?"

Mia told him about Sector Nine and blowing up the supply room to secure all the weapons and ammo. "Hopefully not too much got destroyed. There were a lot of food and water barrels down there as well as weapons. They've been stockpiling for awhile."

Jack rubbed the bridge of his nose. "Damn it."

"No use beating yourself up about it now. The question is, how are we going to fix it?"

An older woman with silver hair and blue eyes sharp as tacks stepped from the group and cleared her throat. "Excuse me? Can we leave? We were told to go to the Basin Territory and find a woman by the name of Mia. You wouldn't happen to know her, would you?"

Cooper must have given the stranger her name. "As a matter of fact, I'm Mia. And you are?"

"Oh, how fortunate. My name is Dana. I have some information for you, too, from a man named Cooper."

"I see. And what did Cooper have to say?" She frowned at the woman.

"He always liked the book *A Wrinkle in Time,* Butte's moving west and something about gophers burrowing near a white barn north of you? I took it to mean somebody's got a tunnel going but he didn't say so. He wanted to talk in code, so I left it in code." She blinked rather innocently, though a curious spark lit behind her eyes.

Mia about choked over the name of the book she'd read to Cooper all those years ago. Dana had definitely talked to Cooper. "If you're heading to Basin it's about three hours south of here. But I have to let you know, the borders are closed."

"That's what I said. He said you'd let us in." She folded her hands in front of her and waited. Her people shifted behind them. There were about sixteen total—she'd finally counted—a mix of men, women, and children. All were painfully thin. All were wary as hell and had rearmed themselves, including the woman in front of her.

"Why didn't you try and shoot those two?" Mia nodded toward Sarah and her companion, both of who were groaning on the ground. Jack stuffed a gag in each of their mouths.

Crooked teeth shone out of Dana's almost feral smile.

Easy does it, she's a survivor. Especially at her age.

"No bullets. All those guns are for show. Keeps most away. Not all, but most. Are you going to let us camp on your border? Or do we need to find another place? That mongrel horde in Montana is gettin' mighty antsy for my taste."

Mongrel horde. Mia choked. "I'd be careful. That woman, there, is the leader."

Dana's eyes narrowed on Sarah, her smile turning even more unruly. "Is she now?"

"Don't get any ideas, she's our prisoner." Mia squinted at Jack. "Well? I believe Cooper sent them. What do you want to do?"

His eyes roved over the group. Children huddled next to the adults, eyes wide and wary. The adults glared back with a fierce intensity, their eyes reflecting years of hardship and determination. "Where did you all come from, originally?"

"Northern Idaho. Those Montana folks started sending scouts our direction. Started taking people from a nearby settlement. We decided it was best to move on. We don't have ammo. We have seeds and each other. St. John had water and we were there for a few weeks before we ran into Cooper. He warned us it might not be safe there, soon. So, here we are."

It was all said matter of factly with no self-pity in her voice or trace of deception. The woman in front of her could have pleaded, and begged, but she stood her ground and waited. Mia had no doubt that if they told her no, she would move on, take her group, and find someplace else without another word. Definitely a survivor.

"Tell you what. You continue on south toward our northern most gate and tell the guard on duty, his name is Tim, that I gave permission to stay there at the campsite for a couple of nights. Tell him Peta would approve. That should give us enough time to get some other things figured out. Then, we can sit and talk. Sound good?"

Dana raised her chin and looked Jack in the eye. "Will we get water?"

He flipped her a water ration chit. "Two days supply. More if we send you on your way after we talk. That's all I can offer."

Dana nodded her head once. "I appreciate it. Any chance you have milk for the kids? We've been trying to give them the most rations since they're growin' but they haven't had any milk and very little protein since we had to leave our goats behind back home."

Leaving part of their food supply? It must have been bad. Mia interjected before Jack could say anything and threw her another chit. "Enough for the kids while you're there."

"Thank you, ma'am." Dana caught the chit out of the air.

"No, thank you for the information."

CHAPTER 19
COOPER

September, 2072

Cooper had found Claire outside a small settlement in northern Oklahoma. There she was, this little girl, no more than five or six years old, curled up in a burnt out car half alive and quiet. So quiet. Her parents had been torn apart by wild animals around the campsite, the car being used as shelter. Nothing much of their bodies remained but gnawed bones. To this day, he didn't know if those wild animals had been creature…or human.

And her eyes. So like his mother's.

Cooper had discovered the settlement five miles away. No piles of human remains had lined the razor wire perimeter, and the fifty odd people just looked like they were trying to survive in whatever way they could. At his appearance, they'd almost shot him, but had finally listened. At the sight of Claire they opened the gate.

As newer members of the community, her family had gone out to scavenge and never returned. The leaders had sent a scout but found nothing, figuring the family had just moved on with their daughter. He tried to withhold judgment of Claire's parents. Who in their right minds would leave a secure community when they had a young child?

He'd hung around, caring for Claire. Another young family took her in and Cooper promised to stop in, supplement their meager supplies with whatever he could find. *You can't save everyone.* Daniel's voice. Yeah, but he could save a little girl. He thus started frequent trips to the tiny settlement. He'd leave for months, finding work where he could, avoiding the growing number of scavvies, and helping take care of Claire. Until one day, he arrived to see the settlement packing up. Kansas City had sent scouts. At the sight of him, Claire had run into his arms, crying, begging him to take her with him.

But look where it had gotten them.

Brushing away the spiderwebs of the past, he focused on the present. The rest of the trip into Montana was uneventful. Cooper avoided the few settlements scattered about and kept as far north as possible before dropping south. All had dwindled anyway as their people followed the water and escaped those in Butte. Soon, if Eva was correct, it wouldn't matter where they went, the surface of the world would be dry, except for the salty oceans with their non-working desalination plants.

Jorge gazed out at the mountains. "Beautiful."

"It used to be more beautiful when it rained more than a few times a year." Cooper focused on formulating a rough plan. Stealth was required, he was essentially a one-man army with a green kid and a dog—special though she may be. He huffed out a half-laugh. How the hell had he gotten to this point?

"It hasn't rained for almost a year back home. I almost forgot what a good rain smells like." Jorge absently brushed a hand over Kiva's head.

"When we get to our destination, I need you and Kiva to guard the ATV, hide and shoot anybody who comes near."

"I can help you, though."

"Dammit, Jorge, what was the condition of you coming with me?" Cooper glanced over, glaring at the young man.

Jorge's lips pursed. "You say jump, I say how high."

"Good. Now this vehicle is our fastest way to get out of dodge after I grab Claire. The last time I was here, they hadn't been able to convert any vehicles to solar batteries like Daniel has. There might be some old electric four-wheelers about but nothing as fast as this thing and they may not have even charged them lately. It's not a throwaway, job, kid. You're guarding our escape route."

"Yessir," Jorge grumbled, not mollified.

"And remember if this goes sideways, don't come after me, you get back to Mia and tell her what happened."

"Can I voice my opinion, now?"

"No."

"Too bad. This sucks. You can't be a lone wolf forever, Cooper. People work better together."

Cooper's jaw twitched. "Yeah, well, you're not wrong; these people have done pure evil together, very well, for years. You're not coming with me. You're not equipped as well as I am."

"Maybe so. All I'm saying is two heads are better than one. It's something my grandpa always used to say to me. He kept our community together for years on nothing but pure will and compromise. It couldn't hurt you to try it sometime, that last bit."

Cooper remained silent. The kid didn't know. Couldn't know the horrors that awaited them in Butte. Compromise wasn't in those people's vocabularies.

Cooper parked the side-by-side in a large mechanic's shed next to a grove of skeletal trees two miles from his target. Barns, it seemed, were the name of the game on this trip. As of the last time he was here—had it been eight months already?—the patrols didn't generally come out this far, choosing to stay close to the camp at the old airport and the mining college. No settlements had survived within a half a day's hike, and everybody within a hundred mile radius avoided the area like the plague. With good reason.

During the last leg of the drive, he'd come to a decision. "I need to show you something before I go get Claire. Something I think you should see. Seeing is always different than hearing about."

"You're bringing me with you?"

"Only as far as it takes to see what they have on the tarmac outside the airport."

"Human bones. Yeah, you told me." Jorge tightened the strap of his gun belt. Kiva sniffed around the barn, trotting to Cooper's side when he snapped his fingers.

"Human bones mixed with animal bones. That's not all I want you to see, though."

Along a dense line of half-dead bushes, they hunkered down. He'd approached the Bert Mooney Airport from the southeast. A once lush creekbed, now dry and cracked, smooth stones rich with minerals, surrounded them. The members of the Butte Militia, a name Cooper always cringed at, relied on the razor wire fence and their reputation to keep people out. Infrequent patrols made their way this far, but most of their manpower—and he used the term in its most general definition; there were many humans involved in the upper ranks—were kept close to guard their resources. How Sarah kept them all in line always mystified him, especially when she was gone for large amounts of time. The core leaders, the ones directly under her, worshiped her like a goddess, and went as far as killing anybody who spoke ill of the woman. What she had done to deserve it was never mentioned.

He handed the binoculars to Jorge. "Look close to the air traffic control tower. And by the terminal."

The piles of bones were horrid in themselves. Desiccated piles of both animal—mostly pig—and human. All picked clean and drying in the sun. They would grind the bone down and use it for fertilizer and pig feed. His stomach churned, bile lodging in his throat. Cooper swallowed it down, shoving the thought far, far back in his mind like he'd been forced to do for years.

"What—what are those?" Jorge's voice cracked, just above a whisper. Chained to pens near the control tower stood massive mounds of muscled human flesh, foreheads flattened, and eyes dulled.

"Some of Sarah's elite guard. They're failed past experiments she exploits. Even I hesitate to draw their attention."

"How many are there?"

Cooper shrugged. "A dozen? Maybe more? She's never let me see the full extent of her arsenal. She kept Claire hostage but I think she always knew I'd try and find a way out. My own... strengths are something she needed, or else I would have been pig food a long time ago."

"Are those collars?"

"On the slaves? Yes."

Cooper didn't preach further, didn't elaborate. Silence lay heavy between them as Jorge continued to scan the tarmac and visible areas of the airport through the binoculars.

After they'd returned to the shed and Kiva's happy tail wagging, Jorge broke the dense quiet. "You win. I'll stay with the ATV and keep Kiva with me."

"It's not about winning or losing, Jorge. We'd need a small army to take on this compound and you're not trained for this sort of thing. I'm sneaking in, grabbing Claire, and getting out." He left off the part about administering Shield.

"Then how am I ever going to get justice for my grandpa?" If Cooper hadn't thought him young and inexperienced before, that statement would have clinched it.

"Wasn't it you who just said people work better together? We'll get it figured out, Jorge, but right now is definitely not the time to right that wrong. And the main person responsible is definitely not somebody you would be able to take on by yourself. I will help you do so, I promise, but we're going to need a different plan than a direct attack to do it."

Chill afternoon air drifted through the broken windows. Kiva lapped at a bowl of water and started in on a jerky stick. The dog required little food, a fact that had surprised Cooper at first. Now, he just labeled her as another oddity in an entire series of weird shit that was a part of his life.

Jorge stuck out a filthy hand. "Shake on it."

Cooper grabbed it and shook.

———

The gibbous moon hung low and bright. Its light glazed the landscape in a silvery white glow, perfect for Cooper's enhanced vision. Shadows of the craggy mountains surrounding Butte offered a sharp contrast to the misery in the valley where he now crept. Broken wire here, moveable plank there guided his journey through the slumbering town. He refused to call it a community, even in his head.

Years of survival and preparation had led to this day. Misery. Heartache. Pain and suffering. For both him and Claire. Could he ever be forgiven for the things he'd done in service to Sarah to keep her safe? To keep himself safe? The people he'd enslaved. Killed.

"...for I will forgive their wrongdoing." But would he be forgiven? Regardless of what was in the Bible. He'd take Claire to Basin and leave her, he didn't deserve to be there. Mia would make sure she was raised right.

When had he started thinking Mia could solve all his problems?

Cooper was nothing more than mist and silence. The route he took was planned over many, many months. Daniel again, no matter how much he wanted to evict the man from his brain. *Always have an exit strategy.* Or entrance. Sometimes it was the same difference.

The Cattle Pen, as the guards called it, housed the slaves and those forced to serve the leadership—whether sexual or otherwise. Cooper's own position in Butte had been precarious at best. Neither strictly slave nor trusted leader, he'd never been offered a human favor or requested one. His sole focus had been getting himself and Claire out of the mess he'd found themselves in. He'd held himself aloof. Alone.

The basement door was in a recessed stairway. Unguarded for those who wanted to access their human chattel during the night.

He drew up the hood on his dark sweatshirt, the door closing behind him with a click.

A hallway to the right led into the gloom, but a stairway in front of him climbed to the floor above. He took the stairway.

Had Sarah made it back ahead of him? Was everyone on alert for his presence as enemy number one?

He'd find out if he ran into any of the handlers in the Pen.

They kept Claire on the top floor along with the other "friendly hostages," so dubbed because they were there as a reminder to their loved ones: comply or watch them die.

Cooper ghosted up the stairs to the fifth floor without incident. Sarah was arrogant as hell, no doubt. But so were her generals. That they never figured anybody would or could infiltrate their settlement—especially after Daniel and crew had done that very thing fifteen years ago—suggested nobody had tried since.

He moved quickly through the final room at the very top of the building. Eight floor mats in all, crammed into the room like sardines in a can. Eight vulnerable humans.

Stop, Coop. Get Claire and go.

Tiny heads rested in various positions of rest, some huddled together for warmth, some off alone. These were the ones who couldn't fight back, all victims of a circumstance they didn't understand. Born into such a fucked up world, they would become something harsh and…wrong without intervention.

He stepped with care through the silver-glazed room, searching.

And there she was, asleep under a single, thin blanket, dark, messy hair exploding onto the wood planks of the floor, curled in around herself.

Cooper called her his foster daughter to others, partly in respect for the parents who'd birthed her, partly in respect for the smart, courageous human herself. If he was honest, he loved the little girl as much as if he'd given life to her himself. Maybe years of loneliness had led to the feeling. Maybe losing his parents and becoming an orphan himself at such a young age, in such a messed up way, he couldn't say.

He put his hand over her mouth so she wouldn't alert the guards. She jerked awake with wide, frightened eyes, calming immediately when she recognized him.

Cooper's mouth touched the tiny shell of her ear. "Shhh. It's Dad. Time to go."

Claire only nodded and gripped his neck in a fierce, tight hug.

CHAPTER 20
EVA

August, 2055

Eva dozed off, her dreams wild and scattered, an amalgamation of dead bodies in enormous rotting piles and mushroom clouds blooming in the sky. They soon turned to nightmares of being buried alive under mountains of dirt and rock or hidden deep within a hole surrounded on all sides by molten lava. Specks of sand embedded themselves into her pores as she fought her way through a storm cloud. Each vision more claustrophobic and horrifying than the next. Tide upon tide of misery.

Then a blank gray slate.

Stars appeared, the calm in the eye of a hurricane. Millions and billions of them. Her body zinged, a waking consciousness resumed in sleep. A version of her *abuelita* in a homespun cotton dress, tiny yellow flowers spotting it, and jet black hair in a braid down her back appeared next to her. Stars loomed above, near and far, halos of light among spectrums of blue and white shining in a soft glow. The ground beneath Eva's feet was black as the slices of night between the twinkle of space dust, foot-long stalagmites growing from the rocky ground, their pointy tips reaching for the shadows and slivers of light. They luminesced in spots, moving with the motion of the rock.

"Home." Her *abuelita* said in perfect English, a language she'd never picked up having lived in Mexico her entire life. "My home."

Eva jerked awake, gasping for breath. Her heart clenched hard and then raced, pounding her chest like a hammer. She curled into the fetal position, trying to warm her frozen bones and sinews.

Science ruled her world, though growing up in the church made her realize that not everything was as cut and dry.

The dreams hadn't been this bad in years. After Salvation, when they'd dug out of the MUC, insomnia ruled her life. Days or weeks would pass, Shield and her brain working together to prevent any kind of peace. In the past few years, she found a balance of sorts between awake and asleep. The last few months had blown it up and stomped on it with cleated boots.

The problem was, it didn't *feel* like a dream.

Kel snored in her makeshift bed, belly tight and round like a mountain that had tipped over on its side. She shifted but didn't wake up.

Eva rolled to her back, knees bent. She spread her arms on the filthy floor and breathed. Shield soon compensated for her elevated heart rate and regulated her temperature.

What did it mean? Seeing her *abuelita* like that? Was God trying to tell her something? Or was it something else?

She stood up and stretched, her stomach tight but painless where the knife wounds had been. Weakness still weighed down her limbs but not as bad as right after the knifing. Visions of Daniel's face in the aftermath flashed through her brain.

She needed a plan.

Eva sat back down and closed her eyes, not that it mattered much in the dark, windowless room. A crack of light from under the door was the only illumination, casting the room in a dim gray haze. The darkness would help her think better.

What did she know?

She knew that these people were either psychotic or brainwashed. She'd read a report on Hensley once from Daniel. The man had been a colonel in the army, a brilliant tactician, and charismatic. He could talk a wool coat off a freezing person. Something had happened to him in the First Wave, though, something that had flipped a switch. Her memory gave out, and Eva frowned. It could matter to her current situation, or it could not.

Then, there were the black stones. Even though they looked like the tellurium meteorite, she'd had no reaction to them like the one in the BAC. Maybe they came from a different sample. The stones were small, and the chunk of meteorite from the BAC had been much larger. Maybe they needed to be closer? Or maybe size really did matter in this case. She had to get one of those stones from around the guard's necks and find out.

Then, there was what Kel said about the Conversion. *Consuming your strength.* It had to mean cannibalism. Eva was *not* being eaten by other humans. She would jump on a burning pile of funeral pyres before she allowed that to happen.

———

Eva pretended to be asleep when Kel stirred. The girl grunted, used the bucket in the corner, and then knocked on the door with her weird little taps. It opened, and this time a man, his gray beard reaching to his chest, looked in.

"Bring up breakfast. Nothin' for her," the young woman said.

The guard nodded and closed the door.

Eva opened her eyes. "No food, huh?"

Kel shrugged. "Kind of wasteful, don't ya think?"

"I suppose." Eva's stomach turned, and not just from hunger.

Kel's entire belly tightened, and she let out a long guttural groan, bending over her belly until it stopped. "Dang pains started. Hope it doesn't interfere with me attendin' your Conversion. Seein' as how you were my roommate last night."

"You want to see them eat me?" Eva didn't try to hide her disgust.

The girl frowned, eyebrows drawing together. "It's actually an honor to attend. We see our Chosen grow stronger. It means we grow stronger."

"It's wrong to eat people, Kel. What your leaders are doing is wrong. It's sick and twisted, the opposite of all the good things left in the world. You should have a choice about where you live, who you love, even whether you want to have babies or not. You should get to make your own decisions in life. The Lord gave us free will for a reason."

An ugly look twisted Kel's very young face. "You're wrong. That leads to death. If people have free will, it destroys the world. We consume others who have sacrificed their flesh to protect the righteous. So just shut up."

She didn't know the word salvation, but she knew the word righteous. God, what had this world come to?

"Kel, there is a better way. A different way—"

Eva didn't get to finish. Kel backhanded her with a small fist. It didn't hurt so much as sting.

"Shut your lyin' mouth, you dirty thief. Your body will protect my child's. That is all I need to know."

Eva held her warm cheek. Why had she even tried? *Salvation.* Ha. Was there going to be salvation for any of them in the afterlife?

She kept her mouth shut as the long minutes passed. The click-clack of knitting needles and the occasional grunt from Kel as she had a contraction were the only sounds breaking up the monotony.

Right on time, the door opened to the gray-bearded guard. "Turn around, hands behind you."

It was now or never. She lunged for the small black stone around the man's neck. He grunted, drawing back on reflex. Her fingertips touched the rock, tingles of awareness zinging up her arm.

She didn't hear Kel move until it was too late, and the chair from the corner was smashed down on her head.

The young woman grunted, bending over from the exertion and her labor pains. "Careful, she's a tricky one, Vic."

The man slammed Eva up against the wall and handcuffed her wrists behind her back. "Not happening, gussie. Time for your turn on the table."

Her turn? "What have you done? Where are the others?"

The man just chuckled and frog-marched her out the door.

Now what? Her thoughts raced. They would all die if she didn't get one of those necklaces.

The house had been an old Victorian, possibly a boarding house or nursing home at one time. The halls were narrow and short, almost triggering a bout of claustrophobia. Exposed board planks of the floor and scuff-marked walls punctuated the space between doorways. Like some old western movie from Eva's teenage years, women in various stages of dress and pregnancy leaned against the doorways, watching as Vic pushed her in front of him. She descended a sweeping staircase to a small entryway. Two more guards waited on either side of the door.

One fell in step ahead of her, the other joined Vic in the rear.

They walked along a dirt path through broken concrete that opened onto a field. Ahead, the towering monolith atop the World War I memorial shaded the area in front of it. Sweat popped out on Eva's face and dripped down her neck. So many guards. So many people.

Despair joined the helplessness. It wouldn't work. Her hands were cuffed, and even if she were in full health, even with Shield, she would still have difficulty breaking the chain. And even if she did get free and saved Daniel, Trae, and Coy, how would they fight their way through all of Hensley's Chosen?

Eva shivered.

Her shoulders slumped forward, and the buzzing voices

washed over her. Vic positioned her in front of the concrete throne, the blood altar between her and it. A trail of fresh blood, a brighter red against the black of repeated coatings, dripped down the side.

"This one has proven strong. Our God has talked to me and told me that her Conversion will be for the many. Her strength will protect us all!" Hensley's voice carried across the square.

"Her strength will protect us all!" The crowd's feverish pitch intensified, repeating the mantra over and over until Hensley raised his hands to quiet them down.

Bile rose in Eva's throat, and she struggled against the bonds. *Not like this.* Dios, *not like this.*

Vic shoved her forward.

"I threw him and those other thieves to the hogs." Hensley had pitched his voice so only she and the guards could hear.

Ringing pounded the insides of Eva's head, and the world narrowed to an ugly focus. "What did you say?"

"The war hero died a coward on my slab." Hensley's mouth curved into a wicked smile, and he leaned forward. "The God is smiling today."

Eva collapsed to her knees, a void opening as her world spun on its axis. Daniel dead? No, it couldn't be. It didn't feel right. The bright blood on the altar mocked her.

"Up you go, gussie. Any final words?" Vic hauled her to her feet and tossed her onto the slab, throwing a chain over her mostly healed stomach. Tacky blood adhered to the remains of her shredded shirt, and the rough stone abraded her cuffed hands and arms, the coppery tang burning her nostrils.

Eva turned her head away. Kel's feverish face looked back at her through the crowd, one hand resting on her burgeoning belly. So she came for a piece? Eva squeezed her eyes shut. This was not how it was supposed to end.

Mia. Oh, Mia.

Images flashed through her mind. Mia as an infant in the MUC. Eyes so like her father's, wide and seeming to be aware of the world around her more than any baby should. Mia as a young child, picking strawberries in the field. Mia as she was now, a pre-teen with an attitude. *I can't let her lose both of her parents.*

"This isn't over." She choked out the empty words.

Hensley leaned over, necklace dangling above her, and murmured. "Thanks for the train. And thanks for ferreting that bitch Hope out of hiding, inadvertent though it was. She was coming down to find you. We couldn't let that happen."

The train would lead them to Mia.

Like a crystal on a hypnotist's chain, the black rock swayed in front of her face.

Focusing her entire being on this one act, Eva slammed against the half-tied chain holding her down, using her aching abs to propel her up. Even healthy, she'd never moved so fast. She opened her mouth as wide as she could and ripped the black stone from around Hensley's neck with her teeth, jerking it off the thin leather.

Eva swallowed the rock whole.

CHAPTER 21
EVA

August, 2055

Eva's parents had worked hard to give her and Sarah everything they needed. Sometimes working double shifts, there were days Eva only saw them for breakfast and dinner. At the ages of ten and eleven, she and Sarah would cook the meals, clean the house, and do the laundry besides doing their homework. Once they were old enough, they also got jobs, putting what little money they made into a savings account for the future. Eva knew how to get things done, how to rise up from a losing position and come out on top. She had learned it from a young age. And she'd mastered it in adulthood.

The stone settled into her stomach like a lump of burning slag, warmth radiating throughout her entire body. Sparks of electricity tingled along her limbs, and adrenaline rocketed through her system. Supercharging the enzymes from Shield. A logical part of her brain, something she hadn't retained with the Tau-159 sample from the BAC, told her it needed further study.

But first, she needed to escape.

Hensley slammed her head into the rock beneath her.

A flicker of pain in her skull—there and then gone—was all

she felt. Eva met his eyes, and whatever he saw there made him pause, a split second of—was it fear?—crossing his features. She slammed her forehead into his with another brief flash of pain. Hensley stumbled back, reaching behind himself to grab something from his throne made of rubble and glass-covered meteorite.

Power tightened her muscles, an energy unlike any she'd felt, even with Shield. Eva sat up and jerked her hands apart—once, then twice—slamming against the restraints that held them beneath her and behind her back. On the second wrenching of flesh against metal, the chains gave way with a groan.

One of Hensley's henchmen threw himself on top of her, but it was too late. She grabbed the woman's throat, her fingers squeezing until she felt flesh give away. Blood coated her fingertips. The part of her that remained logical flinched away from the brutality of the action. The part of her controlled by the black stone simmering in her gut was elated. Blood equaled freedom.

She tossed the body away and extracted her other hand, tightening her abs to roll off the slab.

A shadow crossed her peripheral. Just in time, she threw her body off the altar. Hensley brought the butt of a rifle down but only hit the stone with a *ker-chunk*.

Until then, the crowd was far enough away that they probably couldn't clearly make out what was happening. What felt like long minutes to Eva was mere seconds from ingestion to the release of her arms.

She landed on her hands and knees on the ground opposite of the crowd. Hensley, overextended in his thrust of the rifle, was vulnerable.

Eva stood, head taking him in the stomach and feet pushing off from the ground. The two of them fell back onto the throne, and her hands found his neck, digging in deep.

Hensley's eyes widened in shock. He tried to move, but her arms and legs had him in a vice grip along his torso.

Something stung her back. The impact barely registered.

"Tell them to stop shooting or I'll rip your throat out." Eva didn't recognize the deep, raw voice scraping her throat. Some part of her knew she should be worried about what she'd turned into. Not enough to stop. Not that she could now anyhow.

She loosened her hold just enough for him to speak. "Stop... shooting."

"Good. Now have them back off." Eva shifted, using one of her hands to control the man while she felt along his body. Ah, there. A knife. That would allow her more freedom of movement to get out of here. She yanked it out of its sheath at his thigh and brought it to his carotid.

"You...heard her."

"Now, where's this pit? We're going to go see what happened to the rest of my people. Nice and easy." She kept one hand on his windpipe, the knife poked into the thick vein so a trickle of blood dripped down his neck.

Together, they stood, her body glued to his to limit movement.

Venom filled his eyes. "You'll regret this."

"Doubtful, now move." She eased around his torso. The man was about four inches taller than her, but with her new-found strength, he couldn't use it to his advantage.

A susurration of sound crescendoed around them. The observers surged forward.

"Any closer and your prophet dies!" Was prophet even the right word? Blood sacrifices and a cult-like following indicated it was better than leader.

Hensley's Chosen, the beefy men and women with black rocks hanging around their necks, watched her with flat, steely eyes but backed the crowd off.

Kel kneeled on the ground at the front with a mad gleam in her eyes, panting, sweat popping out on her brow. Eva ignored her. She needed to save Daniel and the others—if they were still alive.

The single-minded thought overrode all others, even the

small voice in her head screaming that something was wrong. That all strength came with a price. She shut it out.

"I'm not going to ask again. Where's the pit?"

Hensley licked his lips, a quick darting of tongue. "Behind the memorial."

The monolith of the old World War I memorial had somehow survived the bombing of Kansas City. It shadowed the throne and altar of Hensley's center of power like an unwilling guardian. Representative of the oppression of evil, it was now being used to house it.

Eva lined her legs up with Hensley's to walk behind him. The closer the better. Something else Daniel had taught her; an old martial arts principle.

They walked around the towering structure, the Chosen and a surge of people following at a distance. Somebody had helped Kel to her feet and the young woman hobbled after them with a mirthless smile slashed across her mouth.

The hog pit was giant, at least as big as an Olympic swimming pool, and ten or eleven feet deep. Snorting, snuffling boars and sows stomped through the dust and half-eaten body parts of various creatures; their cloven hooves crunching over the bones of meals past.

Daniel was nowhere to be seen in the bottom—unless the freshly mauled bodies were her team's. No. She wouldn't accept that. He was Dr. Daniel Burgess. He'd survived nuclear war, being buried alive, and years of building a haven amidst overwhelming odds. He couldn't just die as pig food.

"Eva?!"

Was the meteorite making her hear things that weren't there?

"Down here!"

His voice. It was real.

Not a hallucination.

She searched frantically, her hand loosening a fraction from Hensley's neck. He twitched, and she tightened it once again. Best not to get distracted.

"To the left."

Halfway up the wall, on a roughly cut-out ledge almost directly below her and just out of reach of the ravenous pigs. Only Trae sat next to him on the precarious perch. Dried blood coated Daniel's shirt and jeans, his feet dirty and bare. The teenager hadn't fared much better. Shield had healed any wounds, but the remains of what had been done were evident.

Kill. Kill everyone. She tightened her hand, and Hensley gagged, his hands clawing at hers. A roar like a wave washed over her as people filled the space around them. She didn't care. They all had to die. It was only fitting. The people would come, and she would slice all their throats.

"Eva, don't kill him! We need him alive to get out of here." Daniel's words meant nothing. He didn't know. How could he? "Dr. Zapada!"

Another spurt of adrenaline heightened her senses and tightened her muscles. The coppery scent of blood and the rank odor of an unwashed male filled her nose. A beautiful range of sherbet lit the sky. This wasn't the enzyme and its murderous urges; this was all Dr. Eva Zapada and the blood rushing in her ears.

"Think of Mia!"

Mia. Her hand loosened just a smidge. Breath puffed out of Hensley's lungs like a bellows.

Two glowing eyes from the shadows of a pile of rubble across the pit looked back at her. Eva blinked. Nala was still alive. Unbroken.

Not taking her eyes off of the dog on the other side, she yelled out to no one in particular, "Get them out of there. Now."

"Do it," choked out Hensley.

The dog jumped to her feet, still hiding in the shadows. Something about the dog steadied the bloodlust surging through her veins. *Focus on Nala.*

One of Hensley's men threw a rope over the edge, securing it to a bent lamp post.

Kel fell to her knees in front of them, a contraction visibly tightening her belly. The young woman groaned.

A dirty, cold hand touched her arm. "Eva?"

Daniel. She didn't look away from Nala.

"I told you Nala was strange."

The hand on her arm tightened. "We need to go."

"I bet the dog knows the best way." All the noise of the crowd, the God's Chosen, hell, even the crazy ass pig pen in the ground, faded away until it was just her, Nala, and the man she held under her knife. And Daniel's voice. His beautiful voice. "And the pregnant girl."

Hensley jerked and Eva tightened her grip.

"Okay. We'll follow the dog. And bring the girl. Just don't kill him yet. If we do, we won't be able to escape." Daniel's strained voice came from a distance, like through a long, dark tunnel.

I hate the underground. "So we can see Mia. Nala's special, isn't she?"

"Yes, I do believe she is. Let's go. Slowly, Eva."

Her eyes firmly on Nala's, she moved around the pit toward the dog. Daniel and Trae followed her, dragging Kel between them. The girl moaned but was too weak from labor to resist.

"What's wrong with her?" Trae whispered.

Daniel didn't respond.

Trae was young. Nothing was wrong with her.

The pressure in her head expanded.

"What happened, Hensley?" Daniel grated.

"She's going to pay for this."

"You can say that even when she's holding a knife to your throat?"

"The bitch swallowed the damn thing. She'll pay." A gritty half-chuckle escaped from Hensley's mouth.

Their words entered her brain but it was getting more and more difficult to process them. Nala met them at the boundary of a broken building and the trail through the rubble that bordered Hensley's domain. Pretty dog.

Nala pushed against Eva's leg, whining, and a little clarity returned. "Daniel?"

"I'm here."

"I think I did something really stupid." They all resumed walking, Nala right next to her, occasionally bumping her leg with a low whine.

Eva had a vague sense of many people just on the periphery of her consciousness, but they blended in with the destruction around them. Knuckles white, she gripped the knife. Her fingers should have been numb by now, but they pulsed with the need to break Hensley's windpipe. To push that knife through his skin until tendons popped and blood poured…

"Not right now. Let's just focus on returning to the tunnels without our companions tearing us to pieces."

"It's getting harder not to rip his throat out," she gritted out. This wasn't her. This felt more like what had happened the night she'd bombed the black site. The man under her knife gritted his teeth, and she could hear the sound, feel the vibration against her arm.

Breathe. Just breathe.

"Just a little farther."

The world caved in around her. Nothing looked familiar. Everything was suffocating. Her hands shook.

Follow the dog. The mantra played in her mind over and over.

Nala bumped her shin again, almost like she could pick up on Eva's thoughts.

Maybe she can.

Hensley's throat moved beneath her hand. "It'll eat her from the inside out, and there won't be a damn thing you can do to stop it, war hero. Best let me go now so I can put you all out of your misery."

"Where did you even get samples of the meteorite?" Daniel asked.

"Let me go, and I'll tell you."

Daniel's anger vibrated through the air. "You are brainwashing these people, and Lord knows what else. How did you get the damn samples, Colonel?"

The man didn't get a chance to respond. They had reached the hole and rough stairs to the underground tunnel system and were met by Tamara's team armed to the teeth.

CHAPTER 22

MIA

September, 2072

Dana's group shouldered backpacks and their useless guns, herded the children to the center of the group, and continued their trek south. A couple of hours would find them at the North Gate.

Mia regarded the bogeyman—woman—on the ground. Cannibal. Sociopath. Self-centered narcissist. Broken. All words used by her parents to describe her Aunt Sarah.

Mia hesitated a step. She had the fleeting thought that she'd had it fairly easy compared to her parents. Except for a few dust-ups defending their borders and a constant need to keep track of every ounce of water and every pound of food, she really didn't know much hardship.

And yet, her parents had saved so many people, Mia had lost count.

"Back through the tunnel? Or take them aboveground for questioning?" She flipped the unconscious woman from the cavern over onto her stomach. She had bled out. Damn it, she was unShielded. Vomit roiled in her gut. *Weakness gets you killed.* Her father's voice.

She swallowed the remnants of lunch threatening to make their appearance.

"Aboveground sounds good to me. Too much is still unknown on those uncharted tunnels." He jerked Sarah to her feet. "We'll interrogate them at the guard station in Sector One."

"Interesting choice."

"I don't want her anywhere near the dam or the MUC." Jack's lips thinned. Sarah had regained consciousness. She glared, the gag keeping her from saying a word. Shield, it seemed, had already repaired most of the damage to her gut. The bullet would have to be dug out at some point, but Mia figured it could just stay where it was.

She removed her fingers from the other woman's neck and stood. "Dead. The man in the tunnel should still be alive."

Jack handed her the last set of cuffs.

The hatch to the underground system loomed in front of her. Where had they got the covers? Better yet, when had Sector Nine placed them? Regular patrols scouted this area. It couldn't be easy installing such things, especially with the tools they had to use.

Unless they knew the patrol schedules. Which Amrit, Tobias, and Chet all knew.

Mia puffed out a breath of frustration and peered over the edge of the hatch.

And swore.

"He's gone!" She hollered to Jack. The man she'd shot on her way to the surface had vanished. Damn it.

He jerked Sarah's cuffed wrists until she stood and she gave a muffled curse. Jack dragged her to Mia. "He can't have gone far."

"Should I go after him?" God, she had to get over this constant need to defer whenever Jack or her parents were around, especially on security concerns. "No, who knows who else is down there. Let's close the hatch, block it and then send guards down to make sure nothing comes crawling back our way."

Jack gave her an appraising look, the kind she used to get when she trained with him as a teenager and had done something right. "Sounds good to me."

"And we're going to interrogate her right here, right now."

"That's not a good—"

Mia ripped the gag out of her aunt's mouth. "Where did you put the vials of my blood? What did you give my father?"

"Growing some *cajones*, niece. I like it," Sarah rasped.

"Mia, this really isn't a good idea. We need a controlled environment." Jack tried to stuff the gag back in Sarah's mouth. Mia batted it away.

"What are you looking for in the tunnels?"

Jack looked to the heavens. The sentiment had never worked when she was a child. Definitely wouldn't work now.

"Salvation." Sarah tilted her head to the side. Except for her shredded clothes and filth covering her entire body, you'd never know she had been shot multiple times.

Mia bared her teeth. Each moment, the edge of her control slipped farther and farther away. "You're trying to kill my parents, our people. I can't believe it's just for the resources. Unless that is, you want to use them as livestock. You know what's down in the MUC. You were in Lab Twenty-One. You could've taken everything in there and yet, you didn't. What do you want? Does it have something to do with me?"

For the first time, Sarah's eyes widened a bit. In shock? It couldn't be. "They've always hidden their secrets within secrets. The two of them will never change." She leaned forward. "I gave your father Diablo. Good luck with that."

Sarah tensed, breaking the cuffs behind her back at the same time she reared back, slamming her head into Jack's face. He jerked away, recovering his balance but not quick enough.

Mia grabbed for her aunt, but the woman collapsed to the

ground, rolling backwards over her shoulder and popping back up. She sprinted for the hatch and jumped.

Crap.

"Go after her, I'm behind you." Jack gasped, blood streaming down his face.

She slid down into the dark depths of the tunnel. Sarah would be going toward the train tracks. It was her only way out.

Mia sprinted, turning on the headlamp dangling from her neck. Air bellowed from her lungs, thighs burning as she pushed herself to go harder and faster.

The tunnel ended on a single track, the curved ceiling towering above her. Mia stumbled to the edge of the walkway before she tumbled over the edge onto the gravel and metal railway below her.

Jack halted next to her, both of their hearts beating in a rapid staccato.

There. To the left. Metal screeching against metal.

Mia careened around the corner. Sarah was in a converted mining cart, one they used to travel across the Territory.

Too late.

It disappeared into the shadows of the tunnel.

There was no way to catch up.

———

The trip back to the Basin Territory was silent. Guilt and anger warred within her. If they had secured Sarah in Sector One before the interrogation, would it have made a difference?

Mia leaned her head back against the side of the mining cart that took her and Jack back to the MUC. Body sore and tired, bones like hard stones against her muscles, Mia let her eyes close. For just a moment.

The nightmare came fast and unyielding. Flames rose around her as she hung suspended in a cage. The heat peeled her skin and tissues to the bone before her eyes. Blood vessels pulsed in thin red ropes along every exposed sinew and her muscles singed…

"Wake up. We're here." Jack's harsh voice jerked her awake. Sweat poured down her face, the man-made cavern suffocating with its single light above the titanium door and limited space.

It had been twenty-four hours since she'd last slept, it was no wonder exhaustion had won, but that dream had been…had been horrifying. She patted her chest and arms to make sure everything was still intact.

Jack stalked in front of her, opening the titanium security door, each step jerky and angry.

Let him be angry, the moody asshole. At least she'd gotten the name of the poison.

They reached the room where Rani had been nursing her parents. Only her mother remained, half-conscious.

"Mia, love," she slurred.

God, Shield really was taking its sweet time, wasn't it? Did Eva need another dose?

"Mom." She grasped her hand. "Where's Dad and Rani?"

Eva cleared her throat and drew in a hard, rattling breath. "Cryo."

"Shit." Jack shot out of the room.

Mia's eyes widened. "No, Mom, we can't do that."

Her mother swallowed hard, closing her eyes. "Dead… otherwise."

Had her mother told Rani to put her father in cryo? A highly experimental process before the Collapse thirty years ago, it hadn't gotten much safer since—especially with the years of degradation to the machine. Only one person had survived. Many, many had not.

"Mom," Mia breathed.

"Shield…will…protect." Each word was laborious, little more than a whisper.

"Okay." She squeezed her mom's hand, kissing her forehead. "Rest, I'll go check on things."

Dammit all to hell. Doom beat a drum in her chest. Mia wiped away the blood from where she'd chewed at her lower lip. *Shit just keeps piling up.* They couldn't lose her father.

She remembered him showing her how to shoot a gun when she was eight, and sitting across from her at the dinner table, deep lines of concentration furrowing his brow. Their relationship had always been complicated, strained. If he died, she'd never get to figure it out.

She jogged down the hallway toward Rani's lab and all the equipment. Through the courtyard and the cathedral ceiling of the natural cavern, down the hallway, passing the dark eyes of the unused offices. She reached the far end, Lab Twenty-One to the right, Rani's lab to the left.

Voice's echoed out of the latter.

"It's too late to turn back now, I already injected him."

"Are you out of your mind? He's already poisoned, his body won't be able to handle being brought back. Don't you remember what happened to the last one?" Jack's voice boomed.

"Without knowing what he was injected with, we don't know how to help him, if we don't help him, he'll die. There's only a handful of poisons that work fast enough to beat Shield, none of them good, all of them synthesized nightmares from the Resource Wars."

"He was injected with Diablo." Mia forced her body forward toward the man-sized tube Rani had brought into the lab.

"Even more reason to try cryo. We have no antidote here for Diablo. Without cryo or the antidote, he is surely dead."

"There has to be another way," Jack insisted.

"Then find me the antidote. Each day he's in that machine means more cell degradation. Shield can survive, even in those temps, but if we have any chance of bringing him out of it, we need that antidote." Rani crossed her arms, squeezing them tight against her body.

Frost coated a small square of glass at the head of what was essentially a high-tech coffin, her father's face just visible beneath. Mia walked over to the cryo machine and placed her hand over the smooth surface, tracing the outlines of jaw and head on the freezing surface. *Please stay alive. Please.*

Jack threw his hands in the air. "And where the hell are we supposed to find that?"

Rani looked between him and Mia, her lips pursing and brow furrowing at whatever she saw on Mia's face. "The only place it might be is in our sister facility in Virginia."

Jack cursed.

Eva wobbled alongside him, pale and stark holding onto a rolling IV stand. At the sight of Daniel in the cryotube, she crumpled to her knees. "I have the maps. When do we leave?"

"Mom, I really don't think you need—"

"When do we leave?!" The ragged question snapped out of parched lips. Eva's skin tightened around her skull, her brown eyes like fiery embers trapped within a cage of bone.

Had she ever felt that connected to another person that she'd drag her half-dead carcass out of a hospital bed for them? The memory of that moment in the tunnel with Cooper flashed through her mind.

"Our lives have been intertwined for so long—for good or ill. I don't know a world without him in it." Eva's voice was craggy, harsh, pushing each word through a void of grief and anger. Her mother's hands covered her face, the sobs tattered and threadbare. Rani and Jack rushed to keep her from falling all the way over onto the floor.

Mia crouched down, taking Eva's hands in hers. Fine wrinkles had finally started to develop around the knuckles, the nails clipped and neat, a daily activity to keep the Shield growth under control. How much had those hands done? Discovered? Destroyed?

Healed.

"I'll find it, Mom. I promise. You and Dad have done enough for us. It's my turn."

CHAPTER 23

COOPER

September, 2072

The walk back to the ATV in the dark, his daughter's arms wrapped around his neck as she rode piggyback in a thin blanket, warm breath on his face, was nerve-racking. And uneventful.

Too easy.

He shook away the growing sense he'd sprung a trap of some kind. Had Sarah made it back ahead of him after all? The speed of the ATV notwithstanding.

As soon as he hit the brushline, he ran, zigging around debris, zagging around rotting trees. He gave two sharp, low whistles before rounding the corner of the shed. Kiva jumped out of the dark on high alert but at his and Claire's scent, she jumped around like a puppy. Jorge walked from the side of the building, rifle at the ready. Good man.

"Hey." He nodded at Jorge.

Claire slid down his back, bare feet buried in the dust on the floor, and hugged the big dog to her, burying her nose in the rough fur on Kiva's back.

First thing was first. "Claire, sweetie, I'm going to have to give you a shot. It's not like the ones you got in the Cattle Pen, it'll be your last shot ever and cure you forever, okay?"

Cooper snaked the small refrigerated box from the secret compartment in his pack. The green light flashed. He took out the syringe he'd pilfered months ago and opened the box. Shield. His curse. His savior.

"Daddy, will it hurt?" Claire gave a little shiver, wrapping the blanket closer.

Jorge peered closer. "What is that?"

"That is a long story for another time." He drew up the serum and flicked the bubbles out. "Give me your leg, Claire. It'll hurt, for a few minutes, but you're strong. You'll get through it, and then things will get really good, okay?"

She set her brows in a determined nod as if deciding to prove him right and pushed a leg out from the blanket, shivering in the cool breeze. The nightgown barely went to her knees. His stomach clenched. Clothes were next on the list. He grasped her thin thigh, found the femoral artery, and plunged the needle into the vein. Claire flinched but kept a firm hold until all the solution was gone.

"Ow, Daddy, it hurts, it hurts!"

"What did you do, Cooper?" Jorge stepped forward and Cooper waved him back. Kiva whined, sniffing the air.

"Stay back. It's alright, it'll be fine." He needed the words as much as Jorge and Claire did. He held her as Shield worked its way through her blood stream and she flailed and cried out, tremors rocking her thin frame. A part of him shriveled up into a little ball of guilt and agony, wishing he could take hers.

Five long minutes later, Claire calmed, her body relaxing. She fell into a fitful doze, exhausted. It would take Shield a day or two to improve her strength. Only time would tell if had cleared the poison.

Jorge paced back and forth behind the ATV, arms crossed, rifle on his back. Kiva had laid down with head on her front paws and her ears alert as she watched him and Claire through her dark, luminous eyes. She hopped up when Claire calmed, walking over to sniff at her. With a disgusted woof, she turned and hopped into the side-by-side with one leap.

Jorge halted, an angry set to his features. "You gotta be straight with me. What was that?"

"They've been poisoning her. That was the antidote." Not a complete lie, but certainly not the entire truth. Cooper wrapped the blanket around the little girl tighter and squeezed her. She snuggled closer. "I need you to do something for me. Something that I would trust very few people in this world with, especially after what she has gone through. But there's something…vital I need to do while I'm here."

Jorge cocked his head to the side, eyes narrowing. "Don't you dare say it."

"I need you to take Claire back to Basin, take Kiva with you too. She's a good judge of character."

Basin Territory may have many flaws but slavery and hurting people for pleasure weren't on the list. Cooper could live with that. He could put up with Daniel, even Jack, if it meant Claire had a secure place to live. *Hard work and sacrifice will keep the wolves at bay.* Another Daniel-ism. If he was going to return there for good—or as long as Claire was a child—then he needed to bring something to the table. Something that could change the tide in favor of Basin winning any outright conflict with Butte. He needed to retrieve Sarah's cache of antidotes. And maybe try and save more innocent kids.

Anything to go toward Mia trusting him again.

Jorge shook his head. "No. We had this talk. Two heads—"

"I want my daughter out of here, Jorge. I won't be as effective if I have to worry about her well-being while I'm out there doing a little recon." He laid Claire on the bench seat of the side-by-side. Kiva hopped to the floor and whined at him.

"Watch out for them, girl," he murmured to the dog.

Kiva rested her head on Claire's belly and the little girl instinctively placed her hand between the dog's ears. The dog licked her arm and woofed once as if in acknowledgement of Cooper's request.

"How are you going to get back?"

"The ATV spoil you or something?"

Jorge frowned. "You know that's not what I meant."

"I'll find a way, I always do. Now, go, before she wakes up. Take a different route back if you can." Cooper drew out the faded paper map, its creases making it hard to read in places. "Go northwest here, drop down south here. Should take you a little over two days but you may be able to avoid most people. Tell Mia the barrels are a present—or partial payment for the one time in the MUC—and ask her to take care of Claire if I don't come back."

Somebody smart had to train the kid now that she was Shielded—*if* the poison had been eradicated from her blood stream.

The other man shook his head. "I don't like it. This is why you decided to bring me all the way, isn't it?"

Cooper just offered him a thin smile. His heart was shattering wide open at the thought of possibly never seeing his kid again. But she would be safe. She had to be. "You're a good man, Jorge, don't let this world kill that."

———

Something had occurred to Cooper on the way to Montana. Something that had rattled around his brain but never really solidified until St. John. Sarah was looking for something in the Basin Territory. Something big.

And now that Claire was relatively safe, he could focus on infiltrating her power structure and finding out what it was, while he also searched for her store of antidotes. Or find out that he was wrong and everything was as messed up as it appeared.

He was also going to get the rest of those kids out if at all possible. Cooper had no clue how he would transport them, but he couldn't leave them there with the monsters—to possibly turn monster themselves.

Cooper circled the fenced in compound, ghosting past complacent guards and aiming for one of the holes he'd established during one of his many visits over the years. *Always have a plan. Always have multiple escape routes.* The people here may have the scary muscled cannibals but they definitely didn't have the training.

He slipped in through carefully joined wire, replacing each link and took stock. The tarmac was to the southwest of him along with the terminal and control tower used to house the monstrosities and the slaves used to care for them.

To the east, several houses lined the road leading into town and Montana Tech, along with the feeding pens for the hogs, the Cattle Pen with their human livestock, and an old community center holding the workers for the water plant and greenhouses.

When he came here, he was housed at the terminal, allowed to visit Claire once a day where they kept her in the Pen. It was a reminder to him how easily they could feed her to the monsters that lurked like deformed lumps of rage infused clay. He had taken the hint.

Other buildings, especially the university, were off-limits to everybody with the exception of Sarah's most-trusted leaders. But he had been there before, with Daniel, on that fateful day when the other man had blown up half the town. The day he'd blown up innocents along with the monsters. All to try and kill Sarah.

The day Cooper had decided he couldn't stay in the Territory anymore. He had been so young but now he knew. Now he understood Daniel was just trying to protect them all. A few for the defense of many. Was it the lesser of two evils? He really couldn't answer that.

Montana Tech it was.

If the rest of the compound had a dearth of guards, it was

because the Montana Tech campus had an abundance. Men and women, rifles alert at the ready, overlapped their patrol routes. High on top of the buildings, three—no, four—people kept watch. Yep, this is where he needed to search. Now, how to sneak past?

Back when he'd come here with Daniel, they'd only entered the mining sciences building—now long gone—but many others dotted the landscape still intact. He forced his brain to remember the layout.

He crouched beside a house and waited, observing the movement of the guards, the holes, the weaknesses. An hour passed before he moved. If he didn't go now, daylight would ruin his chances completely.

Cooper stayed next to the fence, crouching with the shadows. At the first open space, he waited for a beat. Two beats. At three, the guard on patrol hit the midpoint of his route. Cooper streaked to the first building on the campus.

Harsh emergency lights on solar generators created a different obstacle. He padded to the end corner and peered around. Guard on the west building. A metal door on the side where he hid.

Were they connected by steam tunnels? It wouldn't hurt to find out. Crouching, he duck-walked to the door. Unlocked.

Huh.

He eased it open and a musty smell of dust and old books met his nose. Library.

He listened. No sound of movement. Light from outside shone through windows high up the ceiling. Enough for him to see shadowy stacks through the emergency door hallway. A stairwell to his right and another door to his left. Bingo. Stairs going down to a basement.

The bottom was too dark, even for his eyesight. Was he far enough away to use his penlight? Cooper glanced back behind him, up the windowless stairwell. It would have to do.

The thin beam showed a door, the letter "B" next to it. In an alcove tucked under the descending staircase was a man-sized hatch. He opened it, and rungs descended into the dark.

Cooper put the penlight in his mouth and eased down the ladder. Hopping off into a narrow tunnel, pipes and conduit all around him. If he had wanted to, he could've reached up and touched the ceiling. Dust coated the floor, undisturbed for some time.

The tunnel forked. Left or right? He pictured the layout in his mind. Where the mining sciences building once stood would be to the left. Commons and offices would be to the right.

Even though it had been destroyed, something about the mining sciences building called to him. Left it was.

Every so often, a hatch appeared above him. He didn't investigate, he hadn't gone far enough yet. And then the tunnel ended, a door in front of him.

Cooper opened it and his eyes widened in shock. A train track. Another damn train track.

It extended east to west—if Cooper's internal map was correct. Walls of cement and elevated walkways like back in the Basin—and like Track Three—curved around him. Crap. Another branch of the government's underground tunnel system. It must have been a bitch burrowing into these mountains; taken years. All for access to some of the most high-tech mining research in the world.

Another force tugged at him, compelling him forward.

Something else was down here.

Goosebumps erupted along his arms and neck, a spark like the Seeking amplified.

East first. He had a feeling west connected to Track Three. It seemed all the underground tracks did.

He stuck to the walkway, keeping his penlight as muted as possible, just bright enough for his eyes to pick out the lines of the track and cement of the walkway. Who knew what guards Sarah had posted down here.

The tunnel brightened and Cooper's steps slowed. There was a light somewhere up ahead.

Closed metal doors, a half dozen of them, appeared on either side of the track. At one time, touch screens had operated security for them, but every screen was unlit, cracked and coated with dust. A wall, an enormous white sign with a red circle and slash through it ended the track. An emergency light glowed red in front of it.

A converted mining cart, like the kind they had in Basin Territory, sat on the track.

Cold filled his veins. What in the hell were these people playing at?

It was almost like playing wack-a-mole at the county fair. He could only remember one such event, the summer before his parents brought them all down into the belly of the beast in the MUC, but maybe that's why the memory was so clear. Simple people just trying to regain some normalcy after the First Wave. The energy had been almost frenetic, supercharged, like they all sensed the end was near. Three nuclear bombs around the world could do that, make one do everything at hyper-speed: love, laugh, and play.

At almost six, he hadn't recognized that, but the images of cotton candy, ferris wheels, and carnival games had stuck with him. Cooper didn't hold many images of his parents, but those he had, he hoarded like a dragon protecting precious treasure. Psychology told him he should hate his parents for what they did—who was it, Freud?—but life, grief, and experience had forgiven them a long time ago.

Door number one it was.

More steam tunnel. Probably venturing off to different buildings. Most likely so the professors and scientists working at the college could get down here post-haste when a train arrived. Doors two and three revealed the same.

Door four, though, was a room filled with maintenance

equipment much like where he'd found Rani only a few days ago. It felt like a lifetime.

Door five, another steam tunnel.

Door six. Of course it had to be the last one. A hewn tunnel, rocky and large enough to fit two people side-by-side. *One of these things is not like the other.* Door six for the win.

Cooper turned on the penlight once again, keeping it muted in his closed fist. He itched to draw his gun, but refrained. If he met any guards down here, he'd take them out with his knife. Less chance of ricochet if he missed.

The tunnel wound around, going deeper and farther than he thought it would. He couldn't be beneath the campus—even the town at this point. Were they under the mountain range surrounding Butte yet? His sense of distance at that moment was subpar or less. It could be the mountain range—it could be out in the middle of nowhere.

The main tunnel branched off; he resisted the urge to follow. Whatever lay ahead called to his blood, called to the part of him that was Shielded.

And then, there it was. A cavern, monstrous, enormous. Stalactites clung to the ceiling like daggers pointed to the earth. And in the center, a jet black stone knifed through the air, as big as a car. A sturdy wooden walkway surrounded it.

Energy coursed through him. He took a step forward as if drawn like a magnet.

"I wouldn't do that if I were you. It exacts a price."

Cooper swung around, drawing his pistol. Sarah sat in the shadows, back against the granite wall, legs crossed at the ankles stretched in front of her. Only her eyes glittered in the dim light.

She smiled, a small evil grin. "That won't work in here, even if you take me in the head."

"How did you get here so quick?"

"Oh, just like you, I have my ways. Tell me, Killian Cooper, what do you feel next to it?" She didn't stand up, just eyed the rock in the middle of the room with an inscrutable expression.

"Sunshine and lemonade, lady. That's what I feel." Dread gripped him in its maw and wouldn't let go. He wouldn't make it if he ran back down the tunnel.

She met his eyes head-on. "Funny. I feel fury and pain."

He cocked the pistol, taking a page out of Mia's book. It really *wasn't* necessary with a semi-automatic. "Where are the rest of your goons?"

Sarah clucked her tongue. "You think I'd let them see *that*? You're more of a fool than I thought."

He blinked. "Are you saying you *let* me see this?"

She held up a small device, her voice vile but resolute. "I've been tracking you all along Killian. I *let* you save your daughter."

Claire.

Sarah continued. "I'm saying, you're going to help me."

CHAPTER 24
EVA

August, 2055

Eva's parents doted on Sarah as a child. The youngest and more precocious one of the two, Sarah craved—no, demanded—attention from all and everyone. Sometimes at the expense of Eva.

At five, Sarah had developed meningitis, a childhood disease nobody thought she'd recover from. Fever and headaches ravaged her tiny body, and the lack of good medical care made it next to impossible for Eva's parents to afford the hospital. Thank God for a benevolent boss who saw what was happening. Sarah received the care she needed but was different somehow.

Changed.

During med school, Eva understood. The illness had affected Sarah's brain. Not that it had affected her intelligence. On the contrary, it seemed to do the opposite: made her sharper somehow, more single-minded.

Now, she wondered if this was how a young Sarah must have felt. Brain on fire, fighting for sanity.

"You want me to shoot him, sir?" Tamara aimed her rifle right between Hensley's eyes. Chet handed Trae a gun, jaw set and body tense at what must have been quite a crowd behind them.

An aura had developed around everything, making her eyes water. She blinked back the tears, tremors making her hand tremble. The man under her knife blade twitched in reaction. He hadn't spoken since they'd grabbed Kel. The pregnant woman heaved and grunted on the ground in front of Daniel. Maybe she needed to die too.

Hold it together, Zapada.

"Not until…not until I get answers from him." And not until the flames in her gut and head subsided.

A roar of sound raged in the distance, like the white noise machines before the Collapse, pulsing in time with the screams, shouts, and threats. Somebody fired off a single gunshot, but no other followed it.

Daniel's calm voice cut through the maelstrom. "Walk him into the tunnels. We'll blast the entrance behind us. Can you get him down there, Eva?"

Energy coursed through her body, wanton and wild. She clenched her teeth and simply nodded, words becoming near impossible. Control so tenuous, so thin, it slipped further and further away.

Eva pushed Hensley in front of her, the knife digging a bit more into his neck, the trickle of blood becoming a stream. He winced, but her grip was iron. At least there was that, even if she wanted to rip his throat out with her teeth.

More of their people met them in the cavernous tunnel, the emergency lights casting stark shadows on the curved cement walls. A thud and rattle followed the last person from the stairwell, and crumbled cement chunks blew to either side of her. No more door. She resisted a hysterical giggle.

"I want charges set to annihilate this section of the tunnel in twenty minutes. Scott and Aurelia, you're going to get word to the clean-up crew. Tell them to keep going and we'll catch up soon. We'll have to bypass KC on the return trip. Get that woman to the train." Kel cursed them, spitting and tugging, a contraction tightening her belly till she bowled over. Daniel eyed the man under Eva's knife. "Now, how did you get so many samples of Tau-159?"

Hensley remained mute.

Daniel glared at him, extending a hand to one of their people. Chet. The young man's name was Chet. *So difficult to remember.* He handed Daniel a pistol.

"Eva, let him go, I got him."

The words meant nothing, vowels and consonants strung together into meaningless garble. It accelerated the pounding in her head and the warmth in her stomach. Eva growled, low and deep.

Something bit her leg, and a brief moment of lucidity knifed through her. Nala. Nala had bitten her—just a nudge to break her already healing skin.

Daniel stepped forward, but she shoved Hensley away and toward him as pain sliced along the walls of her stomach and up the nerve ending to her head. She dropped to her knees.

"Trae, take her to the train." Daniel's voice was rough, strained.

"No." She had to hear Hensley's reply. She gripped Nala's fur, the contact enough for a hazy kind of clarity.

Hensley chuckled, a low rasping sound devoid of humor. "Told you. She's already gone, war hero. You let me go, and give me back the pregnant girl, and I won't have my people hunt you down and destroy everything you have."

Daniel looked over Hensley's shoulder to Chet. "Trigger the detonator to the BAC. Only that one."

The young man opened a Velcroed compartment on his vest and removed a detonator. He met Hensley's eyes and flipped the switch at the top of the device. A distant boom rattled the tunnel, dust falling around them.

"You sonofabitch." Hensley charged Daniel, who fired the pistol at the other's leg.

"You see, you were so focused on us that you didn't stop to think I might have other people. You were always short-sighted and arrogant, colonel. Starting your own cult has exacerbated those tendencies. They've laid C4 around your entire camp. Talk, or we'll start detonating them one by one." Daniel kept his gaze narrowed on Hensley.

The man groaned, shoulders heaving, blood drying on his neck where Eva had sliced so close to the artery.

She licked her lips, hands dropping to rest on the ground on either side of her legs, body tensing. Nala growled deep in her chest, head so close to Eva's she could smell the rancid dog breath.

"Arrogant prick. I always figured they blew that entire thing at Diomede out of proportion for their own gain. To rally the troops. You wouldn't dare hurt innocent people."

"Chet, blow the next one."

The young man blinked but followed orders with no hesitation. Another distant boom shook the tunnel walls.

Daniel widened his stance and leaned over the pistol, eyes glittering. "Wonder where that one was? You see, colonel, I'm not the same man I was. None of us are. Tell me where you got the meteorite samples, or I'll have my young friend here, detonate the rest, and you'll not have a settlement to return to."

Hensley flinched, his eyes dark holes in his skull. "General Kaspar's holed up under Fort Belvoir in Virginia. I stole those samples right out from under him and his new 'Western Coalition.' Take care there, war hero, he has a bigger hard-on for those black rocks than I do. Now kill me or let me go."

Daniel blinked at the other man's words, the only outward sign of surprise. "General Kaspar? General Lee Kaspar?"

Hensley didn't reply, toppling to his side half-conscious, a small puddle of blood under his bleeding leg from the gunshot wound. So, he wasn't Shielded.

Eva crawled over and sniffed it. *Mmm.*

"Shit." Daniel holstered the gun and yanked her back before

she could do anything else. "Get her back to the train. I have horse tranquilizers in the back. Use them if you have to."

She growled deep in her throat as two people grabbed her, both unrecognizable. They meant nothing. Hunger made her stomach growl and twist into a knot. Stupid people. They wouldn't listen.

With one swift move, she rose to her feet and swept her two would-be captors to the side. Enough games. Her gaze landed on the dark-haired male in front of her. He smelled familiar, like pine and sweat. He held a gun.

Take it. A voice said in her head. *Take it away from him.*

She stalked over the body on the ground, saving it for later, and swung out an arm to knock the gun out of the familiar man's hands.

He gave a startled grunt and turned with the blow swinging back to elbow her in the face. She shook it off and raised her own leg to kick out. A kneecap to bring him down, neck to take him out after that.

The four-legged creature next to her growled, leaping to grab her leg before she could land the kick.

Eva grabbed it by its ruff and threw it away from her. Wasteful nuisances. Why had she decided to keep it? She gave a long sigh. The stupid animal had given the human male time to regroup, along with the other people in the tunnel she had no names for.

Spinning, she kicked out to take down a blond woman. Next came two dark-haired males she plowed through with little effort. A moment of disappointment creased her forehead as she took in the wary humans circling her position. Weak.

And then she spotted the familiar man striding across the tracks, a rifle in his hands. Silly man. That wouldn't do anything.

She streaked across the ground toward him. *Kill him. Kill him now.*

No hesitation slowed her limbs, and one fist took him in the side of the head, spinning him around. Eva hummed as the whites of his eyes shone, and his cheek exploded open at the impact.

She spun around at a whistle from behind her. Two men and a woman both fired shots, the familiar man crying out to stop. In a flash, she had their guns, breaking their wrists to keep them from picking them up again.

The nasty beast leaped onto her back, and she released a startled huff. Damn animal. Eva reached behind and grabbed it, yanking its snarling body, all claws and fangs, over her shoulder. A sharp, piercing pain stabbed her through the neck, and she swung around where the dark-haired man, stormy hazel eyes flashing in pain, face swelling on one side, held the rifle.

Eva reached up to the dart sticking out of her neck, some clarity returning in gasps and starts. "Daniel?"

He fired again, another tranq dart slicing through the dim tunnel to find its target right in her chest, over her heart.

———

Bleary light met Eva's half-swollen eyes. Weighted chains criss-crossed her arms and legs and fire burned her throat, gut knotting in pain where the black stone still resided. An IV dripped a neon yellow fluid into the tubing ending at her neck. Her carotid was on fire.

"Daniel?" She croaked.

Panic. Utter and complete. She arched her back and kicked out her bound legs but could barely get her butt off the floor. "Daniel? What's going on? Where am I? Daniel?"

She bucked and rolled but barely budged from her position on the floor. There must have been pounds and pounds of chains weighing her down.

Legs appeared at her periphery, and she turned to find Daniel kneeling next to her. "Eva?"

He hesitated before easing closer. An enormous bruise

colored the left side of his face in a swollen blackish-purple, the eye glittering from the folds of skin.

"Get…these…off." Each breath was more difficult than the last, the IV tube vibrating with her struggles.

"Shhh, you're going to hyperventilate." He raised a hand to soothe but it fell away.

"Why am I chained? What happened?"

"You don't remember?" He peered at her carefully, prying each eye open and twisting her head to check the catheter.

"I remember…walking back to the tunnels. After that, it gets fuzzy." Bits and flashes of images drifted in and out. Why wasn't she still under the stone's control?

Daniel's jaw twitched, and he sat back on his heels. "You were out of it for a long while, then."

"Tell me, please." She could reach out and put a finger through the holes in her memory—if her hands were free.

He relayed the conversation with Hensley, the fight with her and subsequent chaining to a large pipe in a small room in the back of the engine, and Nala's part throughout. Each piece of information felt familiar, yet foreign, like she'd watched it all on television without being an active participant.

"Then we blew that tunnel for a straight mile, left Hensley on the other side, and loaded Nala up with us." He gave a sharp whistle, and the dog wriggled into the small compartment. She squeezed between her and Daniel to give Eva a sloppy kiss. "Oh, and we have a brand new passenger aboard. Born an hour ago. Do you remember why you wanted the mother?"

"It's Hensley's child." A vague image of a pregnant Kel flashed through her exhausted brain. The stone stirred somewhere low in her digestive tract. "Will you unchain me now?"

"No. Not till you pass that thing and we have it contained. The horse tranq in the IV bag seems to be helping you maintain some sanity at least."

Eva grimaced. "And how do you want me to *pass* it if I can't get up to go to the bathroom?"

"Eva, you went through us like Moses parting the Red Sea, even after the first two tranquilizers. It took four to put you down and the rest is being pumped into your veins. I don't know what's triggering the enzyme to act in such a way, but this is a small train car. I can't take the chance. When you feel the need, we'll figure it out."

"Are we headed home?" Eva turned her head away, an angry tear rolling down her cheek. Something dark and foreign stirred in her gut, and she swallowed hard. If they had to turn back now, because of her, she wouldn't be able to live with herself.

"We can't. Not if General Kaspar is behind this." Something like fear flashed behind Daniel's eyes. A blink and it was gone. "We have the maps. Tamara was able to retrieve them. I guess our little unintended distraction was enough to get inside the federal building. We need to figure out how to get to the other TMRWS—and see what the general is up to. Now get some rest."

Resignation joined the anxiety, the panic fading. She rested her head on Daniel's shoulder. He scooted closer. Nala whined and curled up beside her on the other side. Sandwiched between the two warm bodies, the train lulled her into a fitful doze.

CHAPTER 25

MIA

September, 2072

Two days. It had taken the Basin Territory Council two days to call an emergency meeting. What back door gossip and deals had gone on before now only they knew. She had tried to call one immediately before, but some of the reps had to finish harvest. And her mother hadn't been strong enough to attend. And it would take several days to ready the train and put together a unit.

And on and on.

Impatience had turned to frustrated anger a day ago.

The Council House had been the main office to a food processing plant in Sector One pre-Collapse. Now it held a large circle of conference tables, the office chairs creaky and old, some held together by wire and duct tape. Democracy—or the notion of it—still circulated in the Basin Territory to varying degrees. For the most part, day to day decisions and operations were decided by a council, the two representatives from each of the ten sectors meeting on a monthly basis. Only Mia's father, Jack, or Eva had the right to veto. Not that anybody had any illusions where the true power lay. With Daniel in cryo, the Council was in a panic.

Except for Sector Nine.

Down to one representative, Carmen sat hunched in her seat, lips compressed, eyes darting around the room. The other eighteen reps were trying to make their disapproval and fear known. Loudly.

"All of the people involved need to be arrested…"

"No trial…"

"To hell with that, everybody gets a trial…"

"…contingency if he doesn't come out of it…"

"Pull in the smaller settlements, if Montana comes…"

Mia banged the gavel once again to no effect. Screw this. Blowing out a breath of frustration, she gestured to Jack and her mother that she was going to get air and escaped the room with some relief. He nodded, standing to add his voice to the mix and trying his best to bring order to chaos.

Eva just sat there, weak and drifting to the side of her chair. Mia had tried to argue with the woman to stay home or in the MUC, but Eva wouldn't have it. Daniel's life was on the line. Everything they'd built was.

The sun dipped in the western horizon, the deep, deep vermillion like watered down blood in the sky. The faint outline of Mt. Rainier stood out in stark relief, a reminder that their section of the world was so, so small in relation to it all.

What horrors did those mountains hide in the remnants of the Eastern Bloc? What horrors were in the west? *Enemies on all sides.*

Mia shuddered, suddenly bereft without her father's strong presence by her side.

A trail of dust from the east caught her eye. A side-by-side, probably from the North Gate. She stepped closer, peering in the distance as it neared.

It was the one she gave Cooper almost a week ago.

A knot curled in her stomach and her heartbeat reverberated

against her ribcage in a quick staccato. Confusion replaced the anxiety when it was a hundred yards away.

There was indeed a little girl in the front seat. Also Jorge and a dog. And a guard from the North Gate. No Cooper.

Crap.

The large ATV stopped beside her.

Jorge's face had a large scratch across his forehead, his eyes harder, more serious than the last time she'd seen him.

The dog, a large German Shepherd, huffed out a low *woof.*

Cooper had said the little girl was ten but her petite frame under a thin t-shirt and coat, wrapped and belted around her body, said younger like she'd suffered a lack of nutrition or exercise. Probably both. A halo of dirty hair—it was difficult to tell what color beneath the filth—framed stark cheekbones and dark, dark eyes. She stared back at Mia with wary interest.

The guard spoke first, "They said they're here to see you. Since they had one of our side-by-sides, I came with to verify, ma'am."

"I know them. I'll have Frank give you a ride back to the gate. Thank you." Mia didn't look away from Jorge's steady gaze.

The guard looked between her and Jorge and shrugged. "Copy that."

He hopped out and walked toward the guard post set up outside the Council House to keep visitors from coming in.

"Where is he?" Mia said.

Jorge glanced at the little girl and back to Mia. Claire rolled her eyes. "I know something happened to my dad. Don't hide it from me."

The dog whined and laid her head on the girl's lap. Claire laced her fingers through her matted fur.

Mia's lips twitched. Good. A little mental grit propelled most people over the major humps of life. What this one had seen, heard, done made Mia cringe. "Jorge?"

He told her about Cooper rescuing Claire, then going back in.

"Why the hell would he do that?"

Jorge shrugged. "Don't know. I thought we'd gotten away, but we were halted about three or four miles out. They didn't try to capture us or rough us up, just held us at gunpoint. Then, a message came over the radio where some woman's voice said she had him. Those bastards smiled and told us to have a nice day. We were allowed to leave, Mia. They have Cooper."

Claire blinked back tears, burying her face in the dog's fur. It licked her leg and peered up at Mia with liquid brown eyes, almost like she understood the conversation and was wondering what she would do about it.

Mia looked away first. Toward the east. Toward the direction that held all the solutions to most of her problems. Her father dying in cryo. Cooper recaptured by the enemy. Her mother weak and withdrawn.

And a bunch of scared, whiny council members unable to make a decision and talking over each other.

Ire burned deep inside Mia. She handed Jorge a couple of ration chits. "I have to take care of a few things. You see that building? Take Claire and the dog there to get cleaned up and something to eat. They'll take care of you. Tell them if they have a problem to come talk to me."

Jorge nodded. "What are you going to do?"

"Have a little talk with the council." And she stalked off back to the Council House.

Jack shouted at a woman from Sector Two. People pointed and punched the air. The entire room burst at the seams in fear and anger. And her mother. Weak and deflated in the chair beside him. Silent, her eyes lost in the distance of her own mind.

Nothing close to the fierce warrior-woman image burned into Mia's brain.

Pragmatic and decisive, Eva's early journals reflected an introspective scientist, capable and willing to speak her mind but definitely not somebody who could lead survivors alongside her father. Not somebody who could take a life if necessary. The

Collapse had changed her, molded her. Defined her new path. Necessity made her so much more than she was. Regardless of where she began.

Mia walked by her mom, squeezing her shoulder as she went by.

Shit or get off the pot. One of her father's more crude sayings, but apropos for the moment. Her parents needed her. Jack needed her. Enough was enough.

Mia climbed onto the board room table at the head. Jack startled, and her mom roused from whatever depths she'd withdrawn to and blinked.

Mia pulled her weapon and fired into the ceiling. The entire room quieted in a blink, mouths hanging open in aghast silence. Carmen's lips twitched from her place to their left.

"Enough! We are not going to solve any problems by yelling and laying blame."

"But—" one of the Sector Five reps began.

She raised the gun again and the man closed his lips and glared.

"We are sending a team to get the antidote for Daniel. I just got word from a trusted source that Montana may be on the move. Their leader, Sarah, just escaped. We're not taking any chances. Sector One leaders, send word to Colville and Craigmont. We're going to pull those settlements in. They're the closest to whatever path Montana may take to get here. Start rationing and checking evacuation procedures to the Inner Territory, and make sure the wall is fully operational."

"What about harvest?" Somebody shouted from the back.

"Harvest will continue until the last possible minute. As of now, all the northern and eastern tunnels are closed. Sector Nine is in quarantine." Carmen made as if to speak so Mia pointed the gun at her, unwavering, "You may say you weren't a part of Gustav's plots, but he has helped the enemy spread discord and lies to many of your people and those around the territory. He has also been stockpiling an awful lot of resources underneath your sector. If we have to evacuate within the wall, Sector Nine will be stationed by the dam. Under the aim of the railguns. Do you understand?"

Everybody shifted uneasily in their chairs.

"With my father incapacitated, I will take his spot. As we're in a crisis, we will move into martial law, and if anybody has a problem with that, I will shoot you and ask questions later. We have an understanding?" Mouths gaped, each of the council members at a loss for words. Good. "Jack said we've become complacent in recent years. I think I finally agree with him. Go prepare your sectors."

Nobody moved.

"Now!"

A quiet rumbling murmured through the room but people started moving. Carmen sat in shocked silence, glaring at Mia.

"You brought this on yourself. Whether by ignoring things, or being an active participant. It's either this or I leave you all out in the cold when or if Montana comes. Go take care of your people. I'll have your guard ready."

"Screw you." The woman stalked from the house.

Mia didn't respond, stepping off the table and turning toward Jack, her heart about to pound out of her chest. She'd done it. She'd taken charge.

Jack smirked and pointed at the pistol still in her grip. "You beat me to it. Nice speech. You do realize you just made all our guards' jobs harder?"

"They were already going to be hard, Jack." Adrenaline drained out of her and she slumped in the chair beside her mother whose eyes were gleaming with something resembling pride. "Sarah has Cooper. His daughter, dog, and Jorge are over at the guard post eating and getting cleaned up."

Jack's face turned serious and he swore. "I told you not to let him go. I told you."

"I would do it again if it meant he got to save his child."

Eva stirred. "I'd like to see them."

Mia frowned. Her mother's voice was raspy, tired. She still needed to ask her about her blood but right now, in this moment, it could wait. "Need help?"

The other woman grimaced. "I'll make it."

Mia and Jack's eyes met. Something was still wrong if Shield hadn't been able to heal Eva already. Understanding passed behind his eyes as well.

A slow shuffle walk to the guard post later, they opened the door.

A streak of brown and black fur and four legs zipped across the room toward Eva, happy barks emitting from canine lips.

The dog wound herself around the woman, vibrating, her tail a fan in the air.

"Nala?" Eva's eyes widened to saucers.

The dog sat and yipped like she had something to say.

"Where did you find this dog?" Her breathy words full of wonder.

Jorge wandered over. "I didn't. She's Cooper's."

"Cooper's?" A hint of a small tilted Eva's lips. The first Mia had seen in days. "I'll be damned. I thought she was lost. Or dead. You know, she has Shield in her blood? I tested it once. What does he call her?"

"Kiva." Jorge gestured for the little girl behind him to come forward. "This is Claire."

Eva stretched out a hand. Claire peered around Jorge's back. "You look like her. Is it true she's your sister?"

Sunlight filtered through the loose strands of Eva's hair like a halo. "Yes, but I'm not like her."

Claire shuddered. "She's horrible. Will you save my daddy?"

The air left Mia's lungs. Jack answered first. "We'll try."

They would?

The little girl nodded but still didn't approach Eva. "Thank you. May I finish eating?"

She ran off before anybody could answer. Kiva or Nala gave a low woof at Eva, then took off after Claire.

"We're going to go save Cooper?" From the first time she had met Cooper, a spark had ignited within her—a sense of purpose that transcended her own fears and uncertainties. He had told her the truth this time, and trusted her with Claire. That counted for a lot.

"I am. Along with Jorge since he knows where to go. We need to recon what's going on in Montana anyway." Jack gave a half-shrug and grinned. "You, on the other hand, are getting a team together and finding that antidote for your father. Daniel has the answers, but if we can't revive him…I don't want to think on that. We'll get the antidote and ready ourselves for an inevitable attack. This time we won't be caught flat-footed. Eva, you're staying here. Keep everyone in line."

Mia snorted. "I thought I was in charge?"

"Haven't you figured it out, girl? The reason why we operate so smoothly is that your parents and I all know when to give in to each other."

Mia smiled and opened her mouth to tell Jack he was full of shit but an earth-shattering explosion thundered from the north, ripping through the stagnant air like a vengeful beast unleashed. In an instant, the world was thrown into chaos.

CHAPTER 26
EVA

August, 2055

t took another day before the devil stone—as she started calling it—passed through the depths of her colon and was birthed into the light of day. Cleaned up and stored safely inside a mason jar, the marble-sized nugget—a hole bored through one end for a necklace or thread—glared back at her menacingly. Eva could *sense* it, even through the glass that should've neutralized the rock's effects. Faint but there, it swirled in her mind like a river eddy.

Nala bumped her head against Eva's hand, and she patted it, thankful for the canine dragging her thoughts away from the excruciating pain of the last several days.

She placed the jar back into the padded duffle and zipped it up. Another day, and they'd be caught up to the clearing crew. Why hadn't it burned a hole through her innards like Hensley had told them it would? It certainly hadn't been pleasant, but according to him, she should be dead. Either Hensley lied, or Shield somehow offered some protection.

Eva hunched her shoulders. She didn't want that loss of

control ever again, but maybe…maybe others did, especially when power came with it.

Daniel dropped into the seat next to her, the train's motion making them both sway until their bodies brushed against each other, side by side, hip to hip. Eva rested her head against his shoulder, a sense of safety sitting comfortably with the ever-present attraction.

Shield had repaired most of the damage to his face, and only a yellow sheen remained.

"What's going on in that head of yours?" Daniel's forehead crinkled slightly in concern, and his hand rested on her leg. She leaned further in, taking in the scent of him, so familiar. Hazel eyes studied her, lips so close. Her heart pounded in her chest, and his mouth twitched, eyes darkening in response.

An uncomfortable cough sounded from the aisle and both she and Daniel blinked up at Tamara, the trance broken.

"Sorry, uh, the crew wants to know if we can stop and stretch our legs? There's a hub coming up in another couple of miles." Tamara glanced between her and Daniel, trying to keep the smirk off her face and not succeeding.

Daniel cleared his throat, and the mask was back in place. "That sounds good. Full grid sweep as soon as we stop."

"Yessir." Tamara gave each of them one more knowing glance, then turned to make her way back through the seats, hands steadying herself on top of each one as she moved to the front.

Eva crossed her arms. She didn't mince words or acknowledge the tension between them. For once, she'd let him wonder. Back to business. "It might take more money than you have for my thoughts, Daniel. My biggest concern is what if there's another source of the enzyme? That each TMRWS has its own individual sample. I've given it a lot of thought, and I'm not completely convinced that rock in the black site is simply a meteorite like we've been defining it."

Daniel took the abrupt shift in stride, a fleeting look of relief flashing across his face. "Then what do you think it is?"

She shook her head. "I don't know. Remnants of an extraterrestrial device? Leftovers from the asteroid that killed the dinosaurs? Something else completely? I just know that most molecules don't react the way the enzymes in Shield are reacting with the enzymes in the raw samples of Tau-159 in Kansas City. They're mimicking the white blood cells in our immune system. It's as if one is a foreign invader that the other instinctively needs to destroy. The only difference is, they continue fighting each other—or possibly enhancing each other. I won't know until I'm in the lab."

"We've seen that reaction before during the Year of Hell. But an ET, Eva? Seriously?"

"You know what I mean. How the hell is that meteorite buried so deep beneath the surface back home? Where's the impact crater? One that size would have left a mighty large one, even if it happened thousands of years ago, we should still see some evidence. That borehole was man-made. I can almost guarantee it after reading those texts from Montana Tech you brought back from the mining school. What if that hole was meant to be a cage?"

"In the end, does it matter? Where it came from, I mean?" Something flickered across his face, there and gone. Guilt. It had been guilt.

Eva tightened her hands where they cradled her elbows. "I think it does matter, Daniel. If it's from an ET, we don't know its true nature. If it's naturally occurring on earth, maybe we can limit the negative effects. We need to find out who discovered the samples, when, and how many sources there are."

He regarded her, and she saw the struggle behind his eyes—a struggle very few witnessed—between military commander and hard-nosed scientist. "I don't disagree, but we need to protect our people as well, protect Mia."

"Because she's our daughter? Or because of what she hides in her blood?" She clipped each word and narrowed her eyes on his face.

"Both, Eva, do you think me so unfeeling? You of all people..." He let the thought drift away like dandelion fluff before continuing, "If there are more sources of the enzyme, the most likely place is going to be near the TMRWS machines, like at home. We start there, regardless of anything else. If we don't stop the drought, it won't matter in the end who we're protecting or where the damn enzymes came from."

With that statement, Eva could agree.

———

Luxury. Pure and simple. No chains weighed down Eva's limbs, no overwhelming hate filled her heart. That other presence, constant since the black site, felt asleep. Quiescent. Dormant even.

The clean-up crew had left a message on the wall, a code only those from Basin Territory could read. They were a half-day ahead now. A few small piles of debris dotted the walkways of the hub in an uneven pattern. Nothing to indicate any massive cave-ins. With only two branches off the mainline, it was a good place to rest.

Nala sniffed the ground, cutting back and forth on the raised walkway ahead of Eva. Every so often the dog would freeze and tilt her head as if she heard something in the distance. An odd lack of movement, as still as a statue. Then she'd become animated again, tail wagging and body vibrating with pent-up energy, poking her nose into every available crack and crevice.

Eva was going to study her, too, as soon as she had a lab.

Daniel had set up a folding table by the door to the engine, one of the maps Tamara had retrieved spread out from corner to corner.

"Anything interesting?" Eva peeked over his shoulder. Neat, handwritten symbols were sprinkled all over a map of North

America. Most of the rail lines snaked their way around the old United States branching off the main line, with a few running south and north into Mexico and Canada.

He shook his head, concentrating on sketching some notes, brow furrowed. "There are more than I thought."

Other symbols, one that looked like the symbol for a cell phone tower, the inverted triangle and half circle lines emanating from the top in sound waves, had a capital T above it. Had to be the TMRWS and there were more than a dozen of them spread all over North America. Some TMRWS had small red letters from the Greek alphabet: alpha, beta, tau, omega. She couldn't see the rest. There were also several large black circles, with a white triangle over the MUC, Kansas City, Virginia, and New Mexico.

"What does that mean?" She pointed at the strange circle hanging like the sword of Damocles over their home on the map.

"I don't know."

"But you have an idea?"

He walked a few steps away, pinching the bridge of his nose. "It's complicated, Eva."

"Then uncomplicate it, Daniel."

Shouting and barking echoed from the dark void of the track. Chet appeared, escorting a bedraggled, limping woman, blood splattered on her face, to stand in front of Eva and Daniel. God, she couldn't be much more than a teenager. Nala trotted next to the pair, nose lifted in the air to smell the girl, hackles raised.

"Found her on the mainline. Said she's from the clean-up crew." Chet stood at attention, hand at the young woman's elbow to keep her standing.

The young woman's exhausted, haunted eyes skittered over Eva and landed on Daniel. "My name's Chloe. I was with the track-clearing crew. They're all dead. All of them. It…it ate them, Dr. Burgess. Neil told me to run and to find you, that he'd buy time. I couldn't do anything. I promise I couldn't."

Her legs gave way and Chet guided her to the ground so she

didn't hang from his arm. Tears streaked through the dust and blood on Chloe's face and she curled in around her knees, burying her head in her gore encrusted hands. Deep sobs racked her thin body.

Shock and horror knifed through Eva bringing with it memories she's suppressed since the Year of Hell. The presence inside of her stirred. *Something ate them. Feral eyes and blood dripping to the ground. The smell of rotting death and shit.*

"Snap out of it." Daniel's voice cut through the harsh vision of her thoughts. The hard lines of his face came into focus. He whistled a piercing note and soon the others on their team drifted into the ring of light around the engine.

Determination set his features and Eva's stomach dropped. The last time she saw that look, they were fighting Sarah's crew back in the Basin Territory.

"You can't possibly think about continuing on? We don't have enough people." God, there had been over twenty people on the clean-up crew. If even one of them had turned into…no, she couldn't think like that, not yet. They'd lost too many in Kansas City as it was. As vital as this trip was, they needed to regroup—or go hunting.

Tamara, Chet, and the others regarded the weeping Chloe then waited for Daniel to explain. Concern and loyalty. Trust and compassion. All words that defined this small group of people, some of who had been there since the beginning in the MUC.

"We need to get to Virginia." He avoided making eye contact with Eva. "Hensley said Kaspar's there. He used to be my commanding officer during the First Wave and he has Shield and Lord knows what else. We need to retrieve those samples—or destroy them. But first, Chloe's crew was killed by something up ahead. We may have to go hunting. Any questions?"

The others shook their heads, slower than usual, but unquestionable determination lit each face. *Damn it, Daniel.*

"But, Daniel—" Eva started.

Daniel gathered up the maps and folded the table. "I said load up, Eva."

Chet got an arm under Chloe and lifted her. They disappeared into the engine with the others. Eva and Daniel were the only two still standing in the tunnel.

The light from the windows backlit Daniel framing him in light and shadow. Nala sat at Eva's feet, a faint whine erupting from canine lips. *Two against one.*

"We need to regroup," said Eva.

"We need the element of surprise. He won't expect us yet." The maps crinkled in his fisted hand.

"What are you hiding?" Eva took a hesitant step toward him. "What aren't you telling me?"

The engine powered on startling Nala, and Daniel's entire body tensed. With the exception of the hum, silence encompassed them in a cocoon. They watched each other, an entire conversation without uttering a word.

Daniel broke eye contact first. "It was his fault."

"What are you talking about?"

He shook his head, either in denial, or negation was yet to be determined. "The Collapse was Kaspar's fault and I could've stopped him. No matter what lays ahead, he needs to be taken care of. We've come too far already to turn back now."

In that moment, the presence within her awoke, eager and waiting. But something had shifted in Eva, some strength of will over those insisting, foreign thoughts. She visualized a leash and shoved it in a cage, deep and dark. "I hope you know what you're doing."

"Have faith, Eva." Daniel wrapped his arms around her waist, something he hadn't done for a long while.

"Funny coming from you." She tried to remain angry but couldn't summon the energy with him that close.

"Yeah, but we've figured out worse. We'll do it again. As long as we do it together." Daniel's lips hovered over hers.

"And that is something I can agree with." She said, her mouth meeting his.

The kiss was an apology, an answer to an unspoken question, familiar and strong. Undemanding.

Daniel pulled back, forehead resting against hers. "I forgot to thank you for saving me."

"Anytime."

"Now let's go finish this."

And the two of them boarded the train, Nala on their heels.

To be continued...

All Things Found, Book 3 of *The Territory Series*, coming December 2024. On pre-order now! Click here to reserve your copy.

SNEAK PEEK OF BOOK 3

All Things Lost: The Territory Series

Prologue

Year of Hell: Month Nine
2045
Eva Zapada

Bloody lines slashed through the number seventeen beside the door of the sub-level landing. Eva got close enough to inhale any scent. The chemical smell of paint assaulted her nose. Not blood.

The blade of light from the flashlight swept the hallway in either direction, ending back on the crossed-out number. The gloom settled like a cloak around her, the open doorway in front of her.

She rested her hands atop her burgeoning belly, the baby inside making her wish for a horizontal surface to rest on.

Daniel, the child's father stopped beside her and examined the cryptic message. "Sarah and Natalie won't get far. You should go back. This is no place for a pregnant woman."

"This entire Complex is no place for a pregnant woman. And how do you know the other missing person is Sarah?" The baby kicked again, and she winced at the solid thump against the wall of her stomach. Another two months of this and she'd be internally bruised black and blue.

Daniel's mouth thinned. "Who else is exhibiting symptoms and has disappeared in the last forty-eight hours?"

Nobody.

Damn it.

"She's my sister, Daniel. We control the eventual way out. It'll take at least two more months to clear the rubble from the tunnel to reach the surface." A lump formed in her throat. Two more months until blessed sunlight warmed her face. "There are not very many places to hide, and they'll have to eventually show themselves."

"We can't wait for that. They consumed human flesh, Eva."

She swallowed the bile rising in her throat. Stomach acid burned all the way back down her esophagus. The body had been horrendous, like animals had torn it apart. How human hands and teeth accomplished that level of destruction was mind-boggling—and sickening. So far, they'd kept it from the others.

"What do we tell Killian?"

"He's six."

"He's going to notice his mother is gone. Natalie has seriously overprotected that boy since the Collapse and hasn't been more than a room away since Kyle died."

Died in pain after volunteering to be one of the first people injected with a prototype version of the newest generation of the Shield serum. Health resiliency was the goal of the serum. Its primary versions elicited anything but in their hosts—including Natalie and Kyle Cooper. Even if Kyle's death hadn't been in vain, it ate at her. Now she'd have to tell the little boy his mom was also sick.

Unless they could fix it...

"He'll remember bits and pieces and how he felt but he won't remember the reasons. Trust me. Killian will be fine, I'll—we'll—make sure of it. Now, we need to find Sarah and Natalie's hidey-hole before they do something else."

"You're thinking they found a way into a stable section of this level? Someplace we haven't scouted?"

"Either that or the ventilation. Some of those ducts are large enough to squeeze through and bypass the main cavern."

Eva swept her light once more through the open door. Piles of rubble clogged the hallways and office area, making the room unstable. Through that hallway, there was a workroom and platform for a branch of the underground train track that the old government used to use to move materials and resources undetected.

"Why the slashes? Why make it look like blood?" It didn't make sense to Eva. They had marred the number on the sub-floor that would eventually lead to freedom from where they were all buried alive.

"The prototype isn't allowing them to think straight. They probably don't even know why they did it. Let's go. I'll send a search party to start checking vents." Daniel placed his hand at the small of her back.

Since she'd started the third trimester, Daniel took every chance to touch her. Arm, back, leg. He now guided her back down the man-made tunnel that would eventually lead down to Sub-Level Twenty, the lowest and most secure floor left in the Manhattan Underground Complex beneath the Hanford Nuclear Site.

The two of them stepped across the threshold to a section of Sub-Level Eighteen, a small part of the hallway before another man-made tunnel took them into the main excavation down to level Twenty.

Something clanged above them.

She froze and Daniel unholstered his pistol in one smooth motion, yanking her into a crouch beside him.

Luminescence flashed in his eyes, there and then gone.

A reflection? Eva couldn't give it much thought because Natalie now stood in front of them, dried blood caking her face, hands, and clothes, eyes dark pools in the dim light. They laser-focused on Eva's belly.

Daniel shoved Eva behind him. "Natalie, we can help you."

The woman took a step forward, hands clenching and unclenching, head tilting to try and look around Daniel at Eva. Her scraggly hair hung around her head in strings, a hungry look on her feral face.

Eva reached into the back of Daniel's waistband and pulled out his other pistol, checking the clip. She placed her back firmly against Daniel's, dropping the flashlight at their feet. Sarah was still out there.

His back tensed. "Natalie, think about your son, think about Killian. He needs you."

Natalie clicked her tongue against the roof of her mouth.

Another dragging step forward.

A shadow moved from down the hallway and Eva narrowed her eyes. Natalie and Sarah were trying to box them in like pack predators did with their prey.

"It's not working, Daniel. Too much of her prefrontal cortex has been damaged." Eva murmured, not taking her eyes from the moving shadows creeping her way.

"You don't know that. Another dose of the stable version of Shield could reverse the effects. It's happened before."

Eva's heart squeezed in her chest. "With initial symptoms. Too much time has passed. It's been days."

The shadow avoided the light, the outlines of a human taking shape.

And Sarah appeared. Old blood coated Sarah's hands and clothes but her face was clean, hair pulled back tight in a braid. "So, you're saying, sister, that there is no hope?"

Eva startled at the words.

Sarah shouldn't have been able to talk.

"Maybe for you. You're still talking. Can Natalie communicate?"

A hiss and clattering steps rushed across the floor. Daniel surged forward away from her. It took every ounce of effort not to look. Eva glued her eyes to Sarah, the other woman watching whatever happened behind her back with a cocked head and mild interest.

"Not in any way you would deem tolerable."

Gunshots rang out and Eva backed up until she rested against the wall, kicking the flashlight until it spun, pointing at the melee down the hall. She flicked her eyes to the tableau of Daniel standing over Natalie with his gun, the woman prone on the floor.

Sarah shook her head. "Guess she's not communicating at all, now."

"Come back with us, Sarah, we can help you." Eva tried.

Without luck.

"Listen to your sister. If you're talking, you still have a chance."

Sarah peered closer at Daniel, a sneer replacing the mocking smile.

"Aren't you an interesting specimen." She stepped back and Eva aimed. "I don't think I want any more injections today."

Sarah lunged into the tunnel leading back up to Sub-Level Seventeen. Eva made to give chase, but Daniel grabbed her arm. "She isn't going anywhere and there's nobody up there to harm."

"But—"

"Think about the baby, Eva."

As if hearing the reminder, the baby kicked her in the ribs. The tunnel disappeared into dark and gloom. Much like her sister.

She met Daniel's gaze. "Just promise me you won't kill her. Please."

Daniel rested his hand on her stomach, on the life hidden

there. "I'll see what I can do. Now, go, get more people up here to help me."

She left him standing in the small pool of light from the flashlight, examining Natalie's body.

He had never looked so alone.

ABOUT THE AUTHOR

D.L. Bunch is an author in Southeastern Washington State near the Hanford Nuclear Site. *All Things Hidden* is her second full length novel. She loves adventure, family, and traveling. For more information, check her out at www.dlbunch.com.

ALSO BY D.L. BUNCH

Click here and get the lost chapter, *Cooper and Kiva* by D.L. Bunch with newsletter enrollment. Or visit www.dlbunch.com.

All Things Lost

All Things Hidden

All Things Found-coming December 2024